Down and Out in Bridgwater

by

Dale Bruton

GW00708180

Spire Publishing

www.spirepublishing.com

Spire Publishing - September 2009

First published in Canada and the UK 2009
by Spire Publishing Ltd.

*A cataloguing record for this book is available from the Library and
Archives Canada. Visit www.collectionscanada.ca/amicus/index-e.html*

Designed in Salt Spring, Canada
by Spire Publishing Ltd.

www.spirepublishing.com

Printed and bound in the USA or the UK
by Lightning Source Ltd.

ISBN: 978-1-926635-09-5

FOREWORD

This story was written between February 2006 and the same month the following year. Prior to this I had last set foot in Bridgwater in August of 2005. The last time I returned to Bridgwater prior to publication of this book was May 2008. During this last visit, what immediately struck me was that, in a way that surprised me and made me feel the victim of irony, the story I had written was already dated. For one thing there were a few architectural changes to the centre, which is not unexpectedly a key location in this tale. Also, changes to the law meant smoking in pubs was now prohibited, for example. But what surprised me the most was the atmosphere I experienced, albeit briefly, in 2008 was not at all faithful to that in the story, and was in fact a vast improvement on the generally gloomy caricatured landscape within these pages. Maybe it was just a fleeting impression upon my then largely tourist presence deluding my senses. Or maybe, just maybe, the catharsis of penning this book actually shifted reality itself and recrafted the world I had known – a feeling every impassioned writer, successful or not, will understand very well. Either way, this story is best viewed as being set in the early/mid part of the first decade of the new millennium.

I can, of course, only speculate on the sales and circulation of this publication at this stage, and the reception it receives. But I would like to address a few issues I predict may develop regarding ´negative publicity´ to the potential reader of this work that may already have coloured their attitude towards it, for it is almost beyond doubt the mere existence of these printed pages will have put numerous noses out of joint, whether on the faces of those whom have read it or not.

Firstly, and perhaps most importantly, this book is not designed to be anti-Bridgwater, not meant as an eighty-thousand word putdown of the town for negativity´s sake. The protagonist of the story, as well as numerous other characters in it, are simply individuals struggling with everyday adversity and trying their best to be their best. If there is any demonisation I can be accused of it is primarily aimed at unscrupulous employers, inept officials and aggressive bullies, surely all of whom could be described as deserving targets for criticism and the real enemies of the Bridgwater public by anyone with the best interests of the town's people at heart. Our own inner demons are also addressed in the story, but this is the job of fiction through the world and its history, therefore it would be the biggest insult to Bridgwater's inhabitants to pretend their perfection and tiptoe around credible characterisation for fear they would not have the strength of character to bear it.

Secondly, this book, even if only to a fractitional degree, goes further toward putting Bridgwater on the map, which can only in the long term be another benefit for the people who live there. Even if people take issue with what I have to say, it will give them impetus and a platform from which to launch their own forms of expression which might not otherwise have taken wing. And if their arguments are stronger than mine, they need have little fear that the most just image of the town will be the one which ultimately prevails.

To conclude, I would like to add that upon completing the original manuscript in 2007, I sent announcements about it, plus a precis and sample chapters, to numerous organisations and individuals based in or connected with the town, including members of local governement, arts organisations, and local press. Well in advance of a hundred people I believed to have aspiring positions within the town itself were contacted for feedback, editorial input, suggestions and assistance. Almost without exception this met with no comment or response whatsoever, and to this date, to the very best of my knowledge, only two people have taken it upon themselves to read what I have written and intended to publish, and one of those two people does not even live in Britain. Therefore I gave plenty of the town's inhabitants and even 'string pullers' ample opportunity for comment and guidance, virtually none of which was taken up. So, whatever its accuracies and otherwise, good and bad points, this book is what I feel, for better or worse, the town deserves to have written about it. Anyone wishing to take exception to my story will kindly ensure blame is accordingly shared.

Any mistakes relating to the town's history and geography, and any other factual innacuracies are entirely my own responsibility. All characters are officially fictitious, although every event described has some basis of truth and personal experience from my own decades of living in and being involved with Bridgwater town. I hope you enjoy it.

He who tries to please everybody, pleases nobody
Aesop

It is infinitely more honourable to fail whilst attempting what you most want to do, than succeed at something else
Alex Bishop

1

'Are you absolutely *sure* you'll be alright?' Alex Bishop's mother asked him yet again, her emphatic tone almost imploring him to lie.

'I've managed three-and-a-half decades of survival; I'm sure I can squeeze in a few days more.'

'Well, if you're *sure*,' Joy assured herself. 'And are you sure this is where you want to be dropped?'

'Yeah, this is absolutely fine, thanks. It's only a little way down.' The car had come to a stop on the Cornhill, the picture postcard centre of Bridgwater town, ever equipped with lurking would be teenage gangs, thinly-glossed thrift shops, and Euro-styled toilets where twenty pence would buy you the privilege to excrete where a thousand others had done the same. 'Thanks ever so much for the lift, mum,' Alex said as he threw his grubby self out of the showroom-fresh Ford Mondeo. 'Have a nice holiday, yeah?'

'I will, thank you,' she chirped with obvious excitement, the idea of the Caribbean sun and the company of the new man in her life clearly in the fore of her mind. 'I hope you find somewhere to stay alright.'

'I'll manage,' he tried to promise himself as well. 'I always do, don't I?' he added, wondering when the last time he had was.

'That's true, you do,' Joy replied, accepting the offered get-out-of-here-for-free card. 'Cheery-ho for now then, darling.'

'Bye, mum,' he managed, trying to sound casual, and started walking, turning to wave briefly as she drove past toward tomorrow's holiday and the otherworlds of solvency and financial security.

Alone at last, after spending three hours with his mother since she had collected him from Bristol Airport, grateful for her motherly love and keen interest in his exploits in Spain, but weary and borderline irritable from the almost unceasing interrogation and feed of her adventures of late and to come, he breathed a sigh of relief in the cellophane factory-polluted air. He squinted at the clock hanging outside the jeweller's halfway down Fore Street, but the hour it declared disagreed with the light and was the same it had announced for several months. Two months Alex had been out of the country, two months plus away from Bridgwater town, and yet in the heart of the burg not a second had passed, it seemed.

Alex started walking in the direction of the river, drawing level with the colonnaded dome that had stood as the frontage to the covered market for centuries. It must have been centuries since it was last cleaned, he noted by the faded graffiti, wondering if the pointless misspellings featured JUDGE JEFFRIES WUS HERE in their midst. Lurking around the stone pillars, almost as permanent as the colonnades themselves, were clusters of youths who might or might not be one tangled group. Others were on the opposite side of the U-shaped road that semi-circled the dome, sprawled over and upon and around Admiral Robert Blake. Mr Blake didn't seem to mind, and neither did he mind the milk crate fashioned as a hat upon his head or the bird droppings mottling his slate-grey bulk. He just pointed toward his home, perhaps wishing he could pull himself out of his concrete foundations and return there, or symbolically commanding the oblivious young to return to their own homes like they might have in his day.

Alex glanced at before stepping onto the road, then retreated with a jerk as a Fiat Uno came screeching around the corner from St Mary Street, the car seemingly as hellbent on getting out of the town centre as its occupants were to be noticed. It somehow managed to cling to the road as it swerved the U to the High Street, a teenage boy shouting something from a rear window as loud as it was incomprehensible to Alex, at Alex. Russian rouletteing to the other side in their wake, bag bouncing uncomfortably upon his back, Alex made it to the pedestrianised Fore Street, where the only thing one were likely to get knocked down by was someone else.

He scooted as nonchalantly as he could past the young crowd, past the clock that told the time that time forgot, and came to a halt at the Halifax bank. Howard, their black suited mascot and a man who seemed incapable of entertaining any emotional state beyond orgasmic euphoria, smiled like a shark from the posters in the window. Apparently now was the best time ever to take full advantage of the bank's special packages for customers old and new. Various other employees from various national branches were also pictured along with their names and locations to help the bank robbery go smoothly. Presumably the printing of the names and locations made the multi-cultural propagandists more accountable and thus the bank more trustworthy, but it was a humble withdrawal and a bed for the night that Alex was after, not flexible repayments on a mortgage endowment policy ideally suited to his own personal needs, thank you all the same.

His pockets positively bursting at the seams with forty British pounds to contain, he ambled down King Street, glad to be out of sight of the wannabee young ruffians, in the direction of Dampiet Street. He passed the ghost of Serpents, an incense and tie-dye and cannabis paraphernalia shop that had reopened just before he had left for Spain, and clearly reclosed before his return. The road widened to his left where the staff parking (if considered worth the risk) of Argos and the Bridge Café had its car spaces occupied by wheely bins. The staircases, shared balconies and entrances to flats above appeared tucked away apologetically, as if the address were somewhere at which to be ashamed to live.

Alex reached Dampiet Street, crossed it at an angle, and entered through a red door beneath its unlit welcome light. Unity Club, the sign above the door read, but the people who frequented this place lacked togetherness every bit as much as The Labour Party itself, whom the bar had originally been intended to serve. He walked through the reception hall with its notice board hording trade union posters, charity appeals, and lists of people who needed to be on those lists in order to feel important, and made his way into the otherwise unoccupied bar.

The clock above the bar had not been forgotten by time, although its location knew little of the meaning of the word. It was almost quarter-to-nine, some of the internal lights had yet to be switched on, and the place had opened early, it being less than fifteen minutes past its posted opening hour. Alex plopped his bag down in a corner and himself on a bar stool, deliberately dragging it slightly across the floor as he did. Someone ceased clattering around in the kitchen and entered the bar to see who the early bird was.

The barman and Alex locked eyes for a moment before the former growled 'Tossa!' at the latter.

'Hi, Ken.'

'You just got back?'

'I have indeed.'

'Want something to drink?'

'I was thinking about it. Anything worth drinking in here at the moment?'

Ken Cunningham looked at the bottles, pumps and optics around him, the strain showing as he searched for inspiration. 'Doubt it.'

'I'll have a Guinness then, slightly above incompetently poured, please. And whatever you want.'

'Oh, thank you very much.' Ken set the black stuff in slow motion and continued frowning at the spirits. 'Was it good then? Tossa?'

'Absolutely fantastic. Even better than last year.'

'Oh, I'm glad to hear that. Bet you're pleased to be back here then?'

'Not much choice in the matter, really. I need a roof over my head for now, though.'

Ken blinked sharply. 'North Petherton not there anymore then?'

Alex shook his head. 'Nope, they moved out. Gone their separate ways at last.'

Ken looked like he didn't know what to look like for a second, then turned the tap off to let the Guinness settle, the glass half empty before them. 'Oh dear. Well, you're welcome to stay at our place if you like, although I have to tell you it's quite a houseful at the moment.'

'Oh really? Who've you got staying with you then?'

'Well, Daryl's got one of his friends staying with us now, and I've got a couple of Czech *bastards* that I'm hopefully going to get rid of as soon as I can manage to. I mean, you're welcome to come and stay, especially if you've got nowhere else, it's just that there won't be much luxury or space at the moment.'

'Alright. I'll consider it an option. Perhaps I'll ask Daniel if I could stay at his place. I can't imagine there being much more luxury but certainly a little more space.'

'Yes, that could well be a sensible option. Actually, though, you mmmight want to phone him. He hasn't been in an awful lot recently.'

'Has he not? That's a bit of a change of habit.'

'Yes. I think he might be a little bit down at the moment, I mean by Daniel's standards, which might be a small obstacle but might actually make him happy to have you there for a few days.'

'I'll give him a call. I'm sure there'll be some change for the phone from this, won't there?' He held out twenty of Her Majesty's finest.

Ken stared at the note for a beat then announced, 'I'll get that. Here, make the call for free.' Alex followed him through to the kitchen and payphone, where Ken did whatever was necessary to make the Unity Club the billpayer of the next call.

Daniel's answerphone kicked in with the same message it had half-heartedly regurgitated for years, but when Alex tried to bumble something onto tape that was no longer tape, Daniel the non-recorded kicked in, with a marginally less tired voice. 'Hello, Alex. When did you get back then?'

'Hi, Dan. Just this evening. You about at all tonight?'

'Uuuh, I wasn't planning to, but I might do now I know you're going to be around. You in the club, are you?'

'I certainly am. I thought about knocking on your door first, but I thought you'd probably be here anyway.'

'No. No, no. I've mainly been staying in recently.'

'Oh, right. Is that good or bad?'

A resigned musing chuckle. 'Hard to tell, really. Anyway, how are you? How was your time in…where was it? Spain?'

'Just fantastic. I mean really, two of maybe the best months I've ever had in my life.'

'Oh that does sound good. Anyway, I tell you what, give me half an hour or so, to stick my head under the tap or whatever, and I'll be down there, OK?'

'Alright, yeah, sounds good. Uh, Dan. One reason I wanted to phone you is because I'm looking for somewhere to stay tonight. Is there any possibility I could stay at yours?'

Half a beat of hesitation. 'I don't see why not. Alright, I'll try to make a space and throw the spare mattress down as well.'

'Oh, fantastic. My life is saved another day.'

Daniel chuckled with something more akin to good humour. 'Alright, I'll see you in a bit then.'

'OK, cheers.'

'Cheers.'

Alex returned to the bar, content that his first hurdle stone had successfully been vaulted since his return to Bridgwater. But before the night was over, a fresh obstacle would stand in his way, and this would strike a blow from fate with viciousness equalled by pain.

2

'So where are your parents now then?' Ken asked, sipping a Jameson's. He coughed up a lung then lit a cigarette to help the other on its way.

'My mother's staying in what amounts to a garden shed in some village somewhere while her new house is still being built. Although tomorrow she goes on holiday to the Dominican Republic. My father's somewhere in Devon with a woman I've never met, I really haven't got a clue where.'

'So you're out on your ear now then?'

'I guess thirty-five is a bit old to still be hanging on to the apron strings. Plus the atmosphere at the place was a bit on the thermonuclear side these past…well, these past thirty-five years, really.'

'I know how that feels. So what's the plan now?'

Alex shrugged. 'Try to get some money together and get shot of the place again, I suppose. Hopefully that won't be too difficult. Anyway, how are you?' Alex glimpsed himself in the mirror that ran the length of the bar itself. A stubbly sunburnt tousled-haired man with searching eyes looked back at him with a fancy-meeting-you-here expression.

'Dying.'

'Right, OK. Nice to know someone's chockfull of optimism. So nothing fantastic happening in your life?'

'Not that I've noticed. I'm probably going to be in the same position as you soon. I'm about three months behind on the rent. Daryl's Daryl. I've got some fucking crims for guests. I offered to do them a favour for a few days because they were stuck for somewhere to stay, they haven't offered a penny for rent, and I think they're handling stolen property as well.'

'That doesn't sound like any Czechs I've ever met.'

Ken laughed robustly. He lifted his Lennon-framed spectacles onto his balding grey-haired head and rubbed his eyes. The bar remained empty of any but the two of them. 'Well, good here, isn't it?'

'A swinging Saturday night. I don't suppose you know of a job going in the immediate future then, do you?'

Uninspired, Ken said, 'This one?'

'Well, I guess that's marginally preferable to bathing in napalm, but I think I'll search a bit further, all the same.'

The door opened and a time traveller from the 1970s stepped into the bar. With *Robin's Nest* hair, *Rising Damp* clothes, and *Crackerjack* gusto, he grinned and nodded emphatically at the two seated men. 'Alex! You just got back? Hi, Ken.'

'Hi, Patrick! I have just got back, that's correct. How are you?'

'Fine, absolutely fine.' He almost admonished Alex for the idea it could be otherwise. 'How was Spain?'

'Super. Fantastic. Absolutely brilliant.'

'Oh, good to hear it. Pint of the usual, please, Ken. Tossa you were, weren't you?'

'Tossa I were, Patrick, although Bridgwater I am now.'

'Glad to be back? I doubt it, are you?'

'Well, I'm trying not to be too depressed about it.'

'So you couldn't stay there and do the teaching then? It's just a summer school, right?'

'That's right, just two months of the year.'

Patrick took a sip of the guest ale, leaving plenty of evidence on his moustache. 'That's a shame. So you back to North Petherton tonight then?'

'That's no longer an option. My parents sold the place while I was away.'

'Oh really? Where are you staying now then?'

'Well, actually, Daniel's agreed to let me stay with him for tonight. Beyond that I really don't know at the moment.'

'We haven't seen much of Daniel lately, have we, Ken?'

'No, I mentioned it to Alex already.'

'I think he's got some troubles, by Daniel's standards, I mean. Mind you, he might actually be glad of the company.'

'I hope so. I'm momentarily a bit desperate otherwise.'

'Yeah, I can imagine. Been dead in here lately, Alex.'

'Well, so the evidence suggests. What's everyone doing these days then?'

'Staying in, I guess. Everyone's broke.'

Alex took a long swallow of Guinness. 'Oh, I'm so glad to be back in Bridgwater.' He drained the rest of the stout, then placed the glass on the bar before him. He watched the bubbles oozing down the sides, collecting at the bottom of the empty dirty vessel.

3

It was over an hour since the phone call before Daniel Patten dragged himself through the door of the bar, looking almost literally like he had just stuck his head under a tap. His thin body and creased clothes looked saturated with heavy emotion, gravity seemed to be pooling around his form. One glance told everyone what no-one needed to tell anyone: it was not a good day.

'Pint of ale, please, Ken,' he ordered, almost beseechingly, then noticeably forced himself to join Alex, Patrick and a handful of irregulars where they flanked a table. Alright thens were exchanged with a noticeable absence of eye contact.

Alex didn't dare ask how Daniel was judging by appearances, nor did anyone else present except Patrick, who broke the awkward pause with a vivacious 'How's it going then, Dan?'

'Not brilliant, Patrick,' he mumbled, half-apologetically. There was a look of preoccupation on the faces of most as the group racked their brains to remember whatever they had been talking about before Daniel's entrance, in vain.

'Oh, I'm sorry to hear that,' Patrick chirpily continued, as if it had come as a surprise. 'What's up?'

'Oh, Patrick…' he pleaded with his voice. 'I haven't been in here for nearly a week, I was hoping it might help me shift the focus from my problems, if anything.'

'Oh, beg your pardon.' Patrick held his palms up in supplication. 'OK, let's change the subject,' he suggested, with the deftness of a butcher's knife.

'Get your leg over in Spain then?' Daniel asked Alex, saving everyone else from having to take the nosedive, the ineloquence forgiven.

'I had a nice time, Dan.'

'Yeah? How many??'

'How many nice times did I have?'

'How many women did you shag? Don't play bloody coy with us, you're back in the Labour Club now. This is England, mate.' His breaking smile belied the coarseness of his words.

'I enjoyed myself tremendously.'

Daniel laughed openly and it sounded as welcome as it was overdue. 'God, it must be fucking awful being back here. So, giving North Petherton a bypass on your first night back, are you?'

Alex explained his newfound accommodation crisis for the benefit of everyone hearing it for the first time. 'Shit, that must be disorienting,' Daniel imagined aloud. 'You leave your home of twenty years to find out you can never go back to it.'

'It is a bit of a peculiar sensation.'

'Well, you're welcome at mine until you can find your feet. I warn you, I haven't exactly done much tidying up lately, mind.'

'How long's lately, Dan?' part-time barfly Ian Scott spoke up. 'Since the day you moved in?'

'Well, never mind that,' Alex tried to reassure. 'I've been living in a hotel room full of sand and sweat for two months.'

'Left out the third S, didn't you, Alex?' Ian suggested.

The jukebox kicked in with *Hello, Mary Lou*.

Alex needed another pint, bought Daniel one in return for the favour of putting him up for the while, bought Ken one back, and because it was the way of the world, bought Ian, Patrick and the others present a pint as well from the salary not yet squandered from Spain. Hello, Mary Lou, goodbye twenty quid.

4

Less than half an hour passed before Daniel announced his unexpected early departure. Maybe someone had said something that had upset him; it had proved difficult for any among the assembled not to. He explained he had a headache, although Alex and everyone else present was sure the exit was due to other things going on inside his head.

Alex started to down his pint, a little disappointed that his first night out in England in months would be cut so short, before Daniel pressed a spare key into his hand. 'Stay here, come back when you're ready,' he urged Alex, Alex tried to ensure this was fine with Daniel, and then Daniel left on his own, leaving the half-drunk Alex to make the final 50% of the journey to his goal.

Overtiredness from revelling and travelling soon started to close the door on Alex's consciousness a short while after the club's door was closed for a lock-in. Fortunately, with foresight and cheek in equal measure, Alex had asked Daniel to take his bag of belongings back to his house already. It was, after all, hardly a cumbersome load.

Alex opened the as it was known to its non-Labour locals Labour Club's door, stepped out into the post-midnight dark, and slammed the door behind him with a thud of finality. Sometime while he had been in the club the west had done what it does best, and rained. The roads and pavements made stretched reflections of the sickly amber streetlighting, the after-rain smell drifted off the concrete not quite as fresh as it perhaps ought be.

To the left, Dampiet Street reached to a minor crossroads the town council had fashioned into a dysfunctional mini-roundabout. Foot traffic staggered along St Mary Street, perpendicular to Dampiet, most of it venting an urgent need to show it was angrily pissed. Roughly straight across the roundabout, Friarn Street kicked in where Dampiet bowed out, with Daniel's terraced house at its far end, ten minutes' walk with beer shoes. To the right, past the entrance to King Street, the town library was caged behind railings in Blake Gardens, the road then running parallel to King

Street at Binford Place where it banked the River Parrett.

Alex paused in the lightless doorway for a beat, then decided to take the long way back to Daniel's. The Guinness had made him subtly queasy and the refreshed air was unlike any he had breathed these summer months. He started for Binford Place, surprised he could walk at what to him seemed a straight line, then curved with the road toward the river that helped give the town its name.

As he passed the iron gates standing open at the gardens' entrance, a furtive sound made him glance warily that way. Inky darkness blotted out the town centre park. He maintained his pace, ears alert for further evidence someone was there in the impenetrable shadows. A chuckle issued from an unseen mouth from somewhere beyond the railings, an unwholesome sound born of something other than good humour. Peripheral vision in league with his hearing, he ensured he was not being followed by the denizen of the dark, and carried on to Binford Place, stopping at the roadside wall to look at the river below. The Parrett, an inlet of the Bristol Channel, was roughly the same colour day and night, appearing polluted to a near-Stygian degree. It was a grounding exercise, designed to see how being back in hometown territory was affecting his emotions, but the moment he reached the wall the thing in the grass of the mudbank prepared to attack. The goose honked its warning and Alex could not have recoiled faster had it been a cobra ready to strike. A gull flew past, close to his head, issuing its desolate cry, maybe laughing at the frightened man, maybe encouraging its feathered friend.

Alex followed the Parrett toward Fore Street. Water lapped as if cadavers lolled on the surface of the Acheronian stream. Somewhere a security alarm cried in vain, its omnipresent shrill demanding ears to block it out. He walked along the pavement, past the church the denomination of which he wondered how many people knew or cared. Raindrops beaded on parked cars aligned along the riverside. In the feeble light their synthetic bodies looked covered in organic sores.

A few strides past the church, Bridgwater's Argos lay to the left, its raised ramp entrance lurking just around the corner of a wall. As he approached, Alex heard crying from the area presently concealed, the tears of a female in pain or grief or both. He slowed his pace a little as the part of the building came into view, glancing that way to determine whether or not that was wise. The weeper, surely no more than twenty, was bespectacled and clearly overweight, and she stood accompanied by a similarly aged man. It wasn't clear if this man was causing or easing the tears, and Alex looked away, listening intently as he continued on his way, wondering if he should check she was OK.

'*WHAT YOU FUCKIN' LOOKIN' AT?!?*' threw itself out of the large woman's large mouth, and his question was adequately answered. '*WHAT YOU FUCKIN' LOOKIN' AT?!?!*'

Welcome back to Bridgwater, Alex thought to himself, uncomfortably slowly increasing the distance between the couple and him. Welcome home, my friend. It's like you've never been away.

5

Alex reached the bridge over the filthy water that gave the town its name. He turned left into the pedestrianised Fore Street, this being about the only time of day or night a vehicle of some kind could not be seen on its stretch. In the rain streaked windows, more banks offered present and potential customers' the greatest opportunities thus far in history, travel agents teased with ill-affordable bargain getaways, a greetings card shop reminded passersby of occasions they would rather forget. An emergency vehicle's siren helped it bully its way through a nearby street, from somewhere else a man bellowed to someone presumably nearly deaf, at least by now, that there was nothing going on between me 'n' 'er. Two cars sped over the bridge Alex was leaving behind, their tyres seeming to screech in fear, their exhausts fitted with whatever devices were designed to make the engine sound more powerful but to Alex simply made the car sound full of farts.

He walked back past King Street to his left and Court Street to his right, glancing along each as he drew level with them, noting the gangs of shadows collected in them as if with dark intent. Two men loped past in the opposite direction, the alcohol making their shirt-and-trousers smart selves lurch forward with the effort; a cross-breed of primate. A shop that sold natural foods in synthetic carcinogenic packaging had a window boarded up. A car all but fishtailed around the Cornhill ahead, its occupants clearly wannabee students of the school of hard knocks. A skateboarder clattered across Alex's path with feline grace, dressed head to toe in black.

The crowd of youths gathered around the dome and statue had trebled in size since he had passed by earlier. Teenagers, children, a few adolescents, huddled beneath 'hood' hoods and baseball caps, adorned with the uniforms of gangster rappers and crews and brothers and honeyz, minus jewellery or direction or fame. Nike, Adidas, Reebok, Ellessee; the corporate emblems and conspicuous logos were visible on nearly all, propagating the mass exploitation of the Third and Industrialised World alike. Fashion statements had transmogrified into something like gang insignia; on the gathering the brand names seemed as stark and foreboding as regalia of the Third Reich.

A dozen of so youths were strewn across the area to the left of the dome, their body language staking a territorial claim. The cluster around the besieged Mr Blake gave the illusion they had hoisted him up onto their shoulders. To Alex's right, on the immediate pavement, roughhousing had broken out among four of the males; at least, Alex thought that was what it was – if not, the fighting had become so commonplace it did not even turn the young heads anymore.

Not wishing to be drawn into a wrestling demonstration, deliberately or otherwise, Alex cut through a parting in the throng and quick-stepped his way as coolly as he could to the opposite corner where the road curved into the High Street. He was almost on the opposite pavement when sudden violent movement turned his head sharply toward those under the dome. For an instant he had imagined someone was rushing out from under it at him, but it immediately became clear a couple of barely pubescent girls were jostling over ownership of a bottle of cider. Alex's twitch of alarm had not gone unnoticed, and a few teenage boys slumped upon the dome's steps smirked viciously from beneath the brims of their uniform caps. Alex closed the gap between the corner and himself, longing to be out of sight and hopefully collective mind, when someone bellowed a primitive form of Bridgwaterspeak he instinctively knew had been aimed at him. Loud and as viciously delivered as a punch though it had been, clarity of expression had not conspired with the volume and aggression. Something like a several word verbal assault had manifested as a monosyllabic warcry. Alex kept pacing toward the corner; only steps away now but teasingly far and hardly the threshold to safety for all that.

Clearly undignified at the fact it had been ignored, not that that would have been entirely possible anyway, the intimidating ululation vented itself again, one syllable closer to lucidity of speech, at least in terms of choice of words. '…'in' aaat???' echoed from the dome with disproportionate rage, louder and more demanding than at first. Having spent the majority of the previous three-and-a-half decades living in the area, Alex was accustomed enough to the local dialect to realise 'What you looking at?' was what had been intended to be said, the 'are' omitted as being superfluous to requirements.

It wasn't far to the corner now, probably less than half-a-dozen paces. Before he knew what he was doing, Alex had glanced in the direction of the snarler wearing the expression favoured by all too many locals, an almost permanent sneer. Twenty-four hours ago Alex had been in Catalonia, happily drinking in the gay and carefree atmosphere of the Mediterranean coast, seeing and sensing not a hint of aggression from anyone. And now this. It wasn't even as if he had looked like he had been looking for trouble, he couldn't have been trying to mind his own business more if he had tried. This wasn't just unpleasant, it was downright unacceptable, and in a moment of bravado aided by drunkenness and exhaustion, Alex let the indignation override the fear.

Pausing for just probably less than a step, keeping his voice carefully devoid of anything that could be interpreted as inciteful, Alex opened his mouth and carefully intoned, 'What's that? Your one original line?'

It had been intended as a Parthian shot, hardly more than a jovial rebuke that might just get this dark character's grey matter working.

The snarler, sitting on the steps of the dome along with his peers, either did not hear or did not understand. 'What?' He sounded almost disbelieving.

Alex hadn't planned upon repeating himself. Somehow this shifted the dynamic of the instant, caught Alex unprepared, tilted the balance further out of his control.

For better or worse, Alex repeated himself, wanting it done with and forcing himself to keep his voice as dispassionate as he could.

Whether or not the youth understood this time remained unclear. What was clear was that he had taken it as an excuse to see red.

The boy sprang up from his sitting position like a pop-up toy propelled by its spring. He was quick and sure, alert and in control, not tired and drunk like Alex. He was also surrounded by dozens who presumably were something like a gang. Alex was alone, very alone.

The boy quickstepped himself over to Alex, theatrically having snapped, pride and ego and machismo and peer pressure the petrol pumping adrenaline though his veins. At that instant, adrenaline started to course into Alex's bloodstream as well, sobering him in an instant, signalling the stepping into the danger zone.

The youth approached in such a hurry, Alex wondered if he simply meant to bulldoze straight into him. The boy he had taken for a teenager proved older than at first sight, morphing into an adolescent, twenty-two or –three years old, a 'daddy', a ringleader, a big boy with lots to prove.

There was no getting away from it or dressing it up in a face-saving lie. Alex was positively afraid.

As if it were choreographed and Alex had triggered the cue, teenage boys rushed to block Alex's path, some of them whipping in front of him on bicycles, one on a skateboard, most on foot.

The snarler stood squarely before Alex, taller than him, wiry and with a keen pointed weaselly unsympathetic face. His lips were peeled back in a mocking grin and the teeth in view appeared broken and few, despite the young man's age.

He looked like someone for whom violence was second nature. He looked like someone for whom violence was something of which he was not afraid.

Alex, a pacifist all his adult life, had never been involved in a serious fight.

Dozens of teenagers, scores of youths, thirty, maybe forty, young people surrounded the scene like vultures at the kill. Whatever happened next, Alex expected no sympathy from these, no aide whom might come to his rescue, no solidarity or someone whom might try to break it up. Those faces he did glance as his panicked mind whirled with his eyes were goggle-eyed in expectation of a fight.

And violence was what they were about to see.

6

Thought processes in obvious necessitated hyperdrive, Alex remembered a front-page photograph on the local rag, the Bridgwater Mercury, when CCTV cameras were first installed in the town. It had shown quite clearly the exact area where he now stood, the picture taken from a camera fixed atop one of the buildings opposite. He seized upon this as a straw to clutch at. 'There's a CCTV camera just up there,' Alex stated, pointing toward its source. It may well have been a lame attempt to avoid further trouble, and whatever it was it did not work.

'I don't give a fuck,' was spat back at him through those crumbling tombstone teeth.

Unanticipated, reflex quick, allowing no time for the inebriated Alex to react, the man thrust his arm forward, the heel of his palm connecting squarely with Alex's brow, and Alex's head was whipcracked back, the back of his skull connecting with the brick wall behind him with dangerous force.

You can turn around. You can blink an eye. And your life can completely change.

Alex had suddenly lost all control. He had felt the impact on his brow, felt his neck snapped back with surely not much less force than was necessary to break it, felt the explosion of pain at the weak spot at the back of the head as if his skull had been fractured.

Instantly he felt sick as hell, nauseous almost to the point of vomiting. Instantly he felt dizzy as a spinning top, giddy as a man on a white knuckle ride.

The childhood spectators watched in hushed expectation, passively and detachedly observing the damage done.

Alex's attacker was grinning a wide and unwholesome grin. He sensed his own version of victory, he knew at once advantage was all but solely his. He capitalised on his gains with the strategy and sympathy of a Thatcherite entrepreneur.

An experienced hand made a savage fist and drove itself mercilessly into Alex's face. Alex's brain screamed at his body that something was very wrong, his face could not decide if it was numb or in pain, its structure seemed frozen and as if it had caved in.

The strength was suddenly leeched from his knees, all of a sudden he was too weak to stand.

The third strike hit him in the stomach, and any ghost of a chance he might have had to defend himself was now as elusive as the air he struggled to inhale into his shocked lungs.

This was no way to pass a Saturday night on the town.

No-one among the spectators breathed a single word. Their vigil and audience was silent in its morbid awe. The basest aspects of human nature were feasting upon the scene.

Alex could not breathe, Alex could not think. Alex felt like death.

Gulls kited overhead, their bleak heartless calls like malicious glee.

Wheezing pathetically, Alex managed a desperately shallow breath. He found he was slumped on the wet pavement, his palms on the grit of the ground. Easy meat, no fight in him at all, no threat or challenge or sport for these boys. He had to hope his helplessness would bore them of their game.

And then, in that detached manner that adrenaline-veined moments alone can induce, Alex found his survival instinct taking over, making him do something he had never wanted to believe he would ever do. So disgusted was he with his behaviour, so appalled at his self-debasing act, he wondered how, if he did live through this, he would ever live with the humiliation it would leave.

'I'm sorry,' he heard himself plead. 'I'm sorry.'

It had not been premeditated, it did not even seem to make much sense. He must have said what he said, all self-esteem evaporated in the plea, because his instinct had dictated it was his best option of avoiding further harm. Maybe he was sorry he had not taken the short way back to Daniel's. Maybe he was just a sorry individual, pathetic and weak and gutless and failed, maybe he was apologising to himself.

In many ways it caused him more grief than the damage done by his attacker.

'What??' He felt spittle rain over him as the question was ejected from that close to foaming mouth.

'I said I'm sorry,' he repeated, the last time he felt he was able to. He didn't think he would ever be able to speak such words again.

There came a chuckle, a snort, a jeering chuff. If they decided to put the boot in now, he imagined he would end the night in intensive care.

The gull laughter came in a chorus this time. The birds had gathered to mock the beaten man.

Was there anyone else close enough to see or hear what was happening? Anyone likely to help in any way? Was a closed-circuit camera controller watching the theatre on reality TV?

Alex hoped no-one who would not help would see or hear. His pain and fear and humiliation competed with each other. He did not want to feel any less like a man.

Alex's attacker shuffled away, back to the dome. A few continued to stare, but most of the others took the cue to follow him back to the business of loitering with ill-intent.

He sensed the danger was over, unless of course he was hurt more badly than he was aware.

He tried to pick himself up. He needed a moment more.

He needed to be out of sight and forgotten by this crowd as quickly as he could manage.

He got himself back on his feet, but he felt anything but sure on them.

He half shuffled, half fell, toward the High Street. He made it, he was around the corner; though metres away he was at a different address.

He did not look back.

7

Alex couldn't remember the last time he had felt so low. He felt like all self-respect had been stolen by the crowd and their ringleader, and that he had allowed them to steal it. He felt like he could puke. He felt like he could cry.

Alex had no macho pretensions, no illusions of invulnerability or imperviousness to physical or emotional hurt. He was not in denial of his anguish and pain, on top of the inner seething at the injustice that had been done. He was not the type to just shrug this off, then wander into the sunset with a limp and a sneer. He was intelligent enough to know that was the behaviour of someone who was truly pathetic inside.

He wanted back some of his self-respect. He did not need revenge, but he wanted to claw back at least a little of what had been taken. If he had been even a little more inclined to violence, he might be trying to think of ways of paying back like for like, but to react in this way would hand even greater concessions to those whom had bruised his spirit.

But he felt he had to do something.

He didn't want to think about the fact he had told them he was sorry.

He had to do something if he was to live with himself again.

A little further along the High Street, a narrow alleyway led to Angel Crescent, curving around the Angel Place shopping mall. Alex made shaky progress along this route, unable to control the shakes that seized his body. The way was almost totally unlit, the shouts of those whom had taunted and attacked him came as plain as day from not at all far away. He had to pray they had not tracked or would not follow him, but he could not deter himself from going where he wanted to go.

The night had changed around him. The quality of the air, the scenery, the atmosphere, the internal and the external were territory anew. Shock was taking its toll.

No-one else seemed to be on the streets. Alex had no fear of encountering anyone else, just a healthy wariness of those he was slowly leaving behind. Even to someone who was badly out of control, his vibe must by now have the optimal quality of don't-mess-with-me.

Alex reached Northgate, taking a right, his pace increasing as he neared his goal. He passed solicitors' offices and the Conservative Party headquarters, their self-important facades inconsequential to Alex in his plight. He crossed the road, mounted the pavement, and scrambled across the grass to the police station door. The voices of his intimidators could still be heard, loud and meaninglessly obscene, but they were still where he had left them, where they had left him on the ground.

He had made it.

The door was locked. He rang the doorbell, letting it ring for several seconds. Nothing happened for many seconds more. He pressed it again. Again the same.

The wonders of government funding.

He tried one more time. His resolve was starting to crack, already the iron he had brandished was cooling, already his mission felt like it was losing point.

He let the doorbell of the police station ring for maybe a minute non-stop, thankful all the while it wasn't an emergency or he wasn't fighting for his life.

In a wall-mounted speaker beside the bell, a female voice spoke a single word. 'Hello?' Was that the procedural word, he wondered. The delivery had been flat and unhelpful, as if the speaker had already made up their mind Alex was just wasting their time.

'Hello. Uh...I've just been assaulted.'

'You've just been assaulted, right. And are you injured, sir?' Alex thought he detected just a hint of mockery in that last sentence, as if she were dealing with nothing more than a crybaby.

To be quite honest, I haven't the tools, lighting or ideal conditions to conduct a thorough self-examination right now, was what he wanted to say. 'I'm not sure. I don't particularly think so,' was what he said.

'And have you been drinking, sir?'

'Well...yes. But I'm still the victim of an assault. The person who assaulted me is by the Cornhill, in a gang. They're most likely still there now.'

'I see,' came the matter-of-fact reply. There was the sound of keys being tapped; maybe she was playing solitaire. 'Will you wait there while we try to send someone around to the station to see you?' It was only then that Alex realised the voice did not come from inside the station itself. Was there any point in him mentioning the Cornhill to them? They might have been sitting in Maidstone, Kent, for all he knew. They might have been sitting in Birmingham, Alabama.

Alex hesitated, his hope of the police doing anything to help dwindling fast. 'Is it really worth my while waiting here for someone to show up?'

'Yes, sir, it is.'

'And how long will that take? Can you give me a rough idea?' His eyes scanned the streets and shadows in the direction of the Bugsy Malone crowd gone wrong. It wasn't just the fear of them catching up with him again. He was beginning to feel very stupid talking to this speaker on the wall. If anyone had been watching him, he thought he would have long since walked away.

'We'll send someone as soon as we can, sir.'

'Fine, I'll wait.' He intended to wait ten minutes at the absolute most.

8

Five minutes later, buoying Alex's confidence a little in the act, a police car pulled up outside the station. A PC and WPC got out and looked at Alex in a way that suggested they did not ordinarily get summoned to the station thus. 'You the gentleman who reported the assault, sir?' said the PC.

'I am, yes.'

'And you were the one who was assaulted, sir, is that right?'

'That's right, yes.'

'Did you receive any injuries from the assault, sir?' the WPC asked, her tone a stereotypical brusque and no-nonsense one. Maybe all police were trained to sound entirely sceptical and unsympathetic.

'I don't think I've got any visible marks if that's what you mean. But I will say my head was hammered against a wall pretty frighteningly.'

'Um hm. But you were able to walk here unaided, were you?'

'After a fashion, yes.'

'You been drinking, sir?' the PC again. This was so obviously and poorly scripted, it was exactly like they were a couple of parody stooges in a Christmas pantomime.

'Well, you know I have because you've already been told that on the radio.' He couldn't resist that, but then realised any chance of the police co-operating with him would have largely dissolved as they heard the words. 'Look, I'm really not terribly drunk or anything, and alcohol doesn't play a part in what happened.'

'So how much have you had to drink then, sir?' The WPC again, presumably avenging Alex's comparatively smart mouth.

Alex shrugged in undisguised exasperation. 'Five or six pints. Look, if we go there now, the chances are my attacker is still where they attacked me, on the Cornhill.'

'We can't just go after somebody until we know what the facts of the situation are, sir.'

'I was physically attacked. It was an unprovoked assault. How much detail do you need? I'm happy to talk you through every second of the experience, but by that time my attacker will probably have gone. Listen to me, please, listen to me. I am a pacifist, and if this man attacked me for no logical reason at all, what is he going to do to someone else? There could be other people at risk from him right now while we're wasting an opportunity to stop him before someone else gets hurt or he leaves the scene.'

From the moment the word 'pacifist' had been mentioned, the police officers exchanged a lingering wary glance. Alex didn't know what to read into it. It could have been 'It's clear this guy isn't a bonehead, let's take him seriously' or 'Nutter alert! Nutter alert!' or 'If I had been in the other guy's position, I probably would have smacked him in the mouth myself'. 'What's your name, sir?' the PC enquired, surely later than protocol dictated, likely due to the puzzlement both officers registered.

'Alex.'

'And surname?'

'Bishop.'

'And your address, sir?'

Oh god, Alex inwardly groaned. Another time-wasting exercise. 'I just got back into the country from working abroad today. Tonight I'm staying at a friend's, although I haven't sorted out a permanent address for myself yet.'

The officers couldn't stop themselves from swapping eye contact again. 'I'll tell you what we'll do. We'll drive around there and you can fill us in on the other details on the way.'

They drove deliberately slowly, a fact that did not escape Alex's attention, possibly due to them wanting to hear more of the story en route either for professional reasons or simply for their own amusement, or because they hoped the antagonist would be far from the Cornhill by the time they reached it. Alex managed to condense the whole tale into the time with ease, and whatever they thought of the fact he had a few on board, he felt confident his articulation and non-aggressive personality must have been apparent to them.

They arrived at the Cornhill, and Alex felt nakedly on parade sat in the back of the vehicle as it crawled past the crowd of youths still gathered there. He almost felt ashamed enough to pretend his assailant wasn't there without really looking for them, but a sense of righteousness overrode such feeling, apparently to the cops' disappointment.

'Is he there then?' the PC asked from behind the wheel, clearly not wanting to give the throng a second pass.

'I can't quite tell. Someone might have been him.'

The second painful sweep along the street identified a likely suspect, but Alex needed to get closer still to them in order his myopic eyes could be sure. The police seemed to seethe with antagonism toward Alex.

The three parked and approached a small gathering directly outside KFC, one of whom was standing on a public bench, the visual prime suspect. 'Well, is it him?' the PC almost snapped at Alex as they drew level with them, virtually berating him before the accused.

'Looking for me, are ya?' the youth atop the bench scoffed. It seemed like they had been through a similar routine many times before, and had absolutely no fear of what came next.

'Yes, that's definitely him,' Alex confirmed, flatly.

The adolescent leaped from the bench and took three strides straight toward Alex. 'Yeah? Ya fuckin' pointin' the finger at me, are ya? Fuckin' come on then.' Alex was staggered by his bravado before the officers, who quickly stepped in to prevent him getting any closer. He was at least confident the character sketch his opponent had just painted of himself would leave the police in little doubt as to which party had the monopoly on justice.

'OK, stay by the car, please, sir,' the PC instructed Alex, unnecessarily. Somehow, as if he had murmured an icantation to him, the officer said something to the youth at a volume too low for Alex to hear, and he instantly allowed himself to be escorted a little down the street where they could have a private chat. Alex would like to have known exactly what the policeman had voiced; its effect had been like a conspiratorial whisper. The WPC addressed the others around the bench, while Alex stood self-consciously scrutinised - a target for every young eye to mark.

An economical half-minute later the PC returned to the car and victim of crime. 'OK, I've had a word with the individual. He is known to the police, sir. Apparently he had a row with his girlfriend earlier and was in a bad mood. He's going to come and apologise to you in a minute, and I think the best advice I can give you is to accept his apology and leave it at that.'

'That's it??'

The officer's tone became a little more firm, compensating for its lack of substance. 'We have cautioned the individual, sir. If you have no marks on you to show you've been attacked, there's really nothing more we can do.'

'But my head was viciously bashed against the wall. I could have presently undiagnosed brain damage for all we know. And that's bullshit about the row with his girlfriend and being in a bad mood, you know that.' *You probably suggested that line to him, didn't you?* 'The look in his eyes was malicious glee, and even if he did row with his girlfriend, that justifies nothing.'

The officer was agitatedly craving closure, his gaze shifting back to the now approaching attacker. The female officer flanked him both physically and in attitude, adding her own unhelpful helping of blackcap solidarity. 'You look alright to me, sir. And we're not going to get any witnesses to back you up out of this lot.'

'There's CCTV right by where it happened.' Alex pointed at it just in case the officers needed a little academic assistance. 'The attack is probably on camera.'

'It's not as easy as that, sir. Anyway, here he is. Please, just accept his apology.'

The youth entered the circle, a participant in an age old rite. He extended his hand toward Alex, the officers looking on like coiled springs. Alex offered his own hand.

'Sorry about that back there,' the youth said. The line sounded as bogus as the officers' version of community policing, but it was still the most helpful comment Alex had heard since he had sought the police's help. They exchanged the barest perfunctory boxer's style shake of the hand.

Alex opened his mouth to reply. 'Just leave it at that, sir,' the officers interrupted before he could get a syllable out.

'But I wasn't going to say anything-'

'That's enough! That's enough!' The youth had already turned away. 'Alright, you can go now,' the PC told him, the words letting him entirely off the hook.

'Can we give you a lift somewhere, sir?' the WPC enquired,

insistently. 'I wouldn't advise you to leave here on foot.'

What? You mean to tell me that guy isn't 101% rehabilitated after all? Alex wanted to say. 'You can take me to the Broadway end of Friarn Street,' he said, ensuring none of the continually scrutinising crowd overheard.

They took off down the High Street and the WPC addressed a controller on the police radio. 'We've spoken to both gentlemen involved in the altercation and they've apologised to each other,' was her over-simplification, truth-economising and libellous presentation of the events just passed. The red Alex had seen at the indignity of being attacked in the street paled into near-insignificance at that the policewoman engendered in him.

'Hey, wait a minute,' Alex interjected from the back seat, and the WPC struggled to talk over him and make herself and her own jobsworthy interpretation of the truth what the radio controller heard, inflaming Alex's temper tenfold more. 'I haven't apologised to anyone. I am the victim of the crime here.'

The radio and Alex's nerves crackled in competition, and an urgent message came through that a fight had broken out in St Mary Street, and they were the officers required to attend to the scene post haste.

'Sorry, sir, we have to drop you off here,' the PC urged, the car already coming to an abrupt halt. The fact that these uniforms might be all that stood in the way of someone ending the night in a hospital or worse was what got Alex out of their car, their attitude doing anything but.

He slammed the door of the vehicle to make his point at West Bow crossroads, barely out of the line of sight of those whom had shown no qualms about the idea of hospitalising him. As the car pulled away, siren blaring, Alex realised he had not noted the numbers on the officers' uniforms. Never mind, he would be able to lodge an official complaint with the facts denoting their indentities should he choose to do so. He wondered if he would.

The police disappeared from sight, the feral atmosphere of Bridgwater on a weekend night enveloping him in its heartlessness. He felt like he had been sucker-punched by far more than a thug in the street.

9

Daniel was sat on the sofa in his front room, watching a DVD of his favourite film, *2001: A Space Odyssey*, for what was probably the two-thousand-and-first time. Alex interrupted the intergalactic proceedings to speak of his own epic adventure through the alienation and black holes of the microcosmic town. Daniel seemed shocked, intrigued, and a little relieved to have been distracted from his own inner vacuum, and to learn that at least tonight his own luck wasn't the worst this side of the Milky Way.

'Sorry about the mess,' Daniel apologised, as if sensing it might be one more weight to add to the gravity of the return to England, to uncertainty, and to violence in Alex's world.

'I'm not paying it any attention,' Alex quite truthfully declared. Each man was sprawled out on a two-seater sofa, Alex having had to move a mountain of obsessively retained possessions in order to make this possible. Through a film of dust enough to cover The Moon, they gawked at the screen, at Hal 9000 and the doomed crew of the Discovery, Alex's eyes swapping stars for stars. Satellite gadgetry hovered around the mothership of the plasma screen. Techno add-ons banked like a space shuttle console, wires circulated like blood vessels galore. DVD discs formed towering columns, as out of their cases as they seemed to be control. Video cassettes, all unlabelled, none rewound, waited to be catalogued or shelved or even watched. Games consoles, remote controls, mother-, key- and circuit boards, monitors and disassembled plastic PC casing were a Dystopian panorama of a robot post-war. Unpaid bills, unopened letters, unread free newspapers, and the remains of all but uneaten takeaways formed gravity-defying piles around craters on unnavigatable terrain. A coffee table, poking out of the debris like a half-sunken launchpad, overflowed with dirtied plates spawning lifeforms previously undiscovered, teetered with dishes and ash-filled saucers on the verge of flying off, and papers and filters and butt ends and ash to suggest a tobacconists' had burned to the ground.

'Want another beer?' Daniel asked, holding up the remaining two thirds of a six-pack of room temperature Heineken.

It was about the least appealing variant on said beverage Alex could imagine, but he accepted one with gratitude, knowing as he did so he was well and truly back in Bridgwater town.

10

'So what's gone pear-shaped on Planet Daniel, Daniel?'

Daniel groaned, shifted in his slumped recline, looked like he desperately wanted to talk, and at the same time looked clueless as to how to begin. He rubbed his eyes as he spoke. 'Oh, I just don't know what to do, Alex. I've got no energy, I've got no confidence, I can't stand working at the shop anymore, I'm lonely, I don't want to stay in, I don't want to go out, I feel absolutely dissatisfied with my life, and I can't find either the motivation to make it better or a clear idea of what to do even if I did feel motivated. I keep taking the diazepam, I keep seeing my loony woman, I keep-'

'Loony woman?'

'Shrink. I can't sleep, I ache all over. Oh, it's just…I feel fucking awful, basically.'

'Well, there's plenty of options still available to you. Nervous breakdown, heroin addiction, suicide…'

Daniel managed a charitable wry laugh. 'Thank the lord for your words of wisdom. Feel free to stay as long as you like.'

'No, I'm not going to pretend to have some good advice for you right here and now, and I haven't exactly got enviable circumstances myself right at this moment, anyway. I'm sure we can do our usual bouncing ideas off each other and at least provide some sympathetic ears for a few days, though. I don't see it having any effect but a good one.'

Daniel sighed wearily. Onscreen, *2001* had moved aside for *Big Brother*, the fact almost having become more sinister than the fiction. 'Yeah, I suppose it will stop me from just watching the bloody TV and smoking myself to death and just wallowing in self-pity for a while. Anyway, as you said, I don't envy you. At least at the end of the day I've got this what is at least structurally a roof over my head and somewhere guaranteed as my place to hide away in whenever I need to. Take that away and I don't know what I'd do.'

'I don't know what I'm going to do. But I simply have to take it as fate that not having that is going to force me to get my act together.'

The lukewarm lager kept trickling, the cigarette smoke kept thickening, Alex's nerves settled as his pain subsided, Daniel slumped further in the cocooning cluttered couch. The time kept ticking, the world turned oblivious, and Alex and Daniel rewrote Orwell's prophecy, watching *Big Brother* so it need not watch them. Alex's quantum jumping senses teleported him to late tomorrow morning.

11

Alex awoke in the strong grip of a hangover, with a one-sided headache, as restless as he was fatigued. He lay that way for minutes, maybe hours, in need of water and aspirin and the toilet, but only ever succeeding at getting any of these in a dream.

At 88:88, 00:00 or 21:17, depending on which LCD readout on whichever item of techno-gadgetry that had pushed aside the three-dimensional two-handed clock he chose to believe, Alex woke up for real. The headache had followed him out of his nightmare, a dream that had proved as lingeringly unsettling as it was instantly forgettable. He did not feel nauseous however, at least for the while, so he took this as a good sign, pinning hope on it that his skull wasn't fractured after all. He got up off the sofa to empty his bladder before it carried out its threat to burst.

Daniel had clearly managed what Alex was about to attempt; the climb upstairs. Having exited the front room without stubbing a toe, cutting a foot, or being swallowed whole and alive by the years of detritus and whatever on earth might be lurking beneath, Alex met the challenge of the adjoining room with an emboldened and uninjured stride. The bottom of a right-angling staircase was somewhere in the corner here, but the nights were prolonged in this part of the house due to heavy curtains drawn across the window, cut off from reach by further unjunked junk.

The stairs were located, largely thanks to touch, and Alex proceeded up them, every second step creaking and squeaking in a way that must have been heard and felt in the houses either side. He futilely tiptoed his way to the bathroom, surely making it all but impossible for Daniel to sleep through the act. He made it inside, bolted the door, and turned on the light, steeled for whatever might face him. And steeling himself was something he had definitely needed to do.

It was a bachelor pad bathroom a Turner Prize winner could not have designed. Emptied shampoo bottles, discarded soapcake wrappers, and more toilet roll cardboard tubes than had been transformed into toy components in the entire history of *Blue*

Peter, lay either side of a vague trail to the toilet and washbasin. The linoleum was damp in places, sticky in others; one of Alex's socks had been instantly soaked, the other all but glued to the floor. Further socks appeared attached to the floorsurface, perhaps from others whom had dared this venture and left said footwear behind in order to make their escape. Boxer shorts were also strewn amongst the rubble, as if their soiled selves had slithered in here all on their own. Musty towels blanketed obstructions, laying like stones none dared turn. A dressing gown stretched out like a sheet over a corpse. Paperbacks propped open in puddles lay pulping their fictitious selves. An Arthur C Clarke, reprinted in 1996, set in 2010, lay rotting since 2001. Isaac Asimov trilogies joined the foundation of science fiction artefact. Douglas Adams poked out of the cluttered ground, his name the only thing revealed, like a sinking shrunken tombstone of the dead scribe. Philip K Dick, John Wyndham, Ray Bradbury, Frank Herbert; all waited in vain for the bathroom to be vacant of their broken-spined ghosts.

The bathtub was just high enough to be above the level of the sea of all the bathroom had seen. Green and yellow algae and scale luminesced more than the fluorescent light. A tap dripped, dripped, plinked, plopped, dropped, non-stop. The shower head lay discarded in the floor of the tub; twisted like a post-death, pre-death spasming, snake.

The washbasin had its taps almost inaccessibly obscured by remnants of hygiene control now a riot of rot and decay. Soapscum and pondscum made hybrids in the stagnant shallows. Toothpaste spillages adhered to the enamel like dessicated thrice- striped maggots. Used razor blades cut through the musty air; sprinkles of stubble dressed toothpaste maggots with caterpillar fur. The mirror was less functional than obscured; one's reflection was like an archaeological find. The cold dull tap dripped, plipped, tip-tapped, rapped out its torturous rhythmic rat-a-tat.

And then came the toilet itself. Oh god, the toilet. Alex wondered if there would be any way he could effectively and successfully use it without actually having to look at it at all. That idea proving seemingly impossible, he then wondered if he could actually look at it without seeing it.

With the insistent persuasion of his bodily functions, he finally brought himself to use it. He had been helpless to avoid using it, helpless to avoid seeing it. All he was left with was to pray he was not helpless to avoid thinking about it more than was necessary.

When Alex reached the kitchen, one glance told him there was a theme to be detected in the look of Daniel's rooms. Fortunately he managed to locate painkillers, and swallowed them with water from the kitchen taps. Gaining access to the first requirement of all life on earth had not required the intervention of the Red Cross International, although would have been good survival training for areas where water is not at all easy to find. Alex then set about washing up three or four thousand items of crockery and cutlery, filling a few dozen refuse sacks to capacity, and hacking through fungoid jungles sprouting forth from long left leftovers.

He returned at last to the living room with a cup of economy-priced coffee that no-one should have been forced to drink without being paid serious danger money, a pathetically thin pre-sliced toasted helping of white pointless bread, with a scraping of listeria-promising margarine and Marmite that appeared as old as Marmite was old.

He tried to work the TV with one of the countless remotes he could not help but find. The screen stayed stubbornly blank. He tried to reach the curtains to undraw them, but they were lost in the furthest out-of-reaches of the room. Alex sat in silence in the premature twilight zone, drinking bad coffee and eating crap toast.

Eventually he dozed again, to be woken hours later by the tortured creaking of Daniel's descent of the stairs.

12

' ' **R**ight.'
    ''Right.'
'Sleep alright?'
'Yeah, not too bad. And you?'
'Awfully.'
'Yeah, same as that.'
'So how d'you feel this morning, then?'
'I'm just about OK, I think. How about you?'
'I feel fucking awful.'
'Me too, mate.'
'Coffee?'
'Yeah, alright. I'll make it, though.'
'No, I'll make it.'
'No, no, I can make it, I can make it.'
'What d'you fancy doing today then?'
'I don't know, what do you fancy doing today?'
'Drive down to the coast?'
'Why not? It is Sunday, after all.'
'Isn't it bloody just, mate? Isn't it bloody just.'

13

They arrived in Exmouth mid-afternoon, the tourist attraction showing its bravest effort at being attractive to tourists. They circled the pay and display car park like rodeo riders in Daniel's Hyundai Pony, eventually agreeing that a three-hour ticket would prove ample to allow them to milk the burg of all its charm. They bought charred hamburgers in grease sponge buns, with onions and mustard that was yellow to the point of fluorescence. They perched on the sea wall with 99s, trying to avoid being mugged by the gulls. They eat rubbery cod and a few dozen chips from polystyrene trays. Kevin threw half of his away in disgust, Alex ate from hunger and the fact he had not had said meal in two months or more.

They watched families too young to be dysfunctional or too set in their ways to change put golf balls through clowns' mouths, between windmill arms and into holes in lieu of all the goals that they had always missed. Pedal boats in the shape of swans glided over a crowded pond, a fleeting flight of fancy to dilute the desire to migrate. Dogs urged their keepers up and down the seafront, as blatantly seeking stimuli as their owners discreetly did purpose. A wailing child blackmailed its mother into letting it ride in a car that went nowhere, save for the contents of its coin feed slot. Adolescents cruised past in sound distorting cars, forcing the street to listen to music designed for people for whom music is something they never really listen to. Young couples (strictly heterosexual, of course) held hands or entwined, further embracing Alex and Daniel with the solitude they felt inside. Teenagers minus parents relished the opportunity to feel older than their years, mentally escaping an age they would mourn for once they escaped. Pushchairs and wheelchairs commanded the pavement while the obese in plenitude commanded more.

Alex and Daniel sat themselves down on the sand, looking out at the pretend-its-the-sea, bathing in the English summer sun and wishing they had brought their coats. 'Well, at least it gets us out of Bridgwater for a few hours,' Daniel offered with something like embarrassment.

'It's good to get out of Somerset for a few hours too, although don't you always tend to think of Devon as permanently feeling like a Sunday?'

'It's a good job we picked today to come here then. I suppose you're still on a bit of a high from Spain, though, aren't you?'

'I was until last night.' Alex touched the tender spot at the back of his head.

'What are you going to do about work then?'

'I'll go back to the agencies tomorrow. I'll just take on any old rubbish for a few weeks, squirrel it away and try to find somewhere new to escape to for a while.'

'Where do you want to go next?'

'I really don't know, Daniel. You know me. I don't plan my life, I let life plan me, and that always seems to produce the best results.'

The pair were watching a sailboat cross the water, its metal fixtures glinting in the sun. 'Christ, I wish I had your confidence,' Daniel confided.

'What confidence? Daniel, I don't know whether I'm coming or going, and I haven't got a clue what lies ahead. If it wasn't for the charity of someone like you right now I might be literally sleeping on the streets. I don't want to think about how my life has changed. But I suppose, I hope, the only way is up from here.'

Daniel fished a pouch of tobacco and papers from his shirt pocket. His long thin face studied the apparatus, something smouldering inside him and eating away at his joy like a cancer. 'But at least you can embrace change. It's like you've always managed to fall on your feet whenever you've looked like you had fallen into a rut. You've done your travelling, you've done your working abroad. You seem strong and optimistic. If there's something you really want to do, you're the kind of person who will find a way to do it.'

'Not without a struggle, Daniel. And what achievements have I really managed to achieve anyway? It's all experiences, memories, not that there's anything wrong with that, because that's all that life is made up of anyway. But I've got absolutely nothing to show for my thirty-five years of existence. A few hundred pounds in the bank, full stop. Nowhere to live. No relationship. No possessions.

No strong family base or any particular sense of truly belonging anywhere. No job, no real education, not in any official sense. I'm just a loser at the end of the day. You have a roof over your head, you have a car, you have life savings in the bank. You've got a better base on paper by far from which to do something with your life.'

'But what? What am I going to do? I feel ill all the time, I lack energy. I don't have the confidence to go and meet new people or discover new places, I've hardly been out of Bridgwater my whole life, and it feels late in the day to change my habits now.'

'But if you're not happy with your life as it is right now, what have you got to lose? You don't need to make whopping big changes all of a sudden, just set yourself small goals to begin with, take yourself out of your comfort zone one step at a time. Confidence is like a muscle, yes? We have to gradually build it up, bit by bit.'

'Shit!' It wasn't a comment on Alex's monologue, at least as far as he hoped. The tobacco Daniel had been preparing for smoking had just been sucked up by a passing gust of wind. 'I don't know, Alex. It all sounds so easy to say, for you. But it still seems like parting the Red Sea to put into practice.'

'So does getting out of bed early. Or surviving an eight-hour shift. Or spring cleaning a house. Or learning to use a computer or mobile phone for the first time. Or making love and satisfying a woman. But none of it is really so difficult when we stop thinking about it and actively start doing it. Doing something is always a million times easier than wondering how you're going to get it done. That's elementary.'

Daniel groaned, having finished composing his cigarette at last. 'I suppose…But…'

'I can't roll a cigarette, Dan. I've tried countless times but just don't have the knack. That doesn't mean it's impossible. You know infinitely more about computers than I do. You know infinitely more about astronomy than probably anyone I know. Nothing's really ever as far out of reach as we like to convince ourselves it is, is it? It's only the reaching for it that's the difficult part, much more so than the getting it.'

A frisbee sailed over their heads, turned in a graceful arc above the sand, then returned to its thrower like a boomerang.

'What I need's a girlfriend,' Daniel suggested, blowing smoke into the wind.

'Don't we all? And we're both pretty prime catches at the moment, aren't we?'

'I'm in no fit state to have a relationship right now, I know that.'

'Well, I'm not in much of a position to have a relationship myself either. I think if you work on yourself, everything else follows incidentally.'

'To you, maybe.'

'To anyone. But let's consider the facts again; who's in the best set of circumstances right now.'

'Well, you're not ill, you've got the confidence to get out there in the world, and you don't have a job that's giving you a nervous breakdown.'

'You could quit or change the job, if you really wanted to. Your health would probably benefit as a consequence, as well as your confidence. After that, you develop each of these like a muscle, bit by bit, step by step, as we already talked about.'

Daniel picked up a large piece of flint from the beach, turned it over in his hands, then threw it in the direction of the waves. 'Fancy making a move back then, soon?'

'I suppose. It's getting cold.'

'What you doing tonight then? Labour Clubbing it?'

'I suppose. One more night of non-stop euphoria before getting back to the grinding wheel. You too?'

'Yeah, I suppose I'll brave it again. Let's hope it's a slightly better, and safer, night for us both tonight.'

'Yes. Let's hope indeed.'

14

After dining on shish kebabs, with a scorching overdose of chilli sauce, rich and rubbery forcemeat lamb, and oily sodden pitta bread, the pair eventually managed to drag themselves and for the large part their protesting stomachs to the Labour Club for further self-punishment. It having gone ten before they arrived, they entered through a curtain of smoke and resentment and sat themselves down among everyone else who hated the Labour Party.

'What have you two been up to today then?' Patrick asked them as they were trying to get comfortable.

'Went down to the coast,' Daniel answered, with a shrug.

'What, down in Devon?'

'Yeah, Exmouth.'

'Oh, nice there, innit?'

'Something to do,' Daniel remarked, with a further shrug.

'You have a good day down in Exmouth today then, Alex?'

'The best day in England I've had in months, Patrick.'

Patrick lightly chuckled, thinking about why he was doing so as he did so.

'And what have you done today, Patrick?'

'Spent it down my mum's, of course.'

'Of course.'

'Here, Alex. You hear about the blonde who went to the gynaecologist?' Ian Scott spoke.

'Oh god, not this one again,' Daniel groaned, rubbing his forehead.

'Oh no,' even Patrick cringed. When Ian Scott was in joke telling mode, there were usually two guarantees. One, the joke would be awful, and two, it would be the first of at least a dozen.

'No, but I cannot wait, Ian.'

'This woman goes to the gynaecologist, and says, "Excuse me, Doctor, every time I have sex it causes me a lot of pain. So the doctor has a quick look at her, can't see anything wrong, so he gives her a tube of lubricant.'

Patrick said, 'Oh no,' again, but this time it wasn't because of Ian's joke.

'One week later the woman's back to see the gynaecologist. She said I'm using the lubricant but it still really hurts me to have sex.'

'Oh god,' said Daniel, for the same reason Patrick had said oh no.

'So the doctor has another look at her, can't see anything wrong, and this time he gives her a muscle relaxant.'

'Yes,' Alex urged patiently, turning in his seat to see what had caught Patrick and Daniel's attention.

'The next week the woman's back *again*. She says, "Doctor, I've been using the lubricant and I've been taking the muscle relaxant but it still really hurts me to have sex.".'

An extremely large man had entered the club, with a bald head and an unsteady swagger. He did not look athletically big, but fat big and at the same time somehow solid, a hulking monster of a human being. Whoever he was, he did not look friendly and he did not look like he wanted to be ignored. Alex wanted to enquire about the identity of this newcomer, but Ian was still spinning out his joke, and Alex was in just too polite a mood to stop him in his tracks.

'So the doctor asks her to take her clothes off again. He asks her if she's taken the muscle relaxant today, she says yes, she's taken it. He gets the lubricant and smears it all over her, then he takes his own clothes off and starts giving her one.'

There was some commotion coming from behind Alex, and he turned to see the giant being steadied on his feet – no easy task - apparently having fallen against somebody sat upon a stool at the bar.

'So he keeps on giving her one, she's moaning and licking her lips and shouting more more harder harder and he's thinking he's well away here. So he does her missionary style, doggy style, on top, underneath, you name it they do it and it goes on for about two hours, the best sex either of them have ever had.'

'Christ, he's worse than he was the other night,' Patrick commented, continuing his rapt appraisal of the theatre taking place behind Alex.

'Eventually they finish, lie on his couch smoking a cigarette, and he asks her how it felt. She tells him just fantastic, she never knew sex could feel so good. So he thinks, OK, this woman's obviously cured. So as she's putting her clothes back on he says to her, "So howcome if you were using the lubricant and the muscle relaxant the same as with me, howcome it kept on hurting you to have sex?".'

'Oh god, please tell me he's not coming over here.' Daniel muttered.

'"It hurt me 'cause I kept on getting upset.", she says. "Upset?" the doctor goes. "Yeah it upsets me with every man I've been with for the last month. With every man I've been with for the last month it's been the same.".

'He is. He's coming over here.' Patrick intimated. Alex felt his back itching with tension.

'"In what way has it been upsetting for you?" he asks. "Well," she says, "every time I've had sex with someone this past month, within twenty four hours of shagging me their dick's turned green and fallen off.".'

Alex closed his eyes and sighed. An enormous sausage-fingered dinner plate of a hand landed hard and heavy on his shoulder.

15

Alex turned his head to get a good look at the man that had just become the rest of the universe. The rest of the universe seemed to look down upon Alex as if he were nothing more than a speck in the cosmos, which was exactly how he felt right then. The man's head was as starkly large as it was bald. Small piggish eyes squealed with animal instinct, staring like a frightened beast trapped inside that ruddy meatheaded face. A frown and a sneer had joined together in a cruel wrinkle at the bridge of the broken nose. Snorts of breath escaped his mouth and nose in ragged pants, the bellowing of a bull about to charge. The little of the teeth Alex could see surely spent much of their time clenched together in a barely-controllable rage. The stubby neck, almost as thick as the head and the skin, fused with a mass of muscle and lard and gristle inside the uniform of the closet homosexual, thug, Neo-Nazi, and, just occasionally, simple soccer fan: an England football shirt. 'Ooz this? George fuckin' Michael, innit?' he mocked, in ill humour posing as good humour that was actually bad humour, indicating Alex's liberal growth of stubble. He pinched his cheek between white puddings of a thumb and forefinger to make his joke clearer and slyly cause just enough pain for it to be uncomfortable for Alex. 'Innit, ey? George fuckin' Michael?' He was looking around at the others cosmetically for agreement but clearly wanting to intimidate them into it. Everyone else was pretending to be the only person there who hadn't noticed the newcomer yet. 'Oo're you then?' was demanded of Alex.

In a flat, dispassionate tone that sounded as if it had not been delivered to answer the question cum interrogation, he simply said, 'My name is Alex.' He didn't bother asking the stranger for his own name.

'Alex? *Alex??* Bit of a gay name, innit?'

Alex's gorge threatened to rise. *I get assaulted for walking down the street, now I can't even sit in my local.* He was sure the redness he felt in his cheeks was as much due to mounting anger as increasing embarrassment.

'Oim Bob.' He held his hand up to shake in the manner a stick-up artist would show you his gun.

Alex found himself reaching for it as if in a trance. Of course, he did not want to shake the proffered hand that looked like it was itching to form a fist, but this didn't look like the kind of guy who would take it in his stride were Alex to politely refuse to give him his own. People like this guy did not play by fair rules, and did not listen to reason. Alex expected his hand to be gripped roughly, but what he got was his wrist grasped by an iron cuff-like forefinger and thumb, to be retained for however long this intimidating colossus pleased, which would likely fall just shy of all of eternity.

''andsome lad, inner?' he looked around at his captive, in the wrong way, audience. Most of them were grimacing and squirming in a manner that tried to hide what they were so obviously doing. Alex was aware that all talk behind him had ceased as well. He was now the focal point in the room. How wonderful. When any kind of confrontation occurs, when anyone does something obnoxious or victimising or humiliating in any way, it is always the person they are doing it to that people are most interested in having a gawk at. 'Inner, eh?' he repeated, as an order.

'He's alright. He ain't no harm,' Patrick commented, trying to calm the man and managing to be the most socially adept person present for once. Alex's hand remained securely surrendered, and he was dimly aware of the three fat fingers not being used to encircle and crush his wrist semi-surreptitiously fondling his sweating palm. He was also aware the man was swaying as he stood there, leaning forward now, putting his face close to Alex's, swaying in a way that had those around the table picking up their glasses and cradling them in their hands, just in case the brick wall came tumbling down.

''e's alright, iz er? You ear that, young un? You'm alright you iz, you ain't no 'arm.' Alex's cheek was given a testing and anything but playful squeeze again. This time it burned with pain as much as embarrassment. ''ow come I ain't seen *you* in 'ere before then?' The man's left arm thumped down over his shoulders like a leg of lamb, then squeezed and insinuated itself like a boa constrictor.

Alex took a deep breath, desperately trying to stay as relaxed as he could. 'I haven't been around for a while. I haven't seen you here before either.' As soon as he had got the second sentence out, he wondered if it had been wise. The last thing he wanted to be with this crowbarring insinuator was anything that might be interpreted as conversational.

'Oi've been comin' 'ere for months, oi 'ave,' the man who could only be thought of as Big Bob declared, vainly trying to pull rank. Alex was used to this kind of pathetic pecking order in the club. He had disappeared from Bridgwater for a year here, a year there, several times, and every time he returned to the town and this club, there were always grizzled regulars who were either too addled to remember his face or that had joined the club within that twelve month period and wanted to parade their delusion that they were there first, presumably what was necessary in order for them to make themselves feel somehow important. Alex had been visiting the club since its opening day a few decades ago, but it was anything but a fact that he considered a badge of honour. 'Ain't oi, Pat?' he insisted Patrick confirm for him, erroneously assuming the nickname no-one among Patrick's friends used would further elevate his rank.

Patrick remained on good form. After looking genuinely thoughtful for a moment, he confirmed as matter-of-factly as he dared, 'I guess it must be a couple of months now, Bob, yeah.'

'Yeah, see?' the man must have been floating somewhere between a hard drinking, hard living forty and fifty years, the parameters of guessable age blurred by self-destruction and universal loathing, but possessed the emotional capacity of a delinquent child. 'Where you bin then?' It was about three hairs away from 'What you lookin' at?'.

Alex heard himself mumble a hurried, 'I've been working abroad for the summer. I just got back.' Why was he telling this obnoxious stranger any of this? What was the right thing to do here? How manageable was doing the right thing anyway?

'Abroad? *Abroad??* Where's that then??'

Having little clue as to how to accurately interpret the question, Alex blurted out an 'I was in Spain.' His hand was still very much now a belonging of Big Bob, still very much a toy to be secretly fondled, as if this man were daring him to draw attention to the fact.

'In Spain, 'ey?' he leaned in closer still to Alex, and Alex tried to lean out of the way a little at the same time. 'You bin in Spain, 'ave 'e?' He looked around at everyone else in the bar, not just those at Alex's table, as if he hoped to win some solidarity with his mocking tone. In fact, all anyone else was interested in was the theatre of Alex's squirming and hoping like hell they would not be Big Bob's next victim. 'You wanna know where oi bin 'fore a few month ago?'

Alex was silent, as still and composed as an intimidated man with his hand in the clutches of an ogre could be i.e. blushing and with a subtle case of the shakes.

'Well, oi'll tell 'e. Oi been in prison. 'artcliffe, mate,' he added, referring to Hartcliffe, a prison in the same named district of Bristol, an estate that even a town with such a rough reputation as Bridgwater could only aspire to. Alex was certainly not going to ask Big Bob why he had been locked up there. 'And now oi'm out,' he informed Alex for the benefit of the entire club, clearly not taking any chances that someone might have failed to notice this. He grabbed a firm hold of Alex's cheek again, waggling the painfully pinched flesh. 'Proper George Michael, innit?' He bombastically bombarded the bar with his own forced laughter. 'Ere, oi could do with you tonight, at home with me in moi bed, y' know.' At this point no-one else could bear to look or knew where to look, and just like Alex, no spectator had much clue what to think about this. Alex simply remained silent and as dispassionate as he could, riding the agonising moment out. 'Yeah, oi could do wi' e tonight oi could.' The hand that had clenched his face, the one not clenching his wrist, began moving up and down his spine, slowly and deliberately and disgustingly, while his ensnared palm continued feeling like a fat spider were crawling about on it. Alex had no idea at all where the virtual assailant's narrative was going, and he held his breath as each syllable was delivered. 'Yeah. Oi ain't gay, it's just me telly's remote's broken, and oi can't be bothered to keep gettin' in and outta bed t' change channel.' The laughter that escaped that loud wide mouth this time came with a wind tunnel blast of nauseatingly bad breath. As if that were not insufferable enough, the laugh quickly mutated into a phlegmy wretching cough that threatened to shower Alex's closed-eyed turned away face with all manner of bodily fluids, and followed through on at least some of them. The hand that threatened to drop off remained in the tourniquet grip.

Tonight's barman, and reluctant landlord of the club, Simon Dickson, moved in for the rescue. 'Bob, if you want that round of pool, I've just about got time for it now.' Simon Dickson was about as unthreatening a man as could be encountered, and wouldn't win a pop psychologist award of any year, but his manner, unfazed and straightforward, plus the fact so many depended upon him not banning them from the club so they could keep on the town's cheap cider, meant that when he spoke folk listened.

'Looks like oi gotta go, young 'un. What's yer name again?'

'Alex,' Alex said. *It's a bit gay innit?*

'Say what?' One hand remained climbing and crawling up and down his back, the other doing something to his hand too insensitive to feel it any more.

'Alex,' he repeated, in a borderline shout that took even him by surprise.

'George, you say? George? Yeah, oi thought so. Well, oil leave 'e alone, the top man wants t' ave a game with me.'

'Better come now, Bob, if you want that game,' Simon Dickson reiterated, extremely welcomely and helpfully for Alex.

'Right, gentlemen 'n' ladies,' he emphasised the last word whilst leaning in toward Alex again, giving his cheek a final bit of destruction testing. 'You 'ave a good night. Oi'm gonna 'ave me a game.' He swatted Alex an open-handed clout on the back as he left, forcing the recipient of the gentlemens' friendly gesture to all but go sprawling onto the table before him. As Big Bob finally took his hulking self and presence away, Alex's bruising back began to smart with the blow it had received.

'You alright there, Alex?' Patrick enquired, once he felt it was safe to do so.

'Wonderful, Patrick.' Alex wanted all attention and eyes off him at long last, to at least give his burning red face a chance to cool down a little. Realising that wasn't likely to happen in a hurry, he decided he might as well find out who Big Bob was in slightly more detail. As it turned out, he had joined the club at roughly the time that Alex had been living and working in Prague for a year, done some time in prison when Alex had returned, been in and out of the club again at the time Alex was spending a year in the US, been back to his jailbird haunt again and again released whilst Alex had been in Spain. He had joined after being introduced by another club member, had seemed at least acceptable at first, then had quickly proven himself to be an obnoxious and confrontational bully and pain. Thus far he had yet to overstep the line enough to get barred from the club, which short of murdering the landlord – and even then, of course – almost never happened to anyone. There were two rumours in circulation about Big Bob, whom no-one seemed quite certain of the surname of: one, that he had served a life sentence for murder, and two, that he was ex-SAS and a very potential and able killing machine. The talk then, predictably and understandably enough, turned to Alex revealing his far from pleasant experiences of the night before on his way home from the club.

'Christ, you've had a rough return all in all, haven't you?' Patrick sympathised.

But no-one at that moment could predict just how rough it was going to get.

16

Monday morning arrived in its usual gatecrashing style, spoiling the weekend for everyone. Alex forced himself to get up off the uninviting don't-look-too-closely mattress and duvet-minus-a-cover on the floor of Daniel's spare room while it was still a.m., and finally managed to throw himself out on the street in the direction of employment agencies' offices.

Through an almost discreet entrance in Fore Street, Alex climbed a seedy looking stairway as if entering a Soho walk-up, and made his first visit to Bayley's. A Slovak girl with a tenuous grasp of English and a cleavage it was impossible to ignore had clearly been appointed this week's receptionist. Because Alex had not worked for Bayley's for over six months, the in-house rule was that he fill out all his details again on a labyrinthine form obviously designed by someone who thrived on tedium. None of his details had changed save for his two months in Spain, but despite several attempts to convince them all they needed to do was refer to the details already on record, the rule was apparently as inflexible as it was illogical. Alex managed to get the Slovak to haul one of the back office employees in to see him, where she unconvincingly informed him his old details had been shredded. Realising reason was not a currency these institutions were accustomed to dealing with, Alex managed to get the seemingly interminable form filled out with half-truths, minus supporting evidence which he knew they would forget about in a few days anyway, in order they might offer him work folding cardboard boxes or putting labels onto bottles; work for which they were sure to refer to such details before offering.

Red Arrow thankfully did not have the same in-house policy as Bayley's, and instead went for the theatrical camaraderie we're-your-best-friend-oh-where-have-you-been amateur dramatics bonhomie approach before farming out those on their books to deathtrap sweatshops. They listened to his definite no-nos and vague preferences before feeding him the trademark line of there's-not-much-on-the-books-at-the-moment, trying to soften him up to take any old rubbish they could throw at him, which he realised he would likely end up accepting anyway.

Recruitment West asked if he would like to take an IT skills test, being that Alex considered himself overqualified for blue-collar work and underqualified for the white- variety, just to see if he wasn't better than he thought he was. Seeing as an old friend worked for the agency, they were able to let him take the test there and then. A series of thirty multiple-choice questions and minor tasks flashed up on the screen for him to battle though in thirty minutes. He managed the first four before getting stuck in a process he could not fathom and being clueless as to how to get out of it. After clicking the mouse on every available icon, then experimentally tapping each key to see if it would somehow make something come to his rescue, he stared at the stubbornly merciless screen for five minutes, then stared out the window for five more. Frustration and indignity tightened his jaws. Tail between his legs, he returned to reception to admit his failure and suggest they might try rescuing the PC he seemed to have upset almost as much as it had upset him. Warehouses and production lines for you, my boy, he could almost read behind the receptionist's conciliatory smile.

For good measure, he phoned a Taunton agency he had done a few jobs with, trying to convince himself that menial soul-destroying tasks among the most proletarian of the proletariat would somehow be less depressing in the county capital, though in practice grunt work was simply what the label claimed it was.

Late afternoon a secretary of Red Arrow contacted him to chirpily share the wonderful news he could spend the next two weeks working the graveyard shift making plastic moulds for a whole pound over the minimum wage. Better still, he could start this very night, which in fact was basically mandatory unless he wanted the pleasure to go to someone even more pathetically desperate. He gritted his teeth, reached down deep inside, and told them that yes, he was willing to do what he had once never believed he would ever entertain the likes of doing no matter how low he sunk.

A few garage-bought borderline edible sandwiches and junk food in his bag, enough caffeine in his blood to wake the dead, and with a heart that felt as heavy as it was frenetic, Alex arrived at

SharPak, in the poorly-illuminated heartless heart of a pointlessly named industrial estate. Lucky, lucky Alex.

17

The door to SharPak was closed and locked. There was no doorbell. A security keypad was located next to the door, a device for which Alex had not been provided the code. He tried knocking at the door a few times, but the grinding, hammering, screeching noises of heavy and, by the sounds of it, outdated machinery inside suggested knocking was a futile exercise, and anyone who had spent any amount of time working here was probably deaf by now anyway. He had arrived a few minutes early, having had difficulty locating the address. 22:00, the start time, came and went. 22:14 arrived, and Alex had decided that if another minute passed without someone letting him in, he would turn tail, say a private prayer of thanks, and run like hell away. No such luck. At the crunch time, a group of workers made their exit, and Alex gingerly stepped inside, wondering if he would even survive an hour in such a place.

The first ten minutes inside the building Alex spent as The Invisible Man. A vague and unstaffed cupboard-like office stood next to a brilliantly-illuminated lime-green-painted canteen in which it would have been impossible to hide, and surely no-one would want to anyway. Huge mechanical constructions, twenty or thirty or more, filled the shopfloor, with just enough room for forklifts to barrel through between them, which they did, taking blind corners with blind faith. Several workers attended some of the machines, none of them seeming to notice or care that Alex was stood watching them. Asking someone for guidance was something Alex deemed unrealistic for two reasons. One, he did not want to be macerated by forklifts, and he wondered how anyone possibly avoided this fate as he watched their surely illegally reckless handling. Secondly, this factory was, without doubt of any kind whatsoever, the loudest environment Alex had ever been in.

Cacophonous did not cut it. It was painful, literally painful. The thin shell of the building vibrated with abject noise pollution. There was thudding and grinding, shunting and hissing. There was an immediate atavistic response to the sensory overload and assault that, through casual observation of the employees he was able to see, everyone else was impossibly completely oblivious to. Most of them, he noticed, wore no ear defenders. Surely it must be company policy that such a simple and necessitated practice be mandatory? The very worst sound of all was a rhythmic squealing that reached a pitch that made Alex wince to hear it. It seemed to hit at a bone-deep, primal level that rattled the very psyche. It occurred around every thirty seconds and he could not help but anticipate each repetition, bracing himself each time it came. It was sonic weaponry these people were operating, whatever else it might be in the name of providing some kind of service.

Smell was also impossible to ignore, although greatly overhadowed by the fact Alex thought his hearing must surely be receiving irreparable damage by the minute. Ozone, oil, metal and hot plastic cloyed the air, whilst an undertone of chemicals and solvents offered the promise of fast-accumulating toxicity. A cat would probably die here due to the aural barrage, a dog would likely be instantly sick as its acute sense of smell registered poison after poison. Two weeks here? Would he manage one shift? Would he stay beyond the first break? In fact, it was looking like no-one would notice if he were here or not.

'Agency?' someone barked from behind him, and he jumped. He felt instantly belittled at his response, but assured himself the man who had shouted at him must have done so at quite a volume to be heard at all.

Alex nodded, and said 'yes' for the benefit of lipreaders alone.

The man cocked a thumb in the direction of the office and entered it. Alex interpreted this as an instruction to follow him. Inside the office the man indicated the need to wear a white hat that seemed to be made of felt, presumably to stop contamination of the moulded plastic by hairs. Alex tried to explain he had arrived on time but had not been able to enter the premises, but the man he was talking to, a thin bald checked-shirt and jeans wearing figure around Alex's age, seemed neither to hear nor care. Besides this, even with the office door closed, it was all but impossible to make oneself heard anyway.

The man, presumably a supervisor or shift manager, marched

to a machine with Alex in tow at the far end of the complex. Alex was looking this way and that like The Green Cross Code Man on speed as he weaved his way through the Industrial Age monstrosities, his back itching as he feared a forklift would come speeding from around every corner like a stegosaur, while trying to keep up with the man who seemed utterly without hesitation as he led Alex to whatever fate awaited him up ahead.

Somehow, both men got to a machine alive and, at least bar their hearing, untouched. The machine already had two people busying themselves frantically at its controls, a teenage male and a woman around forty, both of them wearing blue overalls which for some reason were emblazoned with their names, Justin and Denise. The non-overalled man asked, 'Woz yer name?' at Alex several times before he could be heard, and Alex told him several times before the information could be understood. He was left with the overalled pair, who ignored him for a few minutes as they primed the machine to do whatever it was supposed to do, but not before Alex asked for some earplugs or somesuch device. Illustrations instructing employees to wear ear protection were posted on every machine, but every worker visible illustrated ignorance of such vital good advice. Alex understood, as best he could, that ear protection would be fetched for him.

Finally, Denise communicated with barely heard shouts and gesticualtion that Alex would need to line up square-shaped transparent plastic dishes in something like a metal trough, then bag them in tubular black sacks and stack them in a waiting deep cardboard box. All manner of questions started to come out of Alex's mouth, the first an enquiry as to how many such trays should be bagged together, but a dismissive wave of the hand and a 'You'll get the hang uv it,' were clearly all the elucidation a rookie plastics packer needed.

Try and try again, Alex never managed to do what was required of him. He was ever unclear of how many trays to stack at once, the bags refused to open in his fumbling fingers, and the arrangement of the bags in the box became a mess. He lasted half an hour on the machine, annoying Denise nearly as much as she annoyed him, never managing to do whatever was expected of him, in part due to the impossibility of accurately distinguishing human speech from the other omnipresent noises, and partly for a sad fact that Alex had gleaned from the several short-term jobs he had already done in the name of agency work. Too many blue-collar workers, it seemed, lack the skill or the inclination to articulate a lucid instruction. They had often been doing the same job for year after year, or decade after decade, and considered themselves indeed professionals at their unaspiring careers, but ask them to explain what it was they did, day in day out, and the idea of communicating this information in a simple and intelligible sentence was something that perversely seemed never to have occurred to them. Alex was no petit-bourgeois snob, and had in fact been born to working-class parents, but he felt no class loyalty because this was what experience had taught him was grass roots lower-class behaviour and thinking. Whilst despising exploitation of those at the least-affluent end of the social strata, he could not help but feel the last people he would be comfortable with having any real grip on power were the wilfully ignorant, self-destructive and artlessly offensive herds who tolerated this kind of neverending lifestyle, which he did not buy most of them did through necessity at all.

After one of the longest half hours of his life, during which the noise and olfactory pollution threatened to be overshadowed by the antipathy emanating like radioactive ectoplasm from Denise, Alex was ordered to take his first break, extremely impolitely and with the jabbing of a thumb in the canteen's direction.

There were three other men already on their break, all blue-overalled, white-capped clones, all seemingly uniformly post-lobotomised as their conversations speedily screamed forth. A resentful inflammatory looking powderkeg of a Bridgwater male youth was brusquely flipping through a copy of The Sun in disdain. A small-built drone droned on and on in a nasally voice, ceaselessly broadcasting his racist, sexist, homophobic, pro-violence and ridiculously unfounded opinions with as little self-consciousness as self-regard. An obese bespectacled man seemed to serve as a sidekick stooge to the former, staring vacantly into space while giving the illusion of listening, bleating a yes from time to time to encourage the ceaselessly nauseating patter.

'Oi read in there that they 'ad to pay fer a plane to take one asylum seeker back t' where 'e came from. They 'ad to pay fer a 'ole plane outta aar money to send one o' they back!' the oblivious Nazi chuffed, the tabloid he was referring to not having to wish for a more malleable reader of their blatantly racial-hatred inciting slander.

'What would you 'a' done with 'en?' Sun reader muttered, without glancing up from the rag.

'Asylum seeker? *Asylum seeker??* I'd o' put a bomb on the plane, oi woulda. Or chucked 'en out over the ocean without a parachute.'

'Yeah, but maybe he could swim,' Sun reader further provoked.

'Oh, oida made sure it were shark-infested, moind.'

Alex bit his tongue, but didn't know whether not to do this, for his and everyone else in the world's sake. He found himself wondering if any unwitting successful asylum seekers had ever found themselves in here, and sat through a similar conversation.

The half hour proved almost, or perhaps even more, tough on the ears than the tinnitus-inducing mechanised abominations of human rights on the shopfloor. Whingeing about money soon became the principal topic for discussion, but racism and gross presumption were hardly off the agenda. Alex somehow sat through 'Course these days, you want money, all you gotta do is put a load o' black boot polish over yer face, march down the social, 'n' they're bloody chuckin' the stuff at you.'. This, Alex could not help but fume, must be extraordinary news to every black person in the country, as well as every employee of the social services.

Sun reader stood up, his own break evidently over. He returned his paper to his locker, despite requests from the drone to borrow it to read it, or whatever people did with The Sun and if anyone in possession of it were actually capable of reading. 'Fuck off, mate, oi bought that, it's mine. Anyone wants to read the paper, they cun buy one themselves.'

Alex drained the last of his banana milk, a product to which milk and banana seemed to be added to the ingredients as a mere afterthought, and stared into a bare corner of the canteen, seeing there nothing at all.

Just before his break was done, Alex went searching for someone who could provide him some ear protection. The shift manager, or whatever his role was supposed to be, looked up furtively from some paperwork as Alex entered the office without knocking. 'How's it looking with those earplugs?' Alex hollered. He couldn't be bothered with deference any longer, and doubted if he would remain here beyond tonight's shift anyway.

'Yeah, I'll get a pair for you, mate,' was yelled back, the same thing Alex had heard, or thought he heard, an hour earlier.

'I'd really prefer to have a pair before I start back on the machines.' He used his body language as persuasively as he could, and the man with the thankless job title eventually acquiesced and set about finding some. Five minutes later he returned to the office and handed Alex a set of what looked like bright blue plastic headphones, with prominent yellow balls of foam designed to sit over the earholes. Trying to trade dignity for hearing, he tried them on and was stunned at how useless they proved to be. Clearly it was a legal requirement for ear protection to be kept on the premises, but by obviously choosing the cheapest possible, the sound levels must surely significantly exceed the legal limit even when the so-called protection was worn. Alex sniffed a slimy company oozing their way through a legal loophole, then reluctantly made it back alive to the world of Denise and Justin and unfathomable unbearable tasks.

'You ain' on 'ere any more, mate,' Denise hissed, as if to let him know she had personally ensured that were the case.

'Thank the lord for that,' Alex said out loud, without any reason to be cautious.

Alex's next job was working on another hulking piece of metal and grease that looked like it had been around since the time of Brunel. Charlie, someone who had apparently been working there for twelve years and wore no ear protection, showed him how to stack a different shape of plastic tray, the type designed for microwave meals, bag and box these up, with at least slightly less attitude if no more command of his mother language. Alex was monitored for five minutes, seemed to almost have the hang of it, then was left all on his own. Another five minutes passed and the machine malfunctioned. Alex attracted the attention of someone wearing red overalls and looking like one of the plant's engineers/mechanics. The engineer looked at the rows of dials and readouts that would have made a pilot dizzy, then inspected the drums and moulds and plastic film and whatever else was needed to make this torture device exist. Clearly a problem had been located, for the engineer/mechanic let Alex know he had accurately diagnosed whatever the trouble was, using textbook techno-jargon as if he had written the machine's instruction manual himself. 'I don' fuckin' believe it. Look what some fuckin' cunt's been and done there.'

Having zero interest in what the mechanic did or did not fuckin' believe, and in what someone, fuckin' cunt or otherwise, might or might not have done, Alex waited patiently for the problem to be over and the plastic trays to be regurgitated onto the feed belt post haste yet again, one after the other after the other, over and over and over and over, yippee.

'Keep yer eye on it, oim gonna go an' 'ave a fag,' Charlie said, after reporting back for thirty some seconds to make sure Alex could cope. A further five minutes and the machine ceased functioning again. At least it broke up the monotony, or replaced it with another kind. This time no mechanic was in site and, as forklifts were tearing past unheeding, Alex decided to sit tight until someone who knew more about SharPak, and possibly less about everything else on Planet Earth, came into view and could be signalled to.

He waited until Charlie returned, who took one glance at the seemingly unreadable machine, then frantically signalled to his colleagues who came dashing to his aid. Some adjustments were hastily made, but not before Charlie shot Alex a 'I thought you wuz s'posed t' be keepin' an eye on it!?' Obviously it had been a piece of advice Alex had incorrectly, incompetently, and non-telepathically, fallen short of heeding. Another man rushed up to snarl at Alex. 'You could've made the machine explode!' How heartbreaking that would have been, he eventually managed to muse when the shock of this had passed. And clearly the effect this would have had on the machine was of infinite more import than that it would have had on the body of an insignificant agency stooge who just happened to be standing beside it at the time. ''ave another break, mate,' the slightly more clear-headed shift manager suggested, presumably in order to prevent those working under him from doing to Alex what the machine had not.

The third bout of would be working was the final straw. Alex was kept at a safe distance from everyone else and on a machine that was simply too fast by far for him to properly match pace with. Denise, whose name he was also required to stamp onto labels, latched onto this as she pseudo-incidentally vibed her way past. 'You can't go letting 'em [referring to the plastic trays] build up like that!' she lectured through her sneer, further preventing him from attempting to work the thing and thus force him to get even further and hopelessly behind. 'You'll 'ave t' try 'arder 'n that!'

'I'm already trying as hard as I can!' Alex yelled back. He continued seeing her name as he furiously stamped it onto labels. Denise Everidge. Denise Everidge. Denise Everidge. Denise-

'Well, it ain't good enough. You'll 'ave t' try 'arder!'

'I can't try any harder than as hard as I can,' he pointed out to her, a fact she had clearly been daydreaming through during this life school's elementary lesson.

'Well, it ain't good enough!' She all but elbowed him out of the way and took over at the machine herself, trying to belittle him with the amazing swiftness and precision she performed the tasks he had so struggled with; a talent that must have taken plenty of dedication to the most mundane aspects of wasting one's life.

'I'm going to the toilet a minute,' Alex half-shouted, half-muttered, needing an urgent time out and not checking to see if he had been heard or his stepping out approved of. He arrived at the door of the toilet, then found himself walking straight past it, and past the canteen and office and to the exit of the building. He had one fleeting horrific suspicion that he would not be able to open it from the inside without a code, but was flooded with relief when a handle presented itself that did the blessed job.

Alex stepped out into the dark night, finding it was raining hard, half expecting Denise or even a gang of the employees of SharPak chasing after him to drag him back inside or beat him to a pulp in the car park. He did not look over his shoulder to see if this were the case, he did not look back at all.

Within seconds, Alex was liberally drenched. He did not care one jot - in fact, it felt great to be out in the rain. The dreaded cyclic squeal, as if it were from pigs at a production line abattoir where no brain stunning was involved, followed him like a stalker for stride after stride. He realised then he was still wearing his ear protection. He removed it and found his hearing distorted, as if after a very loud gig.

If SharPak were evacuated and the whole place exploded, causing the management to be instantly bankrupted and every employee to irretrievably lose their jobs there, Alex could not think of a better way at that moment of how justice could be so perfectly served.

18

Alex slept through most of the next day. He got up late afternoon, managed another godawful coffee, and remained unable to put the TV or even a radio on, therefore sat in what passed for silence in the untidy house. Despite there being no machete in Daniel's domain, he eventually cleared a path to the curtains to open them in the front room, allowing him to see the state of the place far clearer. Daniel did not return home a few minutes after the computer shop he half-owned, quarterheartedly worked in, and wholly detested, had shut, therefore Alex guessed he must have gone to his parents for dinner – the only place Daniel was likely to be if he were late. Alex took one look at the kitchen, which had virtually returned to its earlier bombsite state, and consoled himself with fish 'n' chips for what passed for his own meal. He sat in silence, ate in silence, and tried to ignore the deafening wail of despair inside his head.

Alex suddenly felt alone, too alone. He felt down on his luck. He felt like he had missed the boat, and that there was no sign on the horizon his ship was coming in. His money was dwindling fast, and he didn't know what he was going to do to survive. The future was uncertain, the present bleak, and the happiness of the past teased him with the fact it was all now nothing more than history, mere memory. He couldn't afford to get depressed, to become reintroduced to that state of being he had spent too many years in the grip of already. For now, he needed his fighting spirit if he was going to pick himself up again; sinking back into the blue and the black would further cement him in emotional quicksand.

He wanted a distraction from the course his thoughts were starting to take. He wanted a little company, and a drink or two would be more than welcome.

He finished all that was edible of his fish 'n' chips, and headed for the Labour Club, for the same fundamental reasons that were the only real reasons people set foot in the place at all.

For a town of around thirty thousand residents, Bridgwater had a large number of pubs – the figure was approaching a hundred, in fact. Alex only drank in two drinking establishments, the rest he deemed borderline unpalatable for any of a short list of reasons. The main reason was usually that the pub was too rough, attracting inarticulate loud inflammable bruisers seeking an excuse to vent their frustrations on anyone they took issue with for groundless reasons. Like tended to attract like, and the aggressive and violent normally ended up battling with the aggressive and violent, be they male or female, but put someone with an unfamiliar face and non-aggressive manner in their midst, the newcomer could easily have a target symbol emblazoned upon their person.

Cliquishness was another trait of Bridgwater pubs; these were not locals where people tended to turn up out of the blue and make casual conversation with shoulder-rubbing strangers. Pubs were often unofficially closed societies, and operated as gathering places for carnival clubs. The carnival was a sort of plebeian freemasonry for the people of Bridgwater – it was a town tradition dating back centuries that had barely evolved in all that time. The original carnival, designed to commemorate the would be blowing up of the Houses of Parliament by Guy Fawkes, featured such guising as white locals depicting themselves as 'niggers' and 'sambos', and the depictions of foreign cultures and races in this event is much in the same vein to this day. Of course, at the time the carnival began, at the beginning of the 1600s, carnival would have been an apt term, although these days procession would be more appropriate. It is one of the great unvoiced jokes amongst local critics of the carnival that the Bridgwater Carnival is, ironically, not an actual carnival, but rather a procession of decorated floats and costumed out-of-shape 'carnivalites', where the spectating public stand in the cold or rain and politely applaud the tightly parametered repeated themes year in, year out, as they labour through the increasingly litter-strewn streets. The other great unvoiced joke is that Carnival night is the safest night in Bridgwater, because all the town's boneheads are safely ensconced on the carts.

The third and final main reason Alex chose to avoid almost every pub in the town was due to the contrived themeing they struggled to suggest and hamfistedly forcefed. There were so many pubs in Bridgwater town, a visitor might initially think they were spoiled for choice, and yet really there is only pub repeated over and over.

It is the west country equivalent of spit and sawdust; curt service, closed atmosphere, bombast and vulgarity from the locals who wanted to project some claim on the place, awful gassy toy beers (or lager, usually pronounced lar-grr), knackered pool tables, darts and skittles teams and carnival clubs, two-a-penny jukebox selections, sometime karaoke, and sometime concerts by what were almost always blues rock bands. A few establishments tried to throw a lick of day-glo paint over the thin veneer, but these were usually just run by thugs in collars and ties who charged extortionate prices for the same cheap chemical thug petrol, and these places were even more likely to erupt into violence than those who didn't pretend they were anything but dens of iniquity.

The Labour Club was, ostensibly, an unforgivable excuse for a watering hole too, with nothing worth drinking, everything worth plugging your ears for on the jukebox, an interior that lacked any aestheticism, and plenty of visitors that could as easily fit in in any of the other pubs that clogged the town. But for Alex it had a certain, albeit sometimes elusive, charm that all the regulars would openly refute and yet returned there again and again because they doubtless secretly felt some pull toward. For the most part it was unpretentious, meaning no-one had to be something they were not to fit in there, no-one had to look a certain part, and no-one had to feel they had something to prove, despite the fact some, like Big Bob, were too ignorant to see this. Also, several of Alex's friends tended to go there on a regular basis, like Daniel, Ken, Patrick, Ian and a few others; even though for all the aforementioned, mates might often be deemed a more suitable term. This was hardly a collection of kindred spirit bedfellows, more like a bunch of disenchanted underachievers who felt safe enough in each other's company that they were not among the violent or intolerably selfish. They were a bunch of semi-intelligent losers and on the one hand they were glad for a little otherwise elusive verbal stimulation whilst at the same time unthreatened by each other's equally unremarkable circumstances and situations.

Tonight, one of Bridgwater's ubiquitous minor-celebrities, Labour district councillor Malcolm Stoodley, and his Czech girlfriend Pavla, were sat at one of the tables beneath an emotional thunderhead in the generally smoky atmosphere. Alex hailed them immediately, and Pavla tried on a smile that didn't quite fit snugly over the frown she fought to contain, Malcolm gave his customary kneejerk nod and averted his eyes. Obviously the mood between them was as it was often enough for it almost ceasing to be noticeable any more in any but a risible way. An argument had occurred and the strains haphazardly papered over – feeling anything but joined at the hip the pair had gone out to show the world how joined at the hip they were in the hope the world might convince them of the same. Alex decided to join them too.

19

'So what are you two doing with yourselves?'

Malcolm looked like he ought best let Pavla answer the question first, prompting Pavla to flash him a look suggesting he ought best not look like he ought best let her go first. Malcolm opened his mouth, and then Pavla beat him to it. 'Well, you know I finished with my studies in Prague now, so I came back here to see Malcolm and to find some work for a few weeks.'

'And how long have you been here for so far?' Malcolm braved needling out of her, capitalising on Alex's presence preventing a public admonition.

'Uh…let me see. I think it must be actually nearly three weeks now…'

'And how much of that time have you spent working so far?'

'Well, they are trying to find something suitable. Anyway, they said I can probably start at Argos later in the week, if I have luck.'

Alex couldn't help but burst into a defusive laughter. 'And what about you, Malcolm? How's luck treating you?'

Malcolm cleared his throat. 'Well, when I'm not doing councillor duties, I've got a driving job, three or four days a week, around the country. It means I sometimes have to spend the night in the cab in truck stops in the Midlands, which is of course a terrible shame.' He glanced back toward Pavla as he finished the sentence, whom was busying herself surreptitiously scowling at the other regulars. 'And what about you? You sticking around for long?'

'Until I can get the capital to escape again, yes. I guess there's not much point in asking either of you if you know a good job.'

'You could always try Argos,' Pavla helpfully suggested.

'I've done my time for Argos, thank you for the suggestion.' Huntworth, a village adjoining Bridgwater that had been mutated into an eyesore industrial estate, boasted the largest Argos warehouse in the country, that was also the largest open plan building in Europe. 'The stories I could tell you about that place.' Alex felt Malcolm's eyes upon him and he quickly bit his tongue.

'But it's OK for a few weeks,' he hastily added.

'So what's up with the teaching?' Malcolm interjected before Pavla could eek more out of Alex about Argos. 'Can't you do that here as well?'

Alex sighed. 'I think it's a bit of a grey area actually. In one sense I'm probably not qualified, and in another I could probably find the work if I really wanted to. I guess what goes against me is the lack of a degree. I'm running on TEFL and bullshit. The less fussy and the more cowboy the employer, plus the fewer the risks posed by bureaucratic necessity, the easier it is to get the work. But, for me, there are a few other considerations as well. I want a break from teaching. It's great when you have three hours work a day and a hotel and half-board in Spain, working for a German con merchants who charge a thousand euros a week for parents to send their spoiled children to have people like me effectively babysit them, but I feel burned out enough by that without getting into something more serious. And I'm only interested in conversational English lessons. I confess I have a gaping hole in my knowledge where grammar analysis is concerned. But also I don't want to spend more time than I have to back in England. I've got the bug, and Spain has only added to it. And the very few plus points about agency work are that there is no interview process and no period of notice. I just want something uncomplicated that will leave my mind free and allow me to get lost again as and when I want to.'

'So Argos it is then,' said Malcolm.

'Argos it isn't, and SharPak it isn't. I think I'm only prepared to work somewhere I haven't yet worked. However unpleasant it might turn out to be, it's at least experience of a sorts, isn't it?'

'Yep. In fact the phrase 'Work makes freedom' gave a lot of people a lot of experience.'

'And now, thanks to people like Argos, how much the world has moved on, right?'

'So you only want jobs you haven't done before?' Pavla tried to confirm.

'At least as far as agency work is concerned, yes.'

'Alex! Just the man I want to see!' All turned to find Patrick had entered the club and was awkwardly bounding toward them. 'Hi, Malcolm! Hi, Pavla!'

'You look like a man on a mission,' Pavla commented.

'I am. A very important one.' When he reached the trio, Patrick leaned close to Alex and spoke in hushed, conspiratorial tones. 'Alex, are you working at the moment?'

'No, I'm not, Patrick. Why?'

'Well, I've got a favour to ask. I'm s'posed to be going to Taunton tomorrow, and the person who was s'posed to be covering the shop for me is ill. I don't s'pose you'd fancy a day in Good Vayoo Records, would you?'

Alex weighed up the prospects on the spot. Patrick was offering him cash-in-hand work he had undertaken on various other low point occasions in the past. It was grossly underpaid, illegal, far from glamorous, and involved being subjected to potentially every social misfit and unemployed anomaly, palatable and often very otherwise, the town had to offer. And Alex was desperate.

'Certainly I'll take it,' he said.

20

Good Vayoo Records was stuck in the same time warp as its owner, Patrick, which was part of its cock-eyed charm. It was one moderately-sized room with a partition at the back, with a doorway screened by a beaded curtain that spent most of the time fallen down. The shopkeeper sat behind a long low storage unit that served as a desk, with sliding smoked-glass doors behind which tapes muddled in alphabetical disorder. Barely presentable display boxes on two sides of the shop were filled with scratched vinyl in tatty covers that yo-yoed in and out of the shop, their sometime owners pawning their collections until the giro came through. It was an Aladdin's cave of temptation for every collector who liked their rarities both unplayable and undisplayable. CDs, videos, DVDs, and even 78s could be found among the rubble, lurking in the dimness and the chaos and the dust. The shop window was plastered in clipart-crafted posters advertising local gigs, most of concerts long gone and thus there to remind one they had been forgotten to be removed, on top of reminding those that bothered reading them that no-one had remembered to attend said events. The posters on the walls were A5-sized depictions of pop and rock idols from the days when Alex remembered it did not feel juvenile to have such paraphernalia on one's bedroom walls. Siouxsie and her Banshees rode the wave of the passé gothic movement years after they had for the large part invented it. Transvision Vamp's Wendy James straddled a powerful-looking motorcycle to prove what fame can do and buy for one. Roy Wood proudly displayed the merits of make-up for men. Lemmy, Adam Ant, even Robbie Williams, flashed their trademark features and struck their unit-shifting poses for the wonder of none quite as much as themselves. The Mission, The Damned, Led Zeppelin, The Cure and The Doors converged like one super- past-it group. The Police looked down upon the shoplifters and addicts who visited the premises en masse. The till was distinctly antiquarian and was surely worth far more than it ever held at any given time. The carpet was so full of toe-snagging holes and tears, it was a wonder anyone entered without tripping or falling, and a wonder that rarely occurred at that.

Alex's shift was set to begin at 10:00, and Patrick phoned to make sure Alex had turned up safe and sound at 10:01. Alex assured him that the shop was still standing, that he had not completely forgotten all the processes involved in keeping the wheels turning at the place yet another day, and omitted admitting he had a hangover. Patrick seemed satisfied enough and informed Alex he would phone again later to check the sky still remained in its appointed place. The shop was due to close at 17:30. If Alex knew Patrick, that particular concerned and considerate call would be placed at approximately 17:29 sharp.

Within minutes of the shop's opening, a small resentful looking man appeared in the doorway, clutching plastic bags filled with what could only be records and videos. There was an agreement between Alex and Patrick that one thing Alex would not do in the shop was to buy stock. That particular headache was far and away more than he was getting paid for. Patrick tried to inform as many of his customers as he could in advance of any time he himself would be out of the shop and thus not buying stock. But there were always a few disgruntled would be sellers, and it was one of Alex's least favourite aspects about covering here. By the way this particular individual was peering around the doorframe in a seething fashion, it was one particular member of the public whom had managed to slip through the grapevine net.

The man lingered where he was for more than a minute, not quite venturing inside. Alex decided to pretend he hadn't noticed him, hoping he would simply go away. After another minute he gave his prickly presence voice. 'Where'z 'e to?'

Alex looked up at the man still stood by the door. 'I beg your pardon?'

'Where'z 'e to?' he repeated, not getting the hint to rephrase his question.

'Are you asking me about the shopkeeper?'

'Yer. Where iz 'er?'

'I'm afraid he's away for the day. He'll be back tomorrow.'

The man tutted. 'Alroit fer some, innit?'

'Isn't it just?' Alex mumbled to himself.

'You buyin'?'

'I'm not authorised to buy stock, I'm afraid, no.'

The man gave an undignified grunt. 'I's good stuff, moind.'

'I don't doubt it, but I'm afraid I can't help you with it personally.' Alex turned on the Bridgwater radio station to learn that Britney had done it again.

'Oi cun always take it up the other place, moind.'

'My friend, if I was you, I would definitely take it up the other place.' Alex flipped open the latest copy of the Bridgwater Mercury, aware his companion was still lingering with intent.

'If oi leave it t' t'moro, there moight not be anythin' left t' sell t' Patrick. If the other place takes it offa me, oi won't be able to come back 'n' sell it t' Patrick t'moro.'

'Well, that'll clearly be Patrick's loss, but that's business for you. You've got to take the rough with the smooth.' In the Mercury, Bridgwater's Conservative MP, whom fellow Conservative MPs ridiculed on webpages aplenty, was taking part in yet another photo-opportunity charity event - a sponsored slimeathon, judging by the look on his face.

'You sure you ain't int'rested in what oi got? Thiz'll be yer last chance.'

Alex breathed a sigh. 'I'm sorry I can't help you, but that's not going to change today. Patrick will be back tomorrow.' With that, he lifted the local rag so his face was hidden behind it.

'Roit. OK. Oi'll be off then.'

Alex riffled the pages of the paper, and finally replaced it on the desk to find the man was gone. But not to find that he was alone.

21

Greg Fisher was a virtual part of the furniture in Patrick's shop, and today was going to be no exception. Greg was a local anomaly that, thankfully, Alex found rather likable, if not entirely fathomable. He was a tall thin spindly spider of a man, well into his forties but looking and acting as a misfit adolescent. His hair was as long and as crazy as was he, and he was tailored by the same two qualities as was Alex: thrift and perseverance to wear one's garments until they were literally falling apart. His attire and self fell just the wrong side of odorous, although Alex was convinced he himself must by now be turning into one of the town's ripest. He had to think of a plan to get his clothes washed somehow, and trying to come to terms with the concept of using Daniel's junkyard washing machine was presently plan Z.

'There's Alex. Hello, Alex. How long you been back then, Alex?'

'Hi, Greg. I got back at the weeke-'

'*Did* you have a *nice* time, Alex?' Greg leaned intimately close enough that Alex felt a fine spray of spittle from his ever-motoring mouth, even though no-one else was in the shop. 'And what about the girls, eh, Alex? Tell me, were there some nice girls there?' He rubbed his hands together gleefully, and sat himself down on the spare stool in a way that suggested he was making himself comfortable for what would hardly be a fleeting spell.

'There were some very nice girls there indeed, actual-'

'I *bet* there were! And what about this place, eh, Alex? Eh? What about this place? Bet you're not glad to be back *here*, are you, eh?'

'I can't claim to be jumping for joy, no.' Stunned to have got to the end of a sentence uninterrupted, and with Greg still silent for what must have passed for a personal record, Alex decided to go for it with a second. 'Anything chan-'

'Where are you going next then, Alex, eh? Where are you going next then?'

'Ummmm...'

'How about back to the States, Alex, eh? Fancy going back there?'

'Well…not-'

'Los Angeles! That's my dream.'

'Greg, when are you going to get yourself there? I presume I'm correct in thinking you still haven't been abroad, right?'

'Go to Los Angeles? *Go to Los Angeles?* Me??' He immediately began fervently looking around for something. Alex knew exactly what it would be before he snatched the calculator up off the desk. 'You work it out, Alex. You work it out. He started striking buttons on the device as if he were trying to kill the thing. 'Right, £75 a week for rent…' He held up the calculator's LCD for Alex to see, should he be having difficulty envisaging the figure written down. The calculator's keys continued receiving their punishment. 'Electric…water…gas…there. Let's round that up and call it another £40 a week. Then there's food…'

'Greg, I know, you've shown me the calculations bef-'

'£25.' He held the LCD too close to Alex's eyes for him to be able to read it. 'That's £140 a week before we've even *started*!' Greg's voice rose an octave as he finished the sentence. 'Do you know what my income is, Alex? Do you know what my income is?'

Alex knew it was a rhetorical question, and that there was no point trying to calm or halt Greg now he was in full flow. Spittle rained from his lips, a fact of which he seemed completely oblivious, as he delighted in reaching what substituted for his point. '£180, Alex! A hun-dred. And. Eigh-ty…pounds!' He paused to let the full impact of his words make no impact at all. '*Los Angeles!*…' His voice rose to a shriek of pantomime theatricality. '*Los Angeles!?!* I've got no chance, Alex. I've got no chance.'

'Come on, Greg, you're not without intelligence. You can make a plan.'

The second would be customer of the day came in, with stock for sale. This one was a twentysomething hardhead with a ripped leather jacket and attitude all over. His face seemed to be imploring others, probably on a permanent basis, not to upset him further because he wasn't in the mood.

'No buying today, I'm afraid,' Greg said on Alex's behalf, Greg clearly having come to the conclusion that Alex must have lost his own voice in the few last seconds.

'You in charge?' was gruffly grunted back at him.

'I'm looking after the place for today,' Alex spoke up before Greg further crowbarred his way in. 'But I'm afraid I'm not authorised to do any buying.'

'Oh…*fffffuck!*' the disgruntled grump grunted. He looked about to kick something, or –one. 'What the fuck am I gonna do now?' he solicited of the other two gentlemen.

'Can't help you. Sorry,' Greg pressed, tight lipped. At least it took the seeing-red focus off of Alex.

'The shopkeeper will be back tomorrow,' Alex stated, hoping it would pacify enough to get the individual off the premises ASAP.

'Tomorrow ain't no fuckin' good t' me, mate. I ain't got fuck all money. I ain't eaten since…fuckin'…nearly forty-eight hours ago.' He held up the nicotine-stained fingers of a beseeching hand to further gesticulate his need.

Greg pointed his own finger in a direction down which the road continued. 'Social's that way,' he stated, possibly gambling his teeth in the process. 'We can't help you here. I'm sorry.'

The man made a sudden movement that made Alex brace himself, and then it was clear the figure was darting smartly for the door, but not before venting a 'Fuckin' waste of fuckin' time, ain' it?' before he left, leaving a cloud.

'Glad to be back in Bridgwater, eh, Mr Bishop?' Greg mockingly intoned while the youth was still barely out of earshot. 'Glad to be back in Good Vayoo Records, eh?'

A corner of a poster suddenly came unstuck, causing Mott the Hoople to droop towards the floor.

'Bridgwater for you, Mr Bishop? Good Vayoo Records for you, Mr Bishop?' With that, Greg stood, and Alex assumed he was about to leave as well. 'I'll go put the kettle on,' he kindly suggested.

22

Greg eventually managed to drag himself out of the shop around an hour and a half after entering it, with a promise to return and check on how things had coped in his absence later. So far the morning had seen quiet traffic, and during a particularly long lull, Alex ventured outdoors to sit in the sun the day had decided to appoint as its ruler for the time being at least.

He stepped out into West Quay and crossed the road to the riverside wall on which he sat himself down, causing the pigeons to strut defensively away then gossip among themselves as to who and what this interloper was. West Quay, at least when viewed from the opposite riverbank, was one of the more attractive – or least unattractive – streets of the town, featuring a huddled line of facades in a collage of history and style, painted in cheerfully contrasting colours; it was a hint of Copenhagen in a dollop of urban decay. Patrick was on good terms with his landlord and had helped Malcolm Stoodley take the third and toppermost of the flats above the shop, and was apparently helping Ken Cunningham, the part-time barman from and full-time barfly of the Labour Club, move into the one just below. As Alex soaked up the precious amount of vitamin D the day had to surrender, casually looking up and down the one-way street to see if anyone was likely to be walking this way, Pavla emerged from the entrance to the flats and shop, clearly having exited Malcolm's flat and carrying Malcolm's bike. She saw Alex and wheeled the bike across the street to say hello. She did not appear entirely happy, which was far from entirely unusual. 'Hello, Alex,' she offered, in a subdued tone.

'Hi, Pavla. You going somewhere adventurous?'

She groaned. 'Probably not. Are you in the shop all day?'

'Every moment I need to be, and not a second more.'

Pavla looked like she was thinking about chewing this over but wasn't quite in the mood for dwelling on the finer points of the English language. 'I might pop in to see you later,' she ventured. She took one wary glance at the world about her. 'I'll probably only be gone half an hour anyway.' Pavla looked preoccupied and off centre enough for Alex not to delay or waylay her any longer, so after slightly strained byes, he watched her pedal in the one-way direction to the town bridge.

The next item of traffic to motor its way along West Quay could already be heard approaching, although it was yet to come into view. The engine-purr increased in pitch, indicating the accelerator had been nailed to the floor, and then, from around the corner of Castle Street just to the right of where Alex sat facing the shop, the cause of the familiar noise came racing into view. Taking the blind corner without any desire to slow down, mounting the kerb and then mowing straight down the pavement itself came another of Bridgwater's minor celebrities: Tailback Sideshow.

Tailback Sideshow was the self-assumed pseudonym of a character called Jim, whom almost no-one, it seemed, knew the surname of. He was one of an almost countless number of Bridgwater residents whom could be referred to, in a way that could be interpreted as both kind and unkind, as harmlessly insane. There seem to be a surprising number of blatant oddballs in the town; degrees of obvious insanity, as it is normally inferred, were so rife as to be virtually ubiquitous. One visitor to the town that Alex knew of had been so gobsmacked by the number and degree of cases, he referred to Bridgwater as being one enormous open mental hospital. Indeed the town had hit the national headlines toward the end of the millennium when the press got wind of the fact GPs were using the acronym NFB in their case notes. NFB translates as Normal for Bridgwater, meaning abnormal for everywhere else, and some emergency damage limitation surgery was required while the local medical profession struggled to hang onto professional decorum, and in some cases their jobs, whilst that particular storm blew over. But for all their foibles, Alex had infinitely more time and respect for the harmlessly insane than those who slotted in amongst the locals and were actually inflammatory timebombs, primed to explode and strike out as randomly as they did irresponsibly once alcohol entered their veins or the emotional balance swayed a little off centre, or simply when they next sensed any kind of challenge – and these were by far more in abundance than anyone who could more readily and officially be blighted by society. Anyway, Alex himself had

had the moniker of 'weirdo' hurled at him on several occasions, for no discernible reason other than that he clearly had not been programmed and hardwired with the standard Bridgwater chip on his shoulder. Weird as a word came from the Anglo-Saxon *wyrd* and was strongly connected with destiny and being on the spiritual path, therefore Alex soaked up the label almost as if it were a well-intended compliment. Let the weird enjoy their weirdness, as far as he was concerned – who, in their right mind, would want to be officially normal anyway?

Tailback, back arched and arms outstretched as if gripping a steering wheel or perhaps handlebars no-one else could see, idled to a near stop as he drew level with the door of the shop. He peered inside, his body moving back and fro a little as he did so, presumably because the handbrake had not been engaged. Seeing there no-one, he turned toward the wall and noticed Alex, whom he vaguely recognised from his time at the shop before. 'Patrick not in?' he called.

Alex shook his head. 'He's away for the day, I'm afraid.'

'When will he be back, do you know?' Tailback's patter was presently without any sign of the out of place at all. An eavesdropper, unable to see Tailback's being in possession and control of an entirely invisible vehicle, at least to everyone else, would have no clue that anything might possibly be amiss at the moment.

'He'll be back tomorrow.'

'OK, thanks.' With that, Tailback gave a cursory glance behind him, indicated with his arm, then swung his transparent roadster back out onto West Quay street. As he did so, another vehicle, this one perceivable in the three-dimensional, but more realistic only for the lazy-minded, world, came rushing from the corner of Castle Street and zoomed straight up behind Tailback. Alex cringed, for a second fearing the worst, but the driver behind applied his brakes just in time, although deliberately not before then, and angrily sounded his horn as Tailback continued unperturbed driving his own set of lead-free-fuelled wheels at not much more than a walking pace. The driver of the car behind continued venting his impatience on the steering wheel as he was forced to comply with the same speed limit as was imposed on Tailback, and shouted obscenities out of his window as he was forced to stop driving at a lethal velocity for a whole several seconds. Tailback seemed oblivious, and it wasn't until they reached the town bridge where Tailback continued straight and the other driver turned left, that the second motorist could continue breaking the speed limit. Tailback disappeared into the distance, his own composure unruffled to the core. Good for him, Alex thought, unashamedly smugly. Good for him.

23

As the exhaust fumes, both visible and invisible, dissolved into the air, Councillor Stoodley exited the same doorway Pavla had minutes earlier. He looked up the street both ways in near comic exasperation, then crossed to Alex. 'Did you see Pavla leave here a few minutes ago?'

'I did, yes.'

'Did she tell you where she was going, by any chance?'

'She didn't, no, although she didn't seem in a particularly talkative mood.'

Councillor Stoodley sighed theatrically and said something to himself. 'She just told me she's gone, left, disappeared for good, exited for ever.'

'Oh, really? She told me she'd be about half an hour.'

A brief chortle escaped the councillor that was either a healthy sign, or quite the opposite. 'Well, half an hour and for ever have felt pretty much the same to me this morning.'

'Oh dear.' Alex dared not venture more, not wanting to become more involved in the interminable soap. He also neglected to mention Pavla had gone, possibly for time immemorial, accompanied by his bike. Councillor Stoodley was an instrumental part of the Bridgwater–Czech twinning and international exchange society. He made it his business to stimulate, manage and organise trips and exchanges, and was passionate about Anglo-Czech relations. Alex was impressed with his overall dedication and ability to realise his plans, although the councillor presently stood before him was unfortunately, for the time being at least, demonstrating the plumbers-have-leaky-taps syndrome.

'Not to worry. I'm sure later on history will have been rewritten once again, and either everything will be coming up roses or we'll have an entirely new disaster to conjure out of nothing then disinvent at a whim.' He pushed his spectacles up onto his nose, then flicked his hair to one side with a hand.

Alex shrugged, unhelpfully. 'We hurt the ones we love the most, and we love the ones whom hurt us the most.'

'Yes, well, thanks for your sympathy and wisdom, Alex. Anything going on with any women in *your* world at the moment?'

'Nothing at all, I'm afraid. I've got having nowhere to live and having no money and having no job to take priority over having no female company at the moment.'

'So planning on a long stretch of celibacy, are we?'

'Thanks. I'm trying desperately to keep depression at arm's length as it is.'

'Didn't you make any money in Spain then? What are you living on at the moment?'

'Unfortunately my employers – International Project, in case you ever come across them - were far from forthcoming with my wages. They still owe me a bundle as it is. Right now I dare not even look at my bank balance. I'm basically living on my wits, Malcolm.'

'Oh. That must be difficult.'

'Thanks again. Oh no, I've got a customer to attend to by the looks of things.'

'Is that so bad?'

'You be the judge,' Alex answered, and Councillor Stoodley turned his head to see who Alex was wearily observing shuffling down the street.

24

Trampy was the less than kind name another daily visitor to Patrick's shop had been given, and considering Alex had no idea what his real name was, the unfortunate pseudonym (of which the poor man was himself unaware, for better or worse, as far as Alex knew) could not help but meld itself to Alex's mental frame of reference.

Poor beleagured Trampy was actually a dear old man who simply had not washed since a time no-one particularly liked to guess at. His hair, his skin, his clothes – it sufficed to say - were simply thick with grime, literally stank to a nauseating degree, and he had even had insects noticeably crawling around in his hair on at least one occasion he had visited Patrick's shop.

What rumours there were about Trampy Alex had listened to time and again. The man visited Patrick's shop to buy rock 'n' roll LPs from the 60s and 70s, although apparently possessed no record player in the stinking house he inhabited, allegedly – and obviously - without any care assistance. He was another Alex bracketed as the harmlessly insane, although apparently – not that this was the kind of rumour that could in any way be substantiated – his condition had in part been caused by his own psychiatric treatment. Alex had heard he had been subjected to ECT – electroconvulsive therapy – to treat relatively minor psychological conditions, and a sadistic employee of the institution that had given him said treatment had made constant references to the man's love of rock 'n' roll while effectively frying his brains, along the lines of 'This'll rock your world' as he gleefully sent the convulsion-inducing voltage coursing through his increasingly damaged body. If it were not true, Alex was nonetheless confident, based on firsthand reports from people whom had themselves received psychiatric 'treatment' at suchlike institutions, that at least this degree of cruelty and gross irresponsibility was very much in existence, if not rife.

Alex was also aware that Patrick, and some others, had expressed concern enough over Trampy's plight and hygienic and physical deterioration to try to alert the authorities to the situation on several occasions. Despite making phone calls to the appropriate departments, the man remained in his state of indignity. Naturally it is not a black-and-white issue of simplicity and uniform procedure when helping anyone with any psychological condition, but Alex's cynical wariness of the care and provision of anyone with any mental health condition suggested to him that the shortfall was almost certainly on the government-funded social services side. Alex himself had sought help when he had first been officially diagnosed as clinically depressed, and for all the lucidity, articulation, able-bodiedness and impetus to get assistance he had blessedly been in possession of, he was astonished at how elusive and un-forthcoming tangible assistance had proven to be. How much more difficult it might be for those lesser-equipped to fight for their own corner and try to pick themselves up out of their rut he could only guess at.

Sometimes Alex wondered where government-, income- and council taxes all went, how it all broke down exactly. It was hardly a secret that the majority of taxes goes directly to fund the military and therefore sponsor the effective orphaning and murdering and mutilating of children in Iraq, for example, but Alex wondered how much overspill was left and what precisely was done with that. He remembered that the pedestrian-signalling part of a traffic lights on the Taunton Road/Broadway roundabout had quite recently been inoperational for three consecutive weeks. Three consecutive weeks is a long time to go without such a basic safety mechanism doing what everyone took it for granted it should do. It was around the same time Alex had been asked by an agency to do a day's work at Bridgwater House while it underwent reconstruction. The job, he was told, was carrying carpet upstairs while the lifts were out of service. Upon arriving on the Saturday morning to carry out said task, he was shocked at the sheer volume of enormous rolls of carpet he was supposed to get up the several flights of stairs. He was also shocked when, upon eavesdropping on a conversation by members of the construction company commissioned to do the renovation work, these professional builders refused to help Alex after being requested to because they claimed the work was too hard. He was also shocked to find he was obliged to walk around areas of the building that all notices declared should not be entered without appropriate safety equipment without there even being safety equipment for him to don. He was also shocked to learn Sedgemoor District Council were only prepared to stretch to the minimum wage payment should he agree to undertake this health and safety legislation-breaking, highly illegal and almost literally backbreaking work. He was also shocked to find that every department on every floor in Bridgwater House was being fitted with an expensive new dishwashing machine, all of which he felt sure would shock every struggling Bridgwater inhabitant on the breadline who sweated and bled their extortionate council tax into these civil servants' coffers, month in, month out.

Councillor Stoodley, whom Alex regarded as one of just a handful of local councillors with a conscience – and certainly not a criminal record for fraud, as with one particular councillor – bumbled something about having to go to Bridgwater House himself and then was off, with his trademark awkward and word-swallowing goodbye, leaving Alex to be the one doing social work for the here and now.

'Hello there, alright?' Alex hailed as he entered the shop after the customer, keeping himself out of physical contact's way and trying his best not to inhale.

'Hello, my dear. He's not in today, is he?'

'Not today, no. Back tomorrow.'

'Taunton he's gone to, isn't it, my dear? Taunton he's gone to?'

'That's right, he's in Taunton today.'

'And how are you, my dear? How are you keeping?' Already the shop was seriously filling up with an odour it was simply impossible to ignore, no matter which way Alex tried to breathe.

'I'm just about fine, thank you. And you?'

'Oh, musn't grumble, my dear. Musn't grumble. The Rolling Stones, my dear. Have you got something by the Rolling Stones?'

'I'll just have a look for you.' Alex went to the section clearly marked with the appropriate initial, which was something those who worked at Good Vayoo Records did so often, they didn't even think twice about it any more. 'The only thing we have in at the moment is *Emotional Rescue*.'

'And how much is he, my dear?'

'That's £3.50, my friend.'

'£3.50 you say.' One of Trampy's hands disappeared deep into his trousers pocket and after some considerable fumbling and jingling, a handful of coins were carefully inspected, handled and counted.

Alex bagged the Stones album and waited as patiently as someone virtually holding their breath could wait while Trampy sorted the correct coinage. Eventually he held it out for Alex to take, with blackened hands, fingers thick with grime, and long yellow clawlike nails. Alex let the coins drop into his own palm, hardly able to stand the wait until he could wash his own hands, which he intended to do the moment Trampy left. No such luck. Another of Patrick's customers arrived at the shop, entering unperturbed by the near noxious fumes. And what this one lacked in repellent smell he more than made up for in odorous personality.

25

Mike the Martian was a self-proclaimed sci-fi fanatic, although for some anoraky sci-fi reason, he always tried to reprimand people who made it sound like 'sigh fie', instead trying to insist it be referred to as SF, which is why Alex always went out of his way to say 'sci-fi' as often as possible in his company. He was a young Tom Baker in Doctor Who mode to look at, but with an ever-present annoying would be know all grin, and an insinuating personality that always thought it had perfect rights to interrupt, needlessly contradict, and outstay its welcome to the —nth degree. Ten minutes in this guy's company certainly introduced one to the concept of time warp, anyway. His conversation revolved about himself and little else for he clearly believed he was the hub the universe circled around. He deliberately tried to speak above or down to any unfortunate and involuntary listener, purposely steered the topic toward subject matter he unqualifiably knew infinitely more about, tried to insist people read his ready stack of unfathomable and incomprehensible short stories, and refused to take a hint that he was simply talking to himself, being tactless, or was boring the bejeezus out of any and all in earshot. The ordeal of his company could be likened to that of an ardent Christian or communist, with a different card to carry but no less of an anorak beneath which to grind an interminably dull axe.

'Ifyoupolarizedthetimecontinuumthegravitationalpullwould-suckmorecustomersintotheshop.' Mike the Martian never seemed to separate his words, the nonsensical babble rolling together as an anybody's-guess stab at something worth saying.

'Oh god. Hello, Mike.'

'Whydon'tyouputasignonthedoorsaying'nohumansallowed'?'

'Will it prevent you from coming in here?'

'No,notatallbecauseIamnotahuman,yousee.'

'No,' Alex groaned. 'Of course not.'

'He'll be back tomorrow, my dear, won't he? Patrick? He'll be back tomorrow, right?'

'Unlesssolarmeltdownbeginssometimewithinthenextfourteen-

hourswhichaccordingtoastrophysicistsitmightalreadyhavedone-
andwecouldbesittinghereobliviousfortheeightminutesittakesforthe
sun'sraystoreachEarth.'

'Tomorrow he'll be back, my friend, yes.'

'Buttomorrowisonlyaby-productofthecollectiveconsciousnesst-
hatinitselfhasnotangibleexistencethereforePatrickcannotreturni-
natimezonethatcanbeprovennottoexist.'

'You will tell him I was here, my dear, won't you? You will
let him know I came in?' Alex doubted, however unfortunately it
might be, that the smell would have dissipated by then anyway.

'Hereisonlyanaxisthroughwhichbipolarplanesintersectcreating-
coordinateswhichcanbemappedthereforeexplicitnessisrequiredto-
decodeaccuratelythehereofwhichyouspeak.'

'I know a few explicit directions myself.'

'I don't know what you're talking about. I don't know what he's
talking about, my dear.'

'It's one thing we can both feel grateful about today.'

'AnywayasIwasaayingIamnotahumanandhumansareonly-
mythirdfavouritelifeformwouldyouliketoknowwhathefirsttwoare.'

'Does it matter either way?'

'Rolling Stones, my dear. Remember to tell him I bought the
Rolling Stones, will you?'

'I certainly shan't forget you've been in, and I certainly shan't
forget *Emotional Rescue* either.'

'Ifllobotomiseyouwithpsychokinesisyouwon'trememberanythi-
ngandcanbereprogrammedasanorganicautomatonservingthewillo
fmyfavouriteandhighestspecies.'

'It is something which I believe someone beat you to a long,
long time ago.'

Nearly twenty-five minutes passed until both Trampy and Mike
the Martian finally exited the premises, leaving behind lingering traces detectable without futuristic apparatus but a nose and
the merest glimpse at Alex's face. Thirty seconds after that Greg
made his own return visit. 'Well, Mr Bishop, fancy meeting you
here.' He took one glance at the otherwise empty shop. 'No-one
here! Wow I bet you're glad for a break from all the nutcases for
a while, aren't you?'

At 17:29, Patrick did not phone as predicted, but instead strolled into his shop. After mumbling something Alex only half-listened to about his own day, he asked how Alex's day was while turning his attention to the takings book. 'You've done well here, Alex. You've done very well. You've earned yourself quite a bit of commission, you have.' After carefully consulting the calculator, he asked Alex if he had a 2p piece. A little perplexed, but not for very long, Alex produced said coin from a pocket and handed it over to Patrick. Patrick counted the wages into Alex's hand, then enlightened him as to what the 2p business had been all about. 'Here we are, here's your commission. Ten pounds, another ten pounds, and another five pounds. There. You earned £24.98 in commission all in all, Alex. I bet you feel pleased with that, eh?'

'You will never know, Patrick. You will never know.'

26

With his newfound wealth, Alex treated Daniel and himself to a takeaway pizza – by Bridgwater standards, this was sheer decadence. Upping the indulgence to a near Bacchanalian degree, Daniel even threw in some more lukewarm cans, of Fosters. They sat, ate, drank and talked in the front room before the moron box; two kings slumped upon their threadbare thrones.

'There's a message for you on the answermachine,' Daniel informed his guest as he scoffed an attempt at Italian-style food self-respecting Italians would scoff at.

'Oh?'

'I'll play it for you.' He operated the device and put it on speaker phone – a process that was a galaxy away from Alex's technical expertise. The TV was muted, *Big Brother* gagged by a remote totalitarian, and a woman struggling to suppress her local accent imposed on their ears.

'Hello. This is a message for Alex Bishop. We've got a position currently available for you starting either tomorrow or the day after if you're interested. It's some light industrial work, starting at seven in the morning until four, with a total of one hour in breaks, which is unfortunately unpaid. The job is in Bridgwater and if you're interested please phone us back and ask for Carrie at Recruitment West-'

'They never actually tell you where the job is,' Alex observed. 'You have to basically agree to it and then it's the last piece of information you get. Well, it's well after office hours now, so I'm certainly not going to start there tomorrow even if I do say yes.'

'Seven o'clock in the morning sounds horrible.'

'You're telling me. But that's the situation I'm in, Dan. I literally can't afford to be too picky at the moment…or anymore.'

'Surely there must be something you can do, Alex. "Light" industrial work isn't you at all. You were born with a brain; you should be using it.'

'Uh…Pot-kettle. Kettle-pot.'

Daniel started to groan, then stifled it by forcing more food an Italian would have to be forced to eat into his mouth. 'You're younger than I am, you've got much more of a fighting chance still left.'

'I've got no acumen, Daniel. No business sense, no capitalistic ruthless streak. And I'd hate the idea of having such a thing, anyway - it's not me. I'm certainly not motivated by money and it seems to me most people who manage to earn material success do so at the cost of selling themselves in the bargain. What's the point of that? People *with* end up having to parade their *withness* to try to convince everyone else they are happier than them in the hope everyone else will persuade them of the same in return. What a sorry shallow joke.'

'Yeah, well, you're not Mr Materialistic, it's clear, and obviously neither am I. But you could certainly elevate yourself above the breadline a bit more. I mean you're interested in what?... Writing?...Travelling? Think how much more time you could devote to writing if you didn't have so many money worries. Think how much more opportunity you'd have to travel. But now you're worried about where you're going to live, how you're going to eat, whether or not you can stomach the next shit job an agency throws at you. You know you're worth more than that. I'm sure there's something you're missing if you look hard enough.'

'Well, why don't you take your own advice and sort yourself out?'

'Maybe that's part of what I'm doing by trying to sort you out. What about going back to school? What about getting a degree? I'm sure you've got what it takes to get one, and surely that would open up far more doors for you?'

'Been there, tried it, didn't fit. They didn't have a degree course in my size. What was supposed to be a non-stop lark was actually one of the worst experiences of my life. I never wanted to get a degree anyway, it's just something society tells you you ought to have in order to get somewhere in life. I think of all the people I know, and there are plenty among those I like the best without a degree, and countless people I've met and disliked who are graduates. The term I spent at uni just confirmed exactly what I already suspected about it. It's about jumping through hoops, doing what you're told, proving you can be an obedient robot. I never rated what the lecturers had to tell us, and besides that I have no sense of belonging in the world of academia. I couldn't get to grips with the whole bureaucratic, organisational side of it, I didn't have a clue what I was doing or if I was where I was supposed to be, or what anything I was subjected to had to do with the subject I was supposed to be learning about or the reason I went there in the first place. I can't concentrate on things that don't directly interest me, I've got no attention span, especially when I'm confused and frustrated, and when anything is presented as mandatory I immediately shut right off, I can't help it. I hate the fact that people judge intelligence or ability by a piece of paper, I wouldn't rate the intelligence of anyone who held to this, and therefore it seems to me a pointless exercise in the first place. You and me are the same in that respect, I think. My obstacles have been handling eczema, dealing with anxiety attacks, obsessive-compulsive disorders, trying to live with depression, not having a practical or organised bone in my body, problems with concentration and attention, not having the money to eat, let alone think or plan or study. And being kept in a perpetual state of poverty by all the above making it so difficult to work or hold down a job. As far as university is concerned, I needed someone to directly support and guide me, to hold my hand a little and show me what to do. As soon as they made it difficult for me, for example with complications regarding my student loan and my finding out I'd spent the first two weeks in the wrong class for my supplementary subject, which I hadn't bargained on having to take anyway, that was like slamming the door in my face and telling me you're not welcome. I'm someone with an artistic bent, and even if I'm no good at it, I'm fuelled by obsession and emotion and the desire *not* to conform. I see no fertile ground for honing artistic genius at university, and however deluded that might be, that was what I had to tell myself was lurking there somewhere in order to get myself there in the first place. No, university is not me, Daniel, purely and simply, and I maintain it's all about production-line certification of what is essentially unqualifiable, and has absolutely nothing to do with a person's true social worth and most certainly wisdom.'

'Well, yes, I basically agree with you, and I expect most people who have been through the university mill would agree with you as well. It's unfortunate that it's what you need to get on in life, which is something we can't really get away from.'

'Yeah, well let them put me in a box marked social reject if that's what makes them happy, I just find it all makes me more stubbornly anti-uni anyway.'

'But at the same time you're involved in the world of academia, aren't you? You're a teacher.'

'I'm a teacher when it suits me to wear the title, although hardly overconfident at it. It's just a way of sponsoring extended holidays. It has its good points definitely, and I do believe I have a penchant for the English language, but it's really not what I want to do in life. I want to be a professional writer, but it's getting a foot in the door.'

'I still think that your non-materialism actually has a bit of a self-defeating effect in practice. You want to be free from the slaving and trappings of material existence, the ratrace, you want to live a romantic artistic life, but your life is governed by want. I'm sorry to make the observation, but you're probably through necessity more dogged by the materialism of life than many who hold down jobs with a degree to back them up.'

'I know, it's a bit of a bummer, isn't it?' Alex drained the dregs of what was the beer market's dregs and looked back towards the muted antics on the screen. *Big Brother* was highlighting the least trivial or more sensational and televisual aspects of a bunch of incarcerated dislikeable individuals of the past twenty-four hours in what for them passed as their effective working day. An adolescent male in a chicken suit was chasing around the 'housemates'' garden after a heavily-tattooed woman with dyed-green hair. After century upon century of invention and technological breakthrough; after war after conflict after revolution; after age after age; with the human race standing on the shoulders of giants; millions of people in the industrialised civilised world were right now glued to a man in a rubber chicken suit running after a woman with green dreads and tattoos. Even though the woman was laughing, there was something intensely sad about the scene and all it symbolised, and Alex found himself having to tear his gaze away in a hurry.

'So what are we going to do with you, Alex? What are we going to do with *me*?'

The man in the chicken suit was now simulating sex with the tattoo-riddled wannabee celebrity.

Daniel crushed his emptied can. 'Fuck it, let's go down the pub.'

'I can't afford it.'

'Neither can I.'

They looked at each other for a moment. In chorus they agreed, 'Let's go.'

27

They went via Fore Street because Daniel wanted to gamble on an ATM en route to the club. As they passed the Cornhill, where teenagers seemed to cluster in shifts, Alex felt his skin prickle a little when he thought of what had happened to him at this location mere days before. He did not care to look that way in conspicuous fashion, to see if he could recognise or be recognised by anyone there, and hoped that by cosmetically breezing by the place he would blow the cobwebs of uncertainty away. Of course, there would be many who would not care to walk past the location at all once they had had a similar experience as Alex, some who might avoid it for weeks or even months. But that was not what self-preservation was really about. Whenever we might find ourselves in unpleasant straits or mean streets, we all climb into cars and think nothing of it, and no statistician obsessed with self-preservation would ever swap the illusory safety of an automobile for their own feet. We all have a tendency to exaggerate or glamorise our personal plights for the overwhelming reason that we like to wallow in self-pity and score points for what we internally know to be cowardice and inertia. People who go out of their way to avoid what is the mere possibility of danger, albeit often dressed as probable for the licence this provides us to be lazy, are exhibiting self-defeatism which is, in effect, the antithesis of self-preservation. Faith and boldness are what lift us out of ruts and the way of peril; to change who you want to be to keep out of danger is the defence of a lifestyle unworthy of defence. It is all too easy to believe that facing down that our cowardice tells us to avoid demands more courage than we have in stock, but nothing takes as much bravery as we thought it would in practice, and the fear we are ruled by when submitting to fear can only inflate our anxieties long-term.

As Alex waited as patiently as he could for Daniel to use the Natwest machine, two boys on bikes accompanied a girl walking toward the town bridge. It was all Alex and Daniel could do to listen to their would be conversation as they passed.

'What we doin'?' one of the cyclists asked, having just fallen into line with the other two.

'I'm gonna beat fuck out of Gemma Davis,' the long curly-haired, shapely and pleasantly attractive girl informed her peer, immediately shattering any illusion of femininity with the subtlety of an exploding windowpane.

'Oh…' the cyclist uttered, as if it were an event so commonplace as to negate all need to comment, which for these young men and woman it very well might be. 'Why?' he added after a long pause, presumably a vague afterthought.

'She got off with my best mate's boyfriend.'

Another 'Oh,' suggesting near disinterest.

And off they went, a trio comprising of a potential female assassin and two male counterparts that would presumably serve well as salivating gawkers whom would confirm the girl bruiser's testimony when she doubtless regaled her Cornhill audience with her sensationalised, inarticulate, sound-effects-and-gesticulation-heavy fantasy of how she single-handedly slayed the dragon that was Gemma Davis: the perfect excuse for an outlet of sadism and viciousness and countless other motives as pure as the water from a Belorussian spring.

Alex and Daniel continued toward the club without commenting on that they had heard. Both having lived in the Bridgwater area most of their lives, such language and attitudes were to them as much part of the scenery as the gull droppings that remained where they dropped or the boarded-up windows of bust-within-a-month shops.

28

The action in the Labour Club was as it almost always was: the clock was ticking while aged drinkers supped away their dregs; solitary drinkers feigned interest in newspapers or made no pretence they weren't there alone for drink; tendrils of thick contraband tobacco smoke wrapped their strangling selves around the bronchioles of every mandatory smoker; darts sailed through the air while their ill-fitting flights soared elsewhere; pool balls clipped pocket corners while the crooked cue handlers cursed above their breath; those at the bar grouped their solitary vigils, tossing non sequiturs one to the other in the hope someone might catch something someone or the other might say.

The money was fast evaporating and thus Alex decided to make it a cider night - a pint of the local bowel-loosener produced at a fermenters where everyone knew someone whom had worked there and had accidentally dropped a spanner into one of the vats which had shockingly completely dissolved once the vats were drained. Only the naïve believed this urban myth with their head; only the inexperienced disbelieved it with their guts.

Alex and Daniel sat down with Patrick - with the exception of Ken the barman, the only regular they could label as a friend - and prepared to engage in their own round of verbal exchanges of the needless to say. Alex and Daniel gritted their teeth while Patrick indulgently talked shop, Patrick obliviously interrogated and Alex desperately tried to change the subject while Daniel reluctantly talked shop, and Daniel and Patrick met with a numb familiarisation as Alex revealed that he was still basically without anything in the way of shop to talk about. Alex started on his second cider and Ken made the three of them four with a manner that left them no doubt he had had one or two too many.

'Hey, I had that stupid little fucker Douggie Evans in today. You know how *thick* he can be, right?'

'I've no idea who you're talking about,' said Daniel, calmly but firmly, immediately sensing Ken's mood.

'I don't know him either,' said Alex.

'I know Douggie, yeah,' Patrick ventured, though looked far from comfortable that he could give such a concession.

'Well, you know how much of a *twat* he is,' Ken continued in the same irrepressible vein. 'Someone started talking about the Berlin Wall, and him - he's so out of touch, he *actually thought* the Berlin Wall separated *East and West Germany*!' Ken then launched into a brief snort of self-satisfied laughter while the other three exchanged guardedly confused looks.

'I thought it did as well,' Patrick ventured, with a resigned shrug.

'And so did I,' admitted Alex, unsure if he was demonstrating gross ignorance of world history or if he had not read the subtext of a political mandate and redefined it according to the bitter and fixed-point intellect of Old Guard communist interpretation.

Daniel, perhaps quietly the cleverest person present, maintained a prudent silence.

'Oh for *fuck's sake*.' Ken buried his reddened face in his hands, and looked, with clockwork reliability, to be about to launch into a no-fun lecture in which years of frustration came to a near head before innocent parties, the comic exasperation in his voice suggesting everyone *must know* what everyone who knew Ken knew no-one else but Ken whom knew.

When he had been a teenager Alex himself had become closely involved in socialism, at least on a local level, but it was a romance that had died by the time he had reached his twenties. That brief immersion into that elite of the intellectually (and often class-based) bourgeois, with their self-referential Bible bashing of *Das Kapital* and other impenetrable, unengaging and imagination-evicting (as opposed to –capturing) propaganda, had taught him invaluable lessons about life and self, but nothing the leftists would ever congratulate him on, for for them congratulation is strictly for those who see red.

In Alex's experience, there were five key ingredients of a radical leftie, none of which made him want to join their ear-bashing, as opposed to shoulder rubbing, rank and file: -

1). Glorification of and susceptibility to violence. There was a cold hole in the heart of the radical red where a tangible machismo complex festered. Bloody revolution was given just the right amount of spin to make acts of mass slaughter that were an inevitable ingredient of it something somehow romantic and heroic. Even smaller scale acts of terrorism given the stamp of approval by leftie extremists were paraded as something to aspire to with that heartlessness and insensitivity that goes hand in hand with fanaticism - essentially the same motivating force that drives soldiers to abuse human rights in the midst of war. And on a private level there lurked a tendency to turn to physical force dressed up as either sorting someone out or, even more sinisterly, jovial fraternising, when emotional sway overshadowed reasoning, as it too often tended to do for these self-perceived academics.

2). Intellectual snobbery. Lefties incessantly quote from their own library and substitute conceptual debate for regurgitation of fact, figure, name, date, time, place – and, of course, always a firm favourite, battle. Few outside their circle (and therefore, of course, puppets of fascism in much the same way fundamentalist Christians view non-believers as tools of Satan) know what the hell they are talking about half the time, and yet they rarely dare question for fear of being branded as displaying gross ignorance and being subjected to another interminable lecture. The most important and meaningful lessons in life are those we find out for ourselves, not something obscure we read in a biased manifesto and then feel impotently outraged when the rest of the world cannot see eye to eye with it. But even trying to communicate this base understanding shared among intelligent non-commies is dangerous, for they have their talking above and down to disguised as the voice of the people to hide behind, and failing that there is their cowardly safety net of the bared teeth and the clenched fist when we cannot be intimidated into accepting that we are the wrong.

3). Materialism. Such machismo necessitates a pretence (and fanaticism in any form can probably best be summed up as pretending to oneself, of course) to understand the world and know what is for the best with the fixed intellect that is arrogance, and arrogance detests not knowing something. For this reason lefties off-handedly poopoo anything that whiffs of the metaphysical, parapsychological, esoteric etc because it dilutes their ability to know all and dictate what's best for the world. Even such concepts as complementary therapy tended to be swept aside as being too 'gay' to represent anything that offered real hope or help as opposed to those whom preferred to offer hope and help with rolled up sleeves and furrowed brows.

4). Philistinism. Because lefties abhor not knowing something, thus they have no time for mystery, blinded to the fact that it is mystery that gives to life its very magic. Unless it falls within the short list of left-wing approved art, reds tend to think of it as below them to have a contemporary or even general understanding of fiction, music, film, poetry, fine arts and they often make the mistake of branding just about everything as controlled by the right, pretentious, or simply trivial in comparison to their dry, brash, blunt battle to create what they have been sleeping through the fact half of the world has just rejected as unstomachable.

5). Infighting. The final straw for Alex was that the lefties' biggest enemies, it seemed, were not the fascists, not the capitalists, not racism or anti-Semitism (and Alex had noted how it was en vogue for reds to badmouth Christianity but defend what is too often the practical gender fascism that is Islam), but the lefties themselves. Take a glance at what has happened in the former Eastern Bloc in very recent history. Hardly surprising given the heroes: Marx, an alcoholic so consumed by his economic theories he could not articulate an idea lucid even to those who call themselves the left in most cases; Lenin, a man who organised armed bank robberies to fund his political manoeuvres; Trotsky, who was killed with an ice pick because he rejected state capitalism and therefore *just had* to be a fascist interloper; and Stalin, widely believed to have been responsible for directly ordering very significantly more deaths than Hitler. Spend any short length of time in the company of the left, see how they squabble over what Marx meant, what Lenin intended, what Stalin did, what Trotsky wanted, why the Communist Party are different from the SWP, the New Labour vs old, and how the Nazis have infiltrated the ranks of the wannabee red, and how allegiances shift left, right and centre with the changing of the crimson tides, and know what left-wing paranoia is – anything *but* an invention by their enemies designed to undermine their credibility. Lefties spend so much time and cause so much self-harm infighting it could be said that they themselves are those whom should be held most responsible for the insipience of global fascism.

Alex was not right-wing any more than left-, for to him capitalism diluted the raw energy and passion of life with whatever market forces could repackage and resell the most effectively, at the same time effecting the least damage to and largest distraction from their shallow, sleazy game. No, capitalism was just fascism wearing a bad disguise, but socialism offered no lasting or satisfying exit, just exchanged one form of oppression for another. The five listed ingredients; the use of violence, smugness and arrogance, obsession with the material, the philistine erosion of art, and the cannibalism that is the philosophy's effective wont, could as easily be an apt description of the extremes of either the left or right, and this is surely no coincidence, for these opponents that see themselves as sworn enemies are perhaps better bedfellows in truth than the knowledge of which would allow them sleep.

Socialism and capitalism can both be allegorised by high intelligence, in that all are their own worst advert, their upholders often demonstrating determination and conviction but little of genuine happiness or compassion. Where politics is not one's profession (and often where it is), one would perhaps be better off focussing one's energy on the struggles that are important in one's personal life, which is usually what a political lifestyle provides a convenient substitute for in the first place anyway.

Ken had apparently finished his seething didactics, and Alex realised he had zoned out during the tense proceedings. He did not feel ashamed. Whatever the Berlin Wall represented, politically, historically, geographically, for the left, for the right, for the right of the left or the left of the right or any permutation thereof, symbolically, realistically or existentially, Alex felt no shame he had not paid attention to Ken's outpouring, for the Berlin Wall was at that moment not the issue, but the fact that Ken, through his attitude, had not earned the right to make himself heard.

Ken Cunningham was, in the broadest sense, a good man, essentially gentle-natured, generous to a fault, helpful, sympathetic, a good listener, trustworthy and concerned, *except* when he got up on his political high hobby horse. It is ironic that perhaps what we perceive as bringing us most in league with the people can be the thing that most divides us from them, and that we tell ourselves is the most radical attitude can be the smokescreen that blinds us from attending to what we most ought.

Ken had only just finished ranting when someone else decided to start their own unwarranted unwinnable war.

29

'Alright? I thought I'd come over and say hello to you men.' 'Hi, Eve, alright?' said Patrick, diplomatically, a hint of wariness in his voice detectable to Alex that he believed Eve, whom he knew only by sight and name, would be oblivious to.

Ken seemed to sober in the moment, and turned his head to look back toward the bar he had neglected, as if just remembering it. 'I'd better get back to the bar, I suppose,' he said by way of excusing himself, and retreated to the other side of that other division line between sense and sensibilities.

The woman remained standing like a vulture over the remains of the group. A forty-some woman, widowed for around a year, clad in black. Life's cruel lottery had taken its toll on the youth she defiantly tried to reel back toward her with the fashion and cut of her evening wear.

'How's you then, Eve?' asked Patrick, simply to break the awkward silence.

'Oh, I'm struggling on. You're Daniel, aren't you?'

'Yep, that's me,' offered Daniel, in a sort of clearing one's throat way. 'Right, I'm going to have a go on the machine.' He stood up and crossed to the no-armed bandit waiting patiently amongst the four-limbed crooks. Alex now sensed he was the focal point, and that Patrick, Ken and Daniel all knew something that he was likely about to find out.

'Who are you then?' was what Alex heard, as if he was back at the mercy of the no mercy police he had gone to in hope of mercy.

'My name's Alex,' he offered, noncommittally, making just the minimum eye contact.

'Who?'

Alex cleared his own throat. 'My name's Alex.'

'Alex?' She seemed to wrestle with the information slightly. He half expected her to follow up with 'It's a bit gay, innit?'

More silence, another pause. Patrick exchanged one be careful glance at Alex then self-consciously sipped from his beer.

'Are you normal?' was Eve's next quizzical conundrum.

As much buying time as anything else, Alex begged her pardon.

'I said, are you normal?'

Normal? Normal as in what? Normal for Bridgwater??

Alex shrugged his shoulders. 'Uh, I'm not sure how to answer that.'

'*I* thought you were horny.'

Alex sat, dumbfounded, catching a look-out-she's-mad look in Patrick's eye.

'Well, aren't you gonna answer??'

Alex pulled a face, beyond the point of caring. 'Answer what, exactly?'

'Are you *gay*?'

Well, I'm not a macho leftie and I've got a bit of a queer name, he felt like saying, knowing it would be lost.

'I should have known you were gay,' was spat at him as if he indisputably was and it were the crime of the millennium. 'You look fuckin' gay.' Presumably that was why she had seemed interested in his sexual attitude seconds earlier.

Eve whatever her surname was took her self and venom back to the table she had come from, surrounded by similar aged women dressed in overtly optimistic fashion; possibly Bridgwater's misandritarians' weekly shindig.

Alex didn't bother ordering another cider. He felt that tonight he could not feel drunk if he tried.

30

Alex did not sleep well at the best of times, but this night had proved especially difficult. Somewhere close to Daniel's house a car's alarm had gone off several times during the small hours, each for around the mandatory minute before it realised its smart chip self was moronically crying wolf. Were Alex ever to be made autocratic ruler of Planet Earth, one of the first changes he would implement would be the complete disablement of every car alarm in existence, for, after all, what possible function could they serve any more in modern society? However, being that his promotion to global absolutist dictator did not look particularly imminent, such noise pollution in the guise of helping one sleep tighter looked like it could safely break into our sleep patterns a good few fragmented nights more.

Leaving the house before Daniel was up, Alex went to Recruitment West to find out what the phone message had been about. Accepting it with both the dread of uncertainty and the burden of necessity, Alex agreed to begin the following morning at Badger Valley Farmers, filling sacks with animal feeds. Wonderful. Another ambition's fulfilment to be ticked off on life's long list. Badger Valley Farmers was a strange name, being as badgers were hardly considered friends to the industry – it had no more sense than them calling themselves after a mole, for example.

Alex took a bus trip to Taunton he could not afford to sign his name on some more pointless forms at the job agency he was enrolled with there. He hoped, alas in vain, that they might offer him something there and then less repellent than tomorrow's start at Badger Valley Farmers sounded.

Alex paced around Taunton, trying to immerse himself in the slightly less choking atmosphere of the county seat, nothing to do, nothing to spend, no-one to meet, nowhere to go, and feeling all the while that he was wasting his time, which he was. A few hours later, with the best of the day's sunlight already packed and left, he reluctantly climbed back onto the bus home, only twenty-one minutes late for its departure which was impressive by Somerset public transport standards.

As the journey wound slowly but dependably toward Bridgwater, like a terminally ill person toward their own final destination, Alex barely noticed the scenery trundling past. 'Ooh, look over there,' one middle-aged woman said to another a few seats away from Alex. 'It looks all...whazizname...rainified.'

Alex somehow tuned this out. With the gravity of the day winding toward its close and the morbid dread of tomorrow's new job looming, Alex hoped the smudged clouds over the Quantocks did not signify rain after all. Alex hoped they portended the end of the fucking world.

31

Alex got off the bus in Taunton Road, unable to stomach the involuntary eavesdropping on inanity so pointless, he wondered how anyone could think let alone voice it, any more. He checked his pockets and discovered less than ten pounds, most of it in annoying shrapnel, remained upon his person. He didn't know what or how he was going to eat tonight exactly, so would need to gamble his luck and peace of mind with the fruit machine that was the Halifax ATM. He hoped his balance might total three in a row other than zero-zero-zero.

He decided to walk through Blake Gardens, a small park in the town centre which featured all the usual trappings plus more: a heavily-graffittied bandstand, benches intact and vandalised, floral diplays, vandalised floral displays, litter, dope smokers, used hypodermics, cottagers, gangs of wilfully-suspect looking youths, and a subtly foreboding atmosphere. It also housed the town library at the edge of the park that bordered with Dampiet Street, although the library entrances were accessible only from the street, which ensured somebody went there. Adjoining the library were the public toilets out of bound to the public for several years. Originally a firm favourite for cottagers, these toilets then met with vandalism enough times that the council decided to take serious action. And thus there came the grand public announcement and virtual unveiling of the innovative concept of vandalism-proof toilets, complete, of course, with those nuances that seem almost unique to Britain: blue IV-user-foiling internal lighting dovetailed against a used needle deposit box. The devil makes work for idle hands to do, and those with an artistic bent forever seek new and exciting challenges, and thus it was the vandalism-proof toilets were vandalised beyond use. The council had them mended one more time and then the same process was repeated. As a result, these conveniences remain to this day a useless monument commemorating the indefatigable victories of mindless destruction and the humiliating impotence of shambolic local government.

For years, a sheltered paved area next to the defunct toilets was a shelter from the elements and drug users and alcoholics' hangout, until eventually the council decided to engage in their own bit of vandalism and wall this up with the cheapest ugliest breezeblock façade they could manage, and thus provide a few more square metres of graffiti to obscure the bigger eyesore of the wall itself. Even the historical-interest feature of a stone arbour had had metal bars fixed across its entrance and windows, the council deciding that if anyone was going to ruin a monument it was going to be them. Like the mentality behind CCTV cameras, some people seem to believe that if you deny 'undesirables' the ability to indulge in anti-social behaviour in one place, the anti-social behaviour and the intentions and social factors that spawn them just magically go away instead of manifesting elsewhere. In the case of CCTV, in the light of Alex's recent experience in the most central location in the town, CCTV did not even seem to succeed at displacing a problem, the evidence screamed.

As Alex neared the gates the council had given up padlocking at night to keep people out of the park, an adolescent male swiftly materialised from behind the thin screen of a hedge and deliberately stepped directly before Alex, blocking his path. For a horrifying instant, Alex thought he had tempted fate a stretch too far and this was the same person as had attacked him on the Cornhill, but a few blinks later it was clear this was someone else, although he got the feeling he was not about to be asked if he ever thought about why we all here or had considered thumbing through a copy of Watchtower.

'Gis 50p, mate.'

'I haven't even got fifty pence to spare,' Alex stated, blandly and truthfully.

'No, mate, I ain't mucking around. Just give us 50p, right?'

'I don't have fifty pence.'

The boy mutated his face into a half-snarl, but a frown dominated. He did not quite seem to know how to continue, especially when Alex was showing neither impatience to get past nor retreating. What Alex would have liked to say was something along the lines of 'I have to take it on faith that you haven't fifty pence, why can't you do the same for me?' or 'Look at my clothes and look at yours, and then tell me which one of has the most,' apart from the more counter-confrontational 'Get out of my way now', but even the first two questions were likely to be lost on or interpreted as the cue for a fight by this example of social plankton currently before him. His sneer remaining to help him keep his ugly face, he moved out of the way in the guise of idly circling Alex, calling a 'Fucking idiot,' under his breath as Alex continued on his way. Well, that told Alex.

From one failed extortionist to another with global success, Alex arrived at the Halifax and held his breath as he got to the front of the internal ATM queue and attempted to withdraw fifty pounds.

He was denied. The onscreen balance flashed up, the coldness and indifference of the digits on the screen rubbing salt into the emotional wound they had carved.

The balance in Alex's Halifax Cardcash Solo account was £33.41.

With what he had in low worth coinage scattered through his pockets, Alex's total wealth was likely to amount to £40.

Aware people were waiting to use the machine after him, and in that way the English born never quite manage to shake off entirely, he took the thirty accessible to him while trying to effect a nonchalant expression.

He tucked the notes carefully into his shirt pocket as he exited the bank, almost forgetting his card altogether. It wasn't much use to him now anyway.

Forty pounds, he thought, as he stepped out into Fore Street, an address that could have been anywhere in any world. Forty pounds sterling. Forty British pounds. Forty quid. About a month's wage for a peasant in the Dominican Republic but less than a week's dole here.

Tomorrow the job at Badger Valley Farmers was due to begin. Friday, the last day of the working week. He would have to wait a further week to be paid and even then he would receive just one day's pay.

He had no credit card (but a wonderful credit card debt), and nothing to sell. He didn't even have a sofa to look behind.

His mother was in the Caribbean. He had no idea where his father was. He had no friends with money to spare, and he thought it too humiliating to ask anyone for a loan he had no idea when or how he could pay back anyway.

Forty pounds to last one week and then, what, another forty pounds at the end of that, for another long week? If he stuck out the day's work tomorrow, that was. What choice was there? The dole? He would be trapped in his current rut for time immemorial, and probably get into it far, far deeper.

He looked to his left, toward Admiral Robert Blake. People were walking along, families with pushchairs and babies, teenagers in logo-flashing overpriced clothes. A businessman hurried along in a suit, a briefcase stuffed with importance in his hand.

Alex turned to the right, looking toward the town bridge. One woman was showing another the contents of her shopping bags. A boy was speaking on a mobile phone. A couple were pushing their mountain bikes along, their hands not supporting their bikes encircled around each other's.

Alex froze in a numb disbelieving indecision. Thirty-five years of life, forty pounds of financial wealth accrued.

He looked at the passing faces again, some of which gave him a lingering look back. He must have looked like he felt.

He tried to see someone he knew. And then he felt like he did not want to be recognised, did not want to be drawn into a conversation. He felt like he wanted to hide, he felt like he wanted to think, but could not see how either could help him in his plight.

Movement. He needed to walk. Alex liked walking, which was just as well as he couldn't drive a car. He liked the feeling of being on the move and the physical process involved. It felt like getting somewhere through effort of will, even if it was an aimless ramble half the time.

He couldn't afford to use up any more energy than he needed to, not now he was on a very strict budget for survival, but for god's sakes, what kind of life is it when you cannot even go for a walk for fear of working up a hunger you cannot afford to satisfy? Besides, whether Daniel was there or not, the littered house of Friarn Street, with its impenetrability by daylight and householder seemingly engaged in permanent psychological self-flagellation would have to wait. Not now, he wasn't ready for them now.

Alex retraced his steps back along King Street. Yes, he was going to brave Blake Gardens again. He almost hoped he would meet the same character as had failed to effectively mug him. Perhaps he could ask him if he could gis 50p.

Once in the park, Alex did not encounter the aggressive beggar, nor anyone else who wanted to give him a hard time and hindered journey to the relative safety of its parameters. He was almost disappointed, which probably meant he had started to think like one of those the behaviour of whom he most detested. Funny how desperation can taint a person's soul. He did, however, have one rather adrenalised moment when a Staffordshire Bull Terrier ran up to him, snapping at the air behind his heels. Desperately scanning the area for the dog's owner, a teenage boy tried to assure him with an ''e ain't gonna 'urt you, mate.'. Tell it to my skidmarks, Alex thought, at last out of snapping distance of the Pit Bull substitute's jaws.

When Alex got to the underpass beneath Broadway he already knew where he was going. He was going to take the canal path, out of the town and an urban environment, away from people en masse. So he could be alone with his deafening thoughts and tortured wasted being.

The underpass stank of piss, and Alex paused to empty his own bladder there, adding to the Bridgwaterisation he seemed to be fast succumbing to. As he urinated, he stared at the graffiti scrawled on the subterranean walls. Someone's initials loved someone else's. An 'I' apparently loved a question mark. Someone was gay. Someone was a bitch. Someone else was fucking dead. All of it, without exception, the most uncensored medium possible for complete and utter freedom of speech, and all of it having absolutely nothing but nothing worthwhile to say.

Alex emerged at the other side of Broadway, at the backs of the houses of Old Taunton Road, on the riverbank opposite Salmon Parade, on the verge of losing it, the edge of tears. He moved onto Old Taunton Road itself, Victorian terraced housing which should have lived and breathed history but instead felt like a past ignored in a couldn't care less town. He plodded on, thoughts buzzing and multiplying with a randomness that was positively insane, and at the same time numb to all the overloading data pinballing through his mind.

He wanted to pull something out of the fabric of reality, to see or encounter something inspiring and helpful, to find an answer to questions he could not even form present itself in the unlikeliest place, a salvation in his hour of need. Cars sat slowly rusting, eco-destructive mechanisations beyond his practical ineptitude to comprehend or control, costing more than he had ever seen or believed he would ever hold in his hands, empty and idle and currently existing only as assets for people who acquired them through means he might never understand.

Litter sprawled across the path like an obstacle course. Litter dropped by people who ate at KFC, who smoked Marlboro Lights, who failed to win the lottery once again. Despite the season, a black woollen glove lay in the middle of the pavement, all the more conspicuous for its being out of time as much as place. Like a tarantula crushed underfoot, it seemed glued to the ground, the middle finger slightly raised as if flipping Alex the bird.

The terraces made way for La Ciotat House on Alex's left and a cluster of new housing on his right, the facades to either side in that glut of ochre, bland red brick. He plodded, plodded, putting one foot in front of the other, not exactly moving very swiftly, and hardly going anywhere it looked worth going. La Ciotat House, a residential premises for the registered disabled over the age of forty, gradually slithered past his peripheral vision like an undignified burden that could only take its time to get out of the way. A miniature industrial estate replaced the residential home, a further eyesore in which able-bodied men came to rot away their wasted lives, and then Alex clambered up to the pinnacle of the humpbacked bridge over the Bridgwater-Taunton canal, the world making him feel so down he had to access reserves to make it to the top like a mountaineer upon a dizzy plateau. What was surely three generations of a family, grandmother, mother and daughter, were staring over the bridge's wall at the water below. The grandmother seemed to be educating her daughter's daughter, an infant held in her mother's arms, to the benefit of ornithology but at the expense of all three's mother tongue. ''ere, Amy, lookit them swans. Look! You see them swans?'

Alex hurried past, head down, staring at the ground, concealing his frown as if ashamed to be seen wearing one. He stepped over the gate at the bank of the canal and went treading heavily in the Taunton bound direction, wanting, perhaps needing, to be away from people, from everyone, just for a while, be it to cry or to think or not to think or just simply because and whatever else. He just knew he needed a time out from the human race. Right now he preffered the company of solitude or, failing that, nature, like the presence of them swans he could see up ahead.

32

Where had it all gone wrong?

Alex blundered on like he always did, following a trail few would choose to journey down without a set agenda, distracted more by the internal than the world that lay around, never totally aware of the getting from one place to the other, but often surprised to find the here and now had shifted in form, leaving the bemused man at the centre of his own life like a castaway shipwrecked on an island of bleak solitude or undiscovered wonders. Around him the world began to two-dimensionalise, as it did when precursing a sinking into depression, the reality becoming surreal as the nowhere and nothing and nobody-ness of one anonymous individual dominated the stage of the theatre the world had become. Birds twittered, a dog barked, them swans glided by. The distant drone of cars going by on the M5. A butterfly jerking up and down on an invisible string. A gentle splash of something in the water (If a fish splashes in a canal and there's no-one around to hear…?). A cloud of clusterflies to be absent-mindedly batted away. The rest of the world just got on with it, it seemed, this unfathomable beautiful dreadful mysterious simple complicated anarchic ordered paradox and perfect correlation of interlocking warring harmonised shapes and forms and textures and sights and sounds and colours and smells of this conundrum that was existence, an indescribable incomprehensible somethingness with no rulebook save for the relative barometers of happiness and sadness, victory and defeat, and the confusion and frustration about which was which, and how but why but no but yes. Why couldn't Alex feel the freedom, the possibilities, the awe; why did the balance always seem to be tipped toward the favour of the other side, or was that too just illusion, just subjective responses to the neutrality of the heartless indifference of nature, the raging war to feel peaceful and secure in a fight that never ended, that could never be won?

Boys sat fishing, a plastic tub of coloured maggots squirming in protest beside them on the grass. The larvae mirrored the spasming thought patterns of the stranger stumbling past, a thirty-five year old inconsequential male perhaps no less a stranger to the person that was himself.

What to do what to do what to do?

Alex let the sadness and emptiness engulf him, turning his stomach, giddying his motor skills, nullifying hope and enthusiasm and drive. Self-pity. A persecution complex upon which none could comfortably bear the burden of blame. Wasn't it all just an accident, a series of wrong choices, bad moves, the weight of circumstance good fortune had incidentally missed? Something did not feel right, there was a taste in his mouth that could not be ignored, the flavour of injustice that slithered away before it could be pinned down. Whatever he was wallowing in, be it a projection of his own shortcomings, or the realisation the world was just an unpalatable mess, he could not keep the darkness at bay; he felt it snowballing inside him, eroding faith and self-respect the more he let it fester, strangling his mental health the more he attempted to push it aside. It was a no-win situation, or that's how it seemed so it might as well have been. He felt downright sorry for himself and worse, and he hadn't whatever it took right then to elevate his plummeting thoughts.

Bitterness tinged the past and the present an opaque negative of gloom. It all, suddenly and without warning, hit home, and hit home hard.

Alone. No home. Nowhere to call home. Nothing to look forward to. Nothing to look forward to on the calendar lying ahead. Snapped back to cold sobriety yet, yet, yet again, finding all the latitude and longitude and longing simply led back to the here and the now and the same. A father who was a stranger, a mother who knew little of his plight, mental and circumstantial, for her own protection and therefore ultimately nobody's good. Welcome to Bridgwater, welcome back, to the reunion with everything he had tried to escape from, tried to rise above, to find himself succumbing to the same base, degrading, undignified struggles of those in aggressive denial of the little they had that was their lot. Home of Blake School, oh sorry *The* Blake School, that torment of his childhood, that torture chamber that had so tainted his attitude toward education, where almost every schoolmate was a roughhousing trial of nerves, and almost every so-called teacher something even worse. Oh, he remembered what they did alright, he wasn't likely to forget it in a hurry. The geography teacher who had hit him repeatedly, hit him about the head until he was dizzy with shock and pain, hit him with the audience of the goggle-eyed class to lap up his humiliation and hurt. And before that, at North Petherton junior school, the class teacher that would indulge in the same antics, knocking him about the head, often before the other children, his lip trembling as he struggled to keep control of his frayed nerves. None of it because Alex had been loud or unruly, none of it because he had been a handful. Oh no, Alex had been far too timid and crushed with shyness, the confidence squeezed out of him by his own father's tripwire temperament and disproportionate misguided anger. No, Alex was simply a misfit, pathologically unable to fit in and keep in line, even though he was petrified of standing out or falling short of impossible expectations. But there were those had posed under the job title of educators whom had seen red at his awkwardness and set him aside as a target for their own wrath, easy prey to vent their own frustrations upon. And then, also at *The* Blake School, the maths teacher and his malicious mocking of Alex's shrinking into his shell, only contributing to the process, and his thin bookishness and lack of enthusiasm for rugby, football, sports. This maths teacher had taken it upon himself to brand Alex a lady and a queer, scoring cheap point after cheap point off of him before the peerage of other boys and girls, making sure he were teased and bullied further because if he wasn't a rugger enthusiast he simply had to be a namby-pamby shirtlifter. And what if Alex had been gay, what kind of damage might have been wrought then. He remembered the behaviour, the specific incidents in detail and the taunts and jibes word by word, a part of the otherwise forgotten past that those whom had victimised him had doubtless long since washed their hands of. Christ, he could sue them if he wanted to, even now, he was sure there would be a way to do so. Maybe he even would one day. But would that be an answer? Who the hell could tell, and who the hell was going to tell Alex? And then, finally, somehow and impossibly, albeit unceremoniously, school days had come to their end. And then...what? He dragged his underconfident shell out into the world, accompanied by the only voices that seemed to come from kindred spirits, that seemed to echo his own jaded thoughts and feelings, that seemed to come from the fringe that he could identify with as unknown unknowable friends – punks. That banshee howl of protest struck a chord with Alex, finally relieving him with the confirmation of his biggest fear – yes, the world really was imperfect and yes, others were also feeling thoroughly disgruntled with the fact. At last, all that angst, all that anger and deep-seated sense of injustice had an outlet, a whole genre of artistic expression to engage with and, united in apartness, fight to change. It had all seemed so credible, so manageable, so like the tide was changing for the first time in history and this was the cutting edge thin end of the wedge with ideas and energy more revolutionary and just than anything else and ever before. Hail to Crass, to New Model Army, to Subhumans, not that mere rabble-rousing commercial venture speeded up rock and roll with contrived sensationalist shock tactics that was the Pistols, but soulful punk with philosophy and conviction and something to say and with a package that gave more than it needed to with the absence of narcissism and shameless self-publicity. Now Alex's desire to strike back at the cruel world had channels, avenues, directions in which anarchy could be organised. Alex embraced pacifism, vegetarianism, the anti-government stances it didn't seem to matter offered nothing as an alternative, the recognition of racism and sexism and the stranglehold these had over the media and marketplace. The opposition to warmongering, to nuclearisation, to sacrificing the removal of want for the sake of having enough artillery to destroy the world countless times over. This was the world of statistics, and harsh ones at that, and demagogy of a political campaign against politicisation. But then the humanitarian got confused with the antisocial, something caused punk to choke on its own malleable righteousness, the bands started to age, spikey-tops grew balding, the anger started to seem pathetic, the world remained as corrupt as it ever had been. And then politics – the sworn enemy of yesterday – became the ally of today, and the manifesto of the red seemed to offer the missing links the heartfelt but clueless punk credo had been spitting at itself for failing to fully locate. Three months was all it took during that period when the red flag was replaced with the red rose for that whirlwind romance to run its course. The seventeen-year-old was far from welcomed into the fold but became a sort of pawn to be pushed and pulled between one warring faction and the other, caught in the midst of their petty and pathetic personality clashes dressed as internationalism's brothers' and sisters' struggle. Solidarity, community, were nowhere to be found, just self-righteous self-satisfied self-referential and spiritually vacuous machismo, choking on its own arrogance and bile, bowing to the pathetic Freudian father substitute and atheists' equivalent of the Christian God; a flag the colour of, and saturated with, spilt blood. And yet he was growing up in the choking sell-out society of Thatcher and her legacy that seems to refuse to die, and he knew too that the right was as equally unsuited to him. The sharp-suited upholdance of selfishness and ruthlessness, the licence for exploitative private enterprise at the cost of true individualism – wolves dressed as lambs behaving like sheep, and that slowburn class genocide that negates ideals and conditions love and dumbs down culture to the lowest common denominator highest profit appeal was as much anathema to Alex as the empty promises of socialism. What was it that someone had once told him? The wheels of capitalism are much less bloody than those of socialism, but far dirtier. Indeed. And from the nuts and bolts of revolutionary struggle there came an urgent need to fill the gaping void left by anarchy and Marxism, and thus the world of the spiritual offered its glittering prizes. The esoteric, riding high on the fads of tie-dyed, incense burning neo-Wiccan quasi-Pagan yin yang West-controlled-Eastern-styled New Ageism elevated him to a higher state of susceptibility and the need to believe. And thus it was the searching and the seeking and the reading and the chilling and the visits to megalithic sites and ley lines and zones of intense energy man and all like that like bullshit but Zen bullshit man, *Zen* bullshit sat him down in the Lotus position on the Lotus blossom that is Buddhism, that beatific flower regally sprouting from life's boggy mire. And after the first encounter at one of their monthly meetings, so Alex too began to meditate as the Nichiren Shoshu Sokka Gakkai sect do, who, of course, refer to their meditation as chanting and not meditation, and their sect as anything but a sect. Having nothing to lose, Alex meditated earnestly, reciting mantra after mantra, voicing cryptic archaic-Japanese sutra after sutra, and sure enough, and make no mistake, something positive and tangible did indeed begin to happen. Confidence rocketing and fortunes improving at speed, so Alex started to experience what only those whom have practised meditation at length can experience; a kind of purification from within, a grasping of one's personal mission, and a tangible comprehension and improvement of one's karma. But the irony was that, while his inner strength and personal development seemed to impossibly blossom in no time at all, thus he started to see the cracks and gulfs in the politics of the group and its meetings, in the whole institutionalisation of the movement that had started him on this journey of self-discovery and spiritual adventure. The further his mind seemed to gape and grasp at possibility and potential, the more poison he perceived in his counterparts, and the less and less Buddhist the establishments that existed under the blanket label of Buddhism seemed to become. He saw materialism where there was supposed to be spiritualism, egocentrism where there might have been community, cliché and surface-skimming labelled as depth, blind acceptance in lieu of faith, the need to control paraded as the desire to grow. Alex was not surprised by this falling apart at the seams as just as he came to consciously recognise this uneasy dichotomy so the honeymoon period of the meditation came to its calamitous end. What had gone so far had been, it now appeared, a window, a portal, to that that is attainable, to the potential and glory that would now require perhaps more courage and effort and tests of faith than Alex had ever entertained the idea of firewalking his way through in order to win back and uphold the delicious dream now so teasingly elusive. As he drifted from his meditating peers, so any ghost of a support base disintegrated, and he was plunged alone into a world forever changed, in which he understood unspeakable treasures are attainable, but at the most unspeakable cost. Snowballing fatalistic personal evolution pulling him hither and thither like a dervish, his concentration, his resolve, faltered, his newfound strength wavered, and he grew bored of the mediation's oft grinding routine. An easier metaphysical fix was sought. And thus, a journey of discovery of drugs and their manifold effects became the new Mecca of his soul. His very first venture was far from subtle, for he began in the class A world of psychotropics, the alleged hallucinogens. Psilocybe mushrooms, gathered from nearby fields, plunged him headlong into another realm with the immediate and ultra-personal sense of euphoria as mediation had, with TV dinner accessibility. With the doors of perception thrown wide and agape, further forays were made into the realisation that the majority of the minions are failing to follow their hearts, are self-deceivers and addicts to distraction from doing what they feel inside themselves they most ought. The near-telepathic insight gleaned from the substance outlawed and scorned for its dissident properties only as a cosmetic veil to keep the masses from the undeniable insight it provides in extremis was tapped again and again until life again chided him for overindulgence and failure to seek out the next rung on the ladder. Confused amongst this lifestyle too were the purveyors of tetrahydracannibinol, the leaf partakers, the dope smokers whom all too easily became dopeheads. Dope was the word that seemed to most accurately summarise that particular subdivision of the drug subculture, for although Alex had experienced enjoyment from the herb, an enhancement of the senses when with one or two close friends, and deepened appreciation of music when hearing it while stoned, the relaxation it provided could all too easily become paranoia when in the company of its less wholesome users in plenitude and finding one's guard had been drastically reduced by the stupefying effects of the drug. Perhaps worse still were the habitual and often daily users, numb to appreciation of the effects due to their lazy overindulgence, the relaxation becoming apathy becoming complacency about their apathy in an ongoing cycle of social inertia. As far as Alex was concerned, show him a habitual dope smoker and he would show you a constant crashing bore. And then, the rift between Alex and the rest of the world feeling deeper and crueller by degrees, with society at large, reactionaries and rebels, the politically motivated and –disenchanted, the drug-addled and the drug-free, the material pursuers and spiritual seekers, everyone and everywhere a door that led back to itself, or that was slammed in his face at the start, thus he floundered without direction or any sense of belonging, without counsel or kin, floating in a tormenting whirlpool of resisting the ratrace and subsequent joblessness and poverty, through loneliness and desperation and absence of a clue and elusiveness of point, then down into an inevitable depression and nervous debility and obsessive-compulsive disorders and loss of confidence and damage to health. For years he trod water through this seemingly endless heartless ocean, dependent on social welfare, alienating himself from his disappointed parents, doing himself no favours but unable to find momentum or impetus or direction and without heart to go anywhere that was not in his empty cardiac chambers. Travel became the manifestation of that lostness inside, the ceaseless questing searching for whatever might prove to be the thing, the ones, the answers he had not known he was specifically looking for all his lifetime. Czechoslovakia had proved to be so much lighter in spirit, less threatening, less front-obsessed than the English. But gradually he recognised a duplicity in the cosmetic, and the Czechs taught him well what a passive-aggressive disposition is, with their utilitarianism of friendship, commodification of social interaction, and over-compensatory gut-reaction to the end of communism, replacing it with an anarchically decadent neo-Thatcherite ultra-rightism. The States had proved more odious than England, in the sunshine belt states of the south east, where they practised a virtual annihilation of Alex's mother tongue, upheld the Second Amendment in one's face, completely depended upon the car as if its absence were a form of social leprosy, displayed microchip-implanted gut-reflex ultra-patriotism, and where the land of the free meant slaving to the lynchpin of accepted responsibility – needlessly, ridiculously long and hard hours of work. Spain was possibly the happiest country to have spent time enough in to be able to say he had lived there, largely due to the climate making depression all but impossible. But here too the seasonal Costa faux-Espana had shown cracks enough that Alex knew he was standing on shifting sands, momentarily dazzled by the holiday romaniticism but with little chance of avoiding the return to England, to Bridgwater, to the exit of summer and the rushed onset of autumn and the falling back to Terra Firma not an inch of which was etched with the promise of shelter anymore. And in the loneliness of those brief migrations, that flight of fancy that always seemed to see its shadow fall first upon the ground where it was about to land, that eagle cry loneliness was dovetailed against feather-in-the-cap memories of females along the way; those several short-lived fiery involvements that had scorched his wings and singed his heels, his habit of easily giving away his heart and plunging deep with another whose breath he had stolen with his gentleness and passion and clear desire to truly love; finally dashing on the rocky bottom of the baser aspects of everyday existence, the intoxication felt by those giddied by his soulfulness and wordiness and dreams surprisingly torn asunder when the wanderlusting little boy lost scribe was revealed to be unable to afford a button for a shirt upon a back, ill-equipped to tie a lace let alone a long-term knot, and dogged by a history of charming then starving the lovers of his past to the point where even he now wondered if it all hadn't much risen above conquests with fanciful aspirations, self-punishment and a will to hurt others wrapped in the romantically-coloured paper thinness of bleeding heart love.

A dog shouted at him to clear off out of it from behind a back garden fence. He jumped, briefly startled from his ferocious thought patterns, surprised to find he was almost at the arch of Somerset Bridge, right on the outskirts of the town. The dog snapped again and Alex locked eyes with it for a second, revealing something of the keen-sensed beast inside that silenced the canine and more domesticated of the two.

It seemed to Alex that the rest of the world had set about organising their own lives while he had been trying and failing to come to terms with what life was. While the multitudes had been busily preparing for the future, he had been busily unable to keep from agonising over the riddles of eternity. He passed under the brick bridge, a simple yet vital invention and construction, forged by hands in seemingly impossible co-operation with each other. He heard the traffic rumbling over the motorway bridge in the nearing distance with concentrated purpose. The ugly unnaturally blue monstrosity of the Argos building straddled the horizon, filled with a thousand acting with the industriousness of a colony of ants. What was it that made this world tick so efficiently, so methodically, predictably, routinely? What was it that kept everybody in this monotonous cycle of drudgery and humbleness, this abomination we call a living the practice of which seems antonymous to the term?

It bloody well beat Alex.

The first few drops of rain flecked his face and he looked up toward their source with an almost unconsciously beseeching expression. The water pressure increased fourfold as if at the turn of a dial, and all at once Alex realised that being where he was he was going to get soaked. 'Have a laugh,' he managed to get out, before looking back down at the ground.

The rain immediately multiplied in force once again above the man in the middle of nowhere.

33

Alex arrived back at Daniel's house in Friarn Street like a drifter carried by a biblical tide. Once inside, Alex discovered Daniel had company, and looked to be in some tense negotiating with the vaguest veneer of camaraderie with his business partner and co-owner of the cursed computer shop. So engrossed were they in the discussion that looked to be a far from happy one, the drenched tramp tramped his squelching self out of the living room and upstairs to the slim possibility of a clean dry towel with barely a glance or look of acknowledgement. Alex was grateful, he wasn't exactly feeling sociable. However, the vibes from downstairs seemed to have pervaded and invaded the upper floor like vines from a black magic beanstalk. Outside, thunder had been electro-magnetised to the rain intensifying to an apocalyptic degree. The unwholesome mumbling of voices downstairs became increasingly argumentative, synchronising the atmosphere indoors and out. Alex didn't feel welcome in the house at that moment. He felt in the way. But the world outdoors was a no man's land, the rain adding to the greyness of it all instead of refreshing the streets and the air. Stuck between a rock and a gritty place.

There were no towels to be found in the bathroom or airing cupboard it housed, save for those drenched and trodden upon on the clutterbucket floor. Instead Alex used one of his own T-shirts to try to dry his hair, learning as he did so that T-shirts made poor substitutes for towels. He braved one look in a mirror and wished it had exploded before it had reflected. He shuddered and sniffed and changed his wet through clothes for fresh ones overdue for laundering. He felt hungry but could not face the kitchen downstairs, knew he would find nothing to eat there anyway, and hated the thought of even entering the kitchen let alone trying to potter around in it. He could have used a hot drink too but didn't want to go down and feel obliged to offer to make the heated debaters something as well. He also felt as if his social skills would be as bare and essential as that that passed for sustenance in the kitchen cupboards.

The rain plummeted in fat drops, splatting against the window pane, distorting the view of the outside world as if the outside world were peering in while pulling a face at him. Needing to drink something, he picked a glass up off the floor, drinking room temperature day old tap water from it, grimacing at the theoretically tasteless liquid.

He would have liked to have had a bath but the bathtub looked like it would contaminate more than clean anyone bathing in it. He could not remember the last time he had felt clean or worn really clean clothes. He could not remember the last time he had eaten a sensible meal. His stomach groaned in protest at the neglect it had suffered, but he was clueless as to how to satisfyingly fill it. He wasn't even really able to afford any more artery-furring, heart valve-gluing takeaway junk food to stave off the hunger pangs and replace them with the feeling of lethargy and unwholesome indulgence.

The room was dimming and not just with the storm. The day was waning, racing like an Olympic sprinter toward tomorrow and the first shift at Badger Valley Farmers. His stomach noisily protested again, another hobgoblin adding to its torments.

Even a half-decent cup of coffee seemed out of his fucking league.

Alex did not know where to go, simply did not know where to put himself. Literally and figuratively.

He sat his dirty self in his soiled clothes down beside his discarded sodden ones upon the Petri dish of a mattress and cover. The voices continued from below, angrier and angrier in tone. The rain continued its desolate timpane upon the window, as cold as it was indifferent as it was cold. No-one was going to be bringing him a meal ticket in the immediate future, no-one was about to magic him out of his circumstantial, situational, psychological, karmic rut.

A tear formed in one eye, but it was not joined by a second. At that moment he craved the release of emotionally letting go, of surrendering to his fragilities and weaknesses, of venting the wounds upon his psyche, bleeding and leaching the poison from his soul.

But, trying to roll with the gut reaction, he somehow found himself unable.

He could not even cry.

34

The Club was The Club was The Club. Ken was working the bar, pouring almost as much of his own money into the takings as of the punters. Patrick was keeping the masses entertained with the latest update of minutiae from Good Vayoo Records, Ian was rewriting the telling and retelling of jokes.

Alex couldn't afford to drink, couldn't afford to get drunk with what was happening first thing in the morning, couldn't afford to pour anything alcoholic onto an all but empty stomach. He opted for a cheapjack gutrot cider.

He sat and shot the shovellable with Patrick and Ian, attempting to distract his thoughts from the knowledge he would be doing such far more literally within a revolution of the clock's fervent hands. His own efforts proved all but fruitless until he was rescued by someone else's intervention and subsequent threat.

Big Bob's shadow engulfed the entire corner of the bar where the three were sitting, then the big guy's butt engulfed the stool beside Alex, straining the seat almost as much as he was about to strain the nerves. Conversation came to an involuntary halt. Patrick squeezed out a 'Hello, Bob' in a voice that tried not to sound heliumised.

'Ooz yer mate?' Bob growled, nonsense and mercy-free, jabbing his thumb at Alex like a spear.

'That's Alex,' Patrick managed through teeth that tried to grin. 'You've met Alex before.'

'Well, my mate don' like 'en.'

Alex sat as silent and still as a statue, momentarily too surprised to have the shakes.

'Which mate is that?' Patrick enquired through a careful frown. 'Eve.'

Oh *what*? Alex's mind reeled as if possessed by the phantoms of ciders yet undrunk. He turned to see the woman who had branded him as first possibly abnormal, then possibly as horny, then definitely as gay, was sat at the table Big Bob must have just left. She was looking over at the proceedings and exchanging sharp looks and pointed comments with fanged, beaked, taloned friends.

'Eve?' Patrick, and Alex blessed him for such, exclaimed, incredulously, and genuinely enough so.

'Yeah. An' oi don' loike people upsettin' moi friends.'

That's something that can't happen often, Alex couldn't help but allow himself to think, a thought that was overshadowed by another thought: Oh heck!

'Alex ain't no harm to anyone,' Patrick further gallantly rescued.

'Well, that's not what Eve says.'

Alex had had enough of being talked about in the third person. It was time to look the monster in the mouth. 'Excuse me, I haven't done anything to upset your friend. If your friend is upset it is because of a misunderstanding, not because of anything I've said or done. I don't come into this place looking for trouble, I've got more sense than to do that.' The big man at last turned to look Alex in the eye, seeming to have more difficulty with the task than Alex had with him. He let Big Bob, and anyone else with vision and a brain, see he meant what he said. Suddenly Alex neither felt nor looked like the smaller of the two.

'Well, oim only tellin' you what oi 'eard,' Big said, but it was already an almost conciliatory would be Parthian shot. The giant was already slithering back to the black clad and their rites that had summoned its presence forth.

Patrick gave one more assurance to Big Bob, and then the nightmare was over, almost as quickly as begun. To celebrate his survival, Alex bought himself and Patrick and Ian another drink, filling himself with more of the poison, pushing himself further toward starvation's door.

35

At ten before seven the following morn, Alex took his sour-butterfly-inhabited-stomached self into Badger Valley Farmers' reception. After three and a half decades of life experience, a not entirely insubstantial number of been there seen that done its, he was surprised at just how much misfortune and desperation can erode the confidence. He could not remember feeling like he did now since his first day at *The* Blake School.

A thin middle-aged man in an imperfectly pressed shirt and tie the wearing of which it was clear was largely pointless to him, introduced himself as the manager, not a Mr Badger but a weaselly Mr Stoat. With minimalist overture he was escorted through a couple of storerooms and into the beast of the machine, a portal through which he quantum jumped, or fell, back into a Dickensian Dystopian hole.

Hulking grain mills flanked the walls and loomed overhead, churning and grinding like giant castanets, needles wavering, valves hissing, a couple of overalled men rallying round and scratching their heads, reading the dials with a look of concern. Primaeval conveyor belts, all wood and iron and caked in dust, trundled sack after heavy sack of backbreaking work and particles to breathe. Pallets teetered in hastily constructed stacks, narrowly missed by a forklift driven by a man on a life and death mission. Vats of agricultural supplies, some with hazard labels, were barrelled between man and machine on trolleys leaving tracks on the inch-thick carpet of dust and desiccation. Orders were barked, warnings yelled, rebukes were fired back. A couple of hostile glances were shot Alex's way by the half dozen men whom had clearly been doing their jobs for a long time and clearly been doing their jobs for too long.

The driver of the forklift was persuaded to sprint over to Alex and Mr Stoat, where he was introduced as the Foreman, otherwise known as Steve. Steve was a stocky man, oozing self-importance and serious job dedication, in filthy jeans and a lumberjack shirt, short hair, hard face, eyes that drilled holes from which there poured no light. Alex was passed from Mr Stoat to Steve like the spare part tool that he was, and the two men went to the room used for breaks – hardly a canteen, hardly a kitchen, hardly a recreational room but somewhere in which the only work that was done was tolerating those on the same break.

'Done anythin' like this before?' Steve asked as they entered the fluorescently-lit would be escape.

What? Shovel shit for peanuts? 'Uh…I've not done anything quite like this before, no.'

'Ugh. What sorta stuff you been doin' then?'

Alex shrugged. What to tell this man. 'Bits of allsorts really.'

'Anyway, here's where you make yerself a tea ur coffee. There's two breaks a day, 'alf 'our each break. Ya got any questions?'

'Is it fun working here?' Alex couldn't help himself.

Steve blinked. 'It ain't too bad, once ya get used to it.'

'OK.'

'Right, I'll see you downstairs once yer ready then.'

Alex didn't know what he needed to do to get himself ready, but accepted the chance to linger in the 'staff room' (?) a minute more, by himself. The yellow-walled harshly lit room contained a table surrounded by chairs, and there was also a sink and worksurface, with mugs and spoons, a kettle and microwave. The table was scattered with The Sun, The Mirror, an Auto Trader and Bridgwater's free mailshot rags. On one wall, the Badger Valley Farmers calendar hung, depicting idyllic country scenes from an antithetic universe to where it now hung. On another wall pouted an A2 shrinkage of Jordan and her breasts, the nipples covered by squares of leopard skin seat covering, the logo of a boyracer magazine unsubtly emblazoning one corner. Alex took himself away from the thoroughly unsexy poster, down to the thoroughly unsexy world of Badger Valley graft.

36

Alex's job description at Badger Valley Farmers was much of a muchness, with just the right amount of twist on the monotony for each machine and customer's needs to keep tedium outdistanced by stress. Sacks were positioned with their openings beneath a funnel, then fed with the appropriate amount of grain or dried produce with the help of either foot pedals or handles. To those whom had worked at the plant ad nauseam ad infinitum i.e. everyone else, the co-ordination required to keep this process smooth and flowing was second nature; to Alex it meant a stumbling lack of synchronisation, grain pouring out of funnels before the sacks were in position, his hands hastily jerked out of the way of industrial clamps he had received no training about the dangers of, and scornful looks and barely under-the-breath grumblings from his new colleagues. Another task was the lining up of the unevenly weighted sacks with a sewing device to seal them shut. Never before had such inventive and artistic needlework found its way onto Badger Valley bagging once Alex was handed the controls. Different machines meant different controls, different customers meant different amounts of filling, different sack materials meant varying degrees of difficulty with the stitching, different workmates meant different degrees and styles of impatience and bad vibes to discourage him even more.

Somehow, in that way that seems all but inexplicable fantasy when we're caught in its invisibly amorphous trap, it came the time for the day to grind to its unceremonious end at Badger Valley, leaving Alex far from enthusiastic about returning on Monday, but thrilled nevertheless to have made it this far.

He took his broke, grubby, physically weary, but appreciative of the fact it was Friday evening, self, back to Friarn Street and Daniel's house, with an appetite-whetting taste of freedom in his mouth about to be diluted by a surprise dish of bitter aftertaste.

37

'I wonder if I could have a word with you about stuff,' Daniel muttered, not very comfortably, as they sat before their finished meal of economy tinned spaghetti on toast before Friday's obligatory helping of Big boring Brother.

'Sounds potentially heavy enough,' Alex replied, and carefully took a swallow of acerbic economy tea.

'Well,' Daniel groaned, 'I hope it's not too heavy.' He licked the Rizla he was preparing to roll. And then Daniel did something that was wildly out of character. He muted the TV – *Big Brother* and all. 'Although there's nothing wrong with your being here, as far as your behaviour or manner are concerned, I'm going to have to ask you to find somewhere else to stay, Alex. It's not like an absolute emergency or anything, but let's say maybe if you could find somewhere else in the next few weeks that would probably be for the best.'

Alex stared at a corner where clutter he had tried to clear had reappeared and reappeared. He shrugged. 'Well, OK. Of course it's clear I wasn't wanting to put upon you longer than necessary anyway. I'll...try to find somewhere else within the next few weeks. I hope I'm successful.'

'Well, obviously I'm not going to kick you out literally onto the street if you haven't found anywhere by then, but...you know what I mean.'

'OK.' Alex frowned, then tried to effect a blank expression.

Daniel sighed, then lit and inhaled some carcinogens. 'I'm having some pretty major problems in the shop right now. I'm really negotiating pulling out of the place as well.' Alex wanted to congratulate him on this, but sensed it was best to keep his counsel. 'I don't think it's going to be an easy thing to resolve. You know I'm only officially living here by myself, and with my business partner and the neighbours able to see who's coming and going, it's probably only a matter of time before someone might blow the whistle on the fact you're here with me.'

'Uh...Forgive me, but I don't understand why you think anyone would do that. I thought you had a good relationship with your neighbours, so you said.'

Daniel sighed again. 'I do, but...I don't want to push the boat out too far. I'm in a bit of a fragile state at the moment-' (*What? A moment that lasts a lifetime?* Alex's unconscious automatically uttered) '-and I'm thinking about going on the sick for a while. The last thing that would help me is for there to be some problem with my landlord or for me to be prosecuted for failing to declare how many people are living here where council tax is concerned.'

'Daniel, wait a minute. I am a guest in your house, no-one else knows exactly when I come and go, and everyone is allowed to have guests come and stay with them from time to time. I am perfectly honestly not living here, I don't actually want to be registered as living here, I'm not living anywhere officially at all – in fact, I probably barely exist officially any more. I'll clear out and give you some space, fine, but please don't let worries about legalities be the cause for me to go.'

Daniel stared at *Big Brother* in muted mode much as he did when the volume was on. 'I'll ask Malcolm what the legal considerations are and when a guest officially becomes recognised as a tenant. I just don't want to take any chances with anything. With respect, it's my home, Alex, it's my decision, and I think two weeks is enough time to find somewhere else, I'm sure there are other people who have fewer problems than me right now-' (*No, actually there aren't, Daniel, everyone has a lifetime's equal share.*) '-who will be able to help you with somewhere to stay for a while too. I'm sorry, I don't want to be a bastard, it's just, things are pretty tough for me right now, the timing isn't exactly perfect.'

'There's no such thing as the right time in life, for anyone, for anything.' (*Oh yes, and irrational fear is your biggest threat, not the bloody local council; the same thing you've allowed to hold you back all your days.*) 'But don't worry about it, hey, I'll find somewhere else, let's just relax for now.'

But Alex did not intend finding somewhere else within the next few weeks. He intended getting out, one way or another, this very weekend.

38

A lex was overdue for a slice of good fortune. On Saturday, one week after arriving back in Britain, he was handed such much needed luck on a plate.

Roy Butcher and Sarah Butler were old friends and colleagues from the halcyon days of the late eighties when Alex was fresh from school and all three were being spoiled in enviable jobs at the town's, and country's oldest, arts centre. Bridgwater Arts Centre housed the only other bar in the town that Alex felt comfortable drinking in, and the whole building had a unique atmosphere of rich lingering presences, cross-cultural fingerprints, and the echoes of old applause that resonated from wing to wing. Alex, Roy and Sarah had worked there during the building's more halcyon days too; a time when plays, concerts and exhibitions managed to draw a crowd, when the community was invitingly and actively involved in both the events and running of the establishment, when interesting people gathered at the place and made it more interesting, when the drama was not restricted to the auditorium but played out in the interaction between the adequate familial staff and unfolded in infighting between the staid and adventurous and head-to-head friction between and within youth group factions and oar-plunging local dignitaries. In the two decades since, the character and atmosphere has been eroded by a more conservative and skeletonised day-to-day running of the place, an idiot council who think cuts to arts funding are somehow going to be for the town's own good, and what seems to be social apathy for anything that isn't mass-media consumerist or interactive in an onscreen one-dimensional way. However, Bridgwater Arts Centre has a ghost, in almost every sense, and no matter what changes have besieged the building, to stand in its auditorium one can feel the history, timelessness, antiquity and passion like a spectral breath upon your tingling flesh. Local government has had designs on closing the premises in Castle Street for many years, and Alex hoped that if this plan ever met with success, they might be haunted by undying voices gravely mourning due to their soulless lack of vision and cold-blooded contempt to the dying days of their useless and meddlesome careers.

Roy, a Tauntonian man around three years older than Alex, had been employed as the centre's technician, and Sarah had been taken on at the same time as a secretary, Alex being the publicist. But the truth was everyone did whatever was needed as needed, no-one particularly understood or lived up to their job titles (particularly Alex), and it was as much a social occasion as a job, far more so in fact, they genuinely happily turned up to each day. Despite being a decade older, in years at least, Sarah had taken to Roy in a romantic fashion, and Roy reciprocated accordingly, and the pair had been together since, living under the same roof in Alfoxton Road on the Quantock Estate, one of the furthest flung and quietest fringes of the town. Alex's contact with the couple had been sporadic since the Arts Centre days, but that in itself was no bad thing, for Alex believed that contact need only be constant and steadfast between friends with whom we constantly need convincing of the bond that we share.

Alex had used his precious small collection of coins to phone the pair the previous evening and arrange to come see them this sun shiner of a Saturday afternoon. He had no idea how he was going to broach the question of whether or not he might be permitted to stay with them a short while, but as it turned out their intuition had proved stronger than he had anticipated, and the offer they provided him went further than he had dared to hope.

'Have you come to beg a favour, Alex?' Roy whimsically enquired as they sipped their teas in the immaculately mown, as was Roy's wont, back garden. In a T-shirt, tennis shorts and trainers, peering through his specs beneath his short crop of boyish hair, Roy wore a mock glib expression, and Sarah giggled good naturedly from her own foldaway antique garden furniture.

'What makes you think I could possibly need a favour?'

'Well, it's been half a year or so since you last popped up, and I gather your circumstances must have changed a bit since then. Plus you're a selfish bastard.'

Alex laughed out loud. It felt as good as it was welcome. 'You know me better than I know myself.'

'What we mean to say is, where are you actually staying at the moment?' Sarah asked, cutting to the chase and mercifully getting to the core of the matter to save Alex from further squirming. Sarah wore a Snoopy T-shirt, shorts and sandals, and wore her impossible to know quite what colour it was naturally hair in a complicated curly style that demanded bathroom time aplenty, frequent hairdressing, and some new ideally-suited-to-her-particular-hair-type products swiftly after each visit, courtesy of her hair svengali.

'In dire straits, on a prayer, at the edge of the abyss.'

'Oh,' said Roy. 'Well, at least the rates are pretty low around there, so I've heard.'

'You're damn right there. That's my life all over, lucky break after lucky break.'

'And where, literally, address wise, have you been sleeping recently?'

'Well, I've been staying with Daniel Patten this past week, since I got back from Spain. I need to pull the plug on that one though, unfortunately. Or not. Whatever.'

'OK. We probably don't want to go into the reasons why. Well, anyway, you're not staying here with us. Looks like you're stiffed.'

Alex smiled and took another swallow of tea, waiting and hoping for a punchline. It came.

'Don't listen to him,' Sarah intervened. 'What we meant to suggest to you is, since I lost dad and mum's in care, the house next door is just standing there empty. It's furnished, and I don't see any reason why it should be collecting dust and empty if someone can breathe some life into it again.' The house next door belonged to Sarah's mother now her father had passed away, her and Roy having lived most of their time at their present address with her parents as immediate neighbours.

Alex didn't know what to say. 'I don't know what to say,' he said.

'How about, I'll see you tomorrow at one, with my suitcase and ready to move in, and look forward to enjoying the delicious Sunday roast Sarah is going to prepare for us?'

Alex smiled, nodded, both looked and felt very agreeably agreeable. He took another swallow of his drink. 'It's a very nice cup of tea you make here,' he declared.

39

S unday lunchtime, while Daniel was still in bed and oblivious, Alex left the house in Friarn Street and carted his small collection of largely dirty clothing to Alfoxton Road. After a much needed large meal of bona fide unprocessed meat and fresh cooked vegetables, not to mention a crisp white wine, and after unwinding and chatting and laughing with his gold-hearted saviours a few hours more, Alex was relieved of most of his soiled laundry, which would receive a good machine washing, shown into the previously unoccupied house, and after being shown what was what, left to his own devices and to settle himself in as best he could. He would not be a legal resident of the property, for council tax evasion purposes, but it would prove a great fully functional squat for an indefinite period of time. It was exactly the breathing space and stepping stone he had prayed fate might provide.

A new single bed, with first day fresh linen, filled up most of the box room where he would sleep. The bathroom had been stripped of its carpet and wallpaper, but the bathtub was clean, and boy oh boy had it been some time since Alex had luxuriated in one. In the kitchen, the oven had unfortunately become dirty beyond use, but the stove tops, kettle and toaster were further welcome gifts from the gods. The living room held lacklustre dust-filmed furniture, in need of upholstering or scrapping, and there was no TV, which suited Alex fine. He did not intend using this room much anyway – there was a good size table and chairs in the kitchen where he could do what may, but one other feature of the living room did catch his sparkling eye. A drinks cabinet had a not insubstantial selection of spirits Alex had been invited to consume as he pleased. There was even a cassette player and radio he could take with him anywhere in the house, and there was the final blessing of a tennis-court-sized garden within which to lounge, read, write, drink and chill the hell out.

Alex had found his way back to faith, or faith had found its way back to him.

40

Monday morning kicked the world in the teeth, shoved the weekend into the vault of history, and demanded subservience to its impersonal indignant demands. And this Monday morning had one particular manifestation to crack the whip on Alex: Mr Badger and his valley full of farmer folk.

Alex arrived, punctual for the need to protect his job until silver crossed his palm, and quickly learned that Friday's induction had been a gentle introduction to the horrors that Mr Badger would deem work. The heat was about to be turned up, and the hand on the dial was a heavy one indeed.

Alex's job for today was stacking the bags that were filled, ready to be shipped to their destinations. The weight of each sack was 20 or 25 kilos, and the sacks were filled at a rate that permitted no rest between each burdening load. The stacks were arranged on wooden pallets, three bags one way, two perpendicular, then reversing the layout for each successive layer, seven layers in all, with a final bag on top, fifty heavy sacks for each pallet filled. What proved most difficult was keeping the stacks a cube shape, for the uneven distribution of the contents, the slippery exteriors of the polythene bagging, and Alex's complete lack of experience, meant the loads looked at best uneven, at worst a tottering accident waiting to happen. It was hard, relentless, physical work, and Alex's recent lifestyle meant he was hardly in peak physical form, and he also decided to keep half an ounce of attention on his back, deciding that even losing this particular job was worth many times an injury to his spine or otherwise. He kept up as best he could, perspiration oozing down his torso, beading on his brow, his arms becoming increasingly shaky from the burden on his muscles. Two and a half hours he worked on the same routine, barely a five minute break waiting for each completed pallet to be forklifted to the loading bay, and none were more impressed than he himself at his stamina and determination. It's funny what desperation can do to a person, and how much reserve we have to draw upon in times of want. And then someone stuck a finger in the soup, and the whole concoction was suddenly stirred into a scalding cocktail of an inedible poison to stew in the forcefed brain.

Steve the foreman marched stolidly over to where Alex was struggling through the third or fourth layer of the somewhere in the double figures pallet of the day, opened his mouth, and shouted.

'*Keep 'em fuckin' straight!*' cannoned out of his brusque inelegant gob with a nerve-jarring, psyche-jolting blow to sense and senses. The words were yelled, bullishly and dictatorially, their impact designed to be as violent and shocking as an on target abdominal punch. It was as if the air turned black with viciousness that left one numb with disbelief.

'I beg your pardon??'

A bag fell off the end of the conveyor belt with a splat onto the floor, Alex having failed to be ready for it in the upset and confusion.

Steve the foreman's face suddenly caught in a dilemma, his expression wavering like a struggling bug stuck between one thing and another. 'Straight,' he implored, the coarseness of his voice now a pathetically fragile screen to hide his own thrown state behind. All at once Alex realised that his own choice of reply, and its almost matter of fact delivery, had been about the best possible response under the circumstances. Steve the foreman emphasised his words by making no-nonsense right angles with his extended fingers. It slightly helped his lack of articulation, vaguely illustrating it was the lack of neatness in the sack stacking that he was incomparably livid about.

Alex said nothing, did nothing, just stared back at the foreman, without confrontation or meekness; what the slap in the face outburst stood the only chance of eliciting, mercifully.

Any moment now another sack was going to end up lying on the dusty concrete floor.

Steve the foreman was turning away and exiting in a hurry. His quickstep ultra-purposeful leaving the scene of his crime was staged with a swagger it was the only thing he could hide his shame behind. He had been caught in the glare of his own unacceptable behaviour, and he knew it.

The second sack hit the deck with the noise of a wounded man going down.

If Alex didn't walk out of here right now, Steve the foreman would have somehow gotten away with his behaviour, and that was not the way in which the unjust should be dealt with. If he walked out of here right now, he would have no tangible way left to put food into his own stomach, and agency jobs that started on days other than Mondays were very few and far between.

The card that had been dealt was grossly unfair, the man whom had dealt it a cheat in the game of life.

Alex picked a sack off the floor, hoisted it up onto his aching shoulders, and tossed it onto the stack in the making, not giving a flying fuck how it might land.

41

Alex's insomnia and stress vied with his physical exhaustion. Almost trying to cling to his trademark inability to sleep soundly, not wanting the clock to reach the hour when he would return to Mr Badger and his circus of horrors, he fitfully succumbed to an uneasy dozing, disturbing and visionary, hardly the reparation sleep was intended for.

Memories and echoes and flashbacks pushed and pulled emotions through nostalgia's tug of war. From the here to the where to the when to the then, 'twixt and 'tween each severed twain, he woke with starts, sweats, tears and resignation, gasps and realisation.

And morphing with the demons in his mind, the sense of a presence, maybe benign, maybe malign, a something in the atmosphere, a visitation from yonder the beyond.

Three unmistakable creaks, in rapid succession, filtered into the room from somewhere near the bottom of the stairs. At once Alex was awake as the midday sun, body frozen, breath held, ears desperate to hear anything but his heart which could but race.

Nothing. No follow up to the sounds, those sounds which had scurried in the downstairs hall. It was as if something had materialised in the house, then tried to home in on Alex's sleeping form in haste, thwarted by his waking in shock, now somewhere in the darkness, its own consciousness a radar with more power and scope than Alex could conceive of.

The seconds became minutes, and it was on the threshold that proffered a return to uneasy sleep the noises began again.

It was a prolonged metallic rasp, as if someone had scraped an industrial file across one of the radiators. Alex awaited the noises of something gurgling in the pipes, some evidence of plumbing stirring after months of disuse, but it just didn't seem or feel like the settling noises of a house by night.

Alex lay in the bed, in the dark, in the new strange and otherwise officially empty house, for as long as he could stand it. He sat, as soundlessly as he could manage, planted a bare foot upon the carpet and made it over to the light switch. He thought he would scrabble around for it, the simple piece of plastic taunting him with its nightmare elusiveness, but his hand happened upon it immediately, and the light worked, and the room and landing were filled with light. Nothing seemed out of place. With the potential excuse for not going to Badger Valley later this morning a supernatural encounter could supply, he was almost disappointed not to be staring the phantasmagorical in whatever it might have in terms of face.

He moved onto the landing and flicked the switch there too. The darkness bolted down the stairs to fester amid the shadows beyond the permeation of the shaded bulb. Through the landing windows, uneasily highlighted by the queasy amber of the street lamps, a small green contained a children's play area, silhouetted so subtly as if barely feeling the need to exist. Alex went to the window as his pale facsimile approached from outside, and studied the bleakness of the all but silent night. No lights burned in any window, no pedestrians made a pointless journey long after everything was closed, not even a car travelled in mysterious purpose along the Quantock Road. The rest of the world, it seemed, had successfully gone to bed and sleep.

Downstairs, a door moved against its jamb, either gently opening or closing. At once Alex remembered the reason he was up, and before that had happened his hairs had turned into porcupine prickles, his skin frozen as his heart pumped ice.

Another wait of several seconds, then inspiration struck. ''ere, Tom, someone's fuckin' about downstairs,' he spoke to an unlikely named ghost of his own conjuring back in the room he had left. The sound of his own voice did nothing to ease him, it was as if he were feeding the darkness with his fear. He almost sensed the echo of his stupidity, a mocking that occupied the rest of the home, smug and omniscient as Alex did its dirty work himself.

He wasn't going to be able to go back to bed and sleep without checking the rest of the house over. That simply wasn't going to happen.

Alex began to descend the stairs.

42

Alex knew a little about the supernatural through first-hand experience. As a small child he remembered vividly ghostly visitations to his bedside, an entire crowd of spectral figures he had felt entirely safe and unperturbed in the presence of as if they represented a guardianship of sorts. When he was eight he experienced an extremely lucid episode of astral travel – his consciousness leaving his physical body and embarking on an independent journey his attempts to recount to his adult peers had been politely but no less bluntly scoffed at. It was a few years later he encountered the theorists and protagonists of the academic study of astral projection and its cross-cultural, deeply historical documentation, and was glad that at least someone in this world would not immediately dismiss such subject matter as impressionable fantasy. Alex's experiments with psychotropics too had opened doorways in his perception that he firmly believed those who dismissed as pure addling chemical reactions in the cerebral cortex – such as the communists and atheists – did so out of fear-fuelled denial and arrogant lusting to nail down the nature of the world. The darkest and most incomparably terrifying occult venture Alex had found himself a victim of was following a particularly mercy-free descent into depression, his existential birthing when the pointlessness and meaninglessness and universal futility of things were all he could see. It was then that a series of nocturnal attacks occurred from something that would only strike when he was alone and defenceless, albeit with a darkly omniscient atmosphere and demi-deific presence undeniable when subjected to its exposure. These dark nights of Alex's soul were the opportunistic moments for an entity of an incubus-like nature to wreak its impossibly antipathetic violence upon the defenceless loner, another supernatural concept Alex learned about after it had targeted him so. For months Alex lived in sheer terror of being alone at night, then somehow he had found an exit at the far end of his nihilistic depression, and crawled through the aperture the demoniacal other it would seem was loathe or unable to pass.

Although far more circumstantially-based, Alex was certainly far from head and shoulders above the weight of depression right now; still, he could not believe that some kind of portal no-one he knew would believe had somehow been prised ajar once again.

'Ah, to hell with this nonsense,' he suddenly called out in a tone that this time managed to embolden him.

He reached the bottom of the stairs, knocked on the light in anger. He went to the kitchen, checked the back door was closed and locked, checked the downstairs toilet. Nothing, no-one, zilch out of place.

He went to the living room. Here, the main light was not working, he needed to cross to a lamp where an entertainment centre might otherwise be perched. He crossed through the dark interior feeling like a living gatecrasher at a get together for the dead. He pushed the button to turn on the lamp, then discovered it was not plugged in.

Alex looked round at the room, forcing his eyes to adjust to the dark. The carpet, the furniture, were dark tones, the curtains were drawn, too little light turned fantasy to reality, too much darkness imprisoned the shadows and locked in fear.

He knelt and felt for the plug. He happened upon it. He groped for the socket. There it was.

He stopped breathing. For a moment it had seemed as if his own was not the only breathing in the living room.

Stupid. And yet, who could not help but feel stupid and succumb at least in part to that stupidity under such circumstances?

What contours there were to be seen remained still as predators ready to strike.

Alex turned his attention back to the plug and socket. He tried to marry them but his skills at marrying electronic circuitry in the dark were about as astute as a practically inept technophobic bachelor's could only be.

The darkness simply loomed abroad, as unhelpful as alienating.

At last he managed to get the plug plugged in and the lamp came to life.

Its glow did not permeate every cobwebbed corner, but clearly there was no other human in the gloomy room. The dusty furniture had sagging cushions and concave indentations in the upholstered backs. They looked occupied even when empty.

Alex was in a house that had belonged to a man whom had recently died. It was a thought that understandably was never too far out of mind. But he did not feel unwelcomed by its deceased occupant, even if that sounded like an arrogant assumption. He simply did not feel it that way.

Alex turned off the living room lamp and downstairs lights. He had reached the foot of the stairs when something in the bathroom made an almighty clatter.

43

Alex tried to see into the bathroom from his vantage point at the base of the staircase. He had a partial view through the doorway, although most of it remained shadowed and unseen.

He decided to take the stairs noisily. Surprised at his boldness, he found himself taking them two at a time. He was in the bathroom, pull cord light switch swinging after being roughly yanked into operation, seeing at a glance what had caused the bump in the night.

The open bathroom window had its loose blinds flapping in the intermittent gusts of breaking and entering wind, and shampoo, toothpaste and toothbrush had decided to take a plunge into the tub. It was either that, or a by now boring common or garden poltergeist.

Alex removed the scattered toiletries and positioned them back on the shelf, dared not glance in the mirror lest he spotted a ghoul over his shoulder or worse still his own reflection, and prepared to drag his own undead self back to bed.

He decided on one more glance out the window before he did.

The moon and stars were in hiding along with the other 6 billion human inhabitants of Earth.

Suddenly something happened, and the real terror, the real beast, the real sum of his fears came to the fore.

Alex began to cry, freely, unstoppably, involuntarily, perhaps for the first time since his return to England and his largely miserable slump down to cold hard earth.

Being granted this house to stay in for an unlimited period had been his first real tangible slice of good luck and taste of freedom since his rearrival; it was a selfless helpful compassionate human gesture he had so needed to have. It was this, probably more than anything else, that had caused the tears to flow. When we are overworked, it is not until the adrenaline ceases to flow that the wall really hits us. When we are stressed, it is often not until the tension has snapped the headache kicks in. When we are down on our luck, it is a slice of good fortune above all else that really puts everything else into proportion.

Alex sat on the stairs, and cried for an age. Eventually he climbed back into bed and cried himself to sleep.

44

Alex and his back and nerves somehow made it to the end of the week at Badger Valley, and with a few out of hours telephoned pleas to the agency, they found him a replacement chore the following Monday. This was not before his eyes had been widened and narrowed by further goings on and revelations in this unhappy valley of animal aggression, however. Steve the foreman had tried it on a few more times with Alex, although Alex had found a sound and dispassionately argued response left the bully seething with an anger that looked as needless and ridiculous as it was, simmering in a cloud of fumes he could choke on all he pleased. One employee, preparing prescription-order concoctions in a blessedly hermetically sealed corner, had confided in Alex that the inflammable far from bright spark was headed for the chop on account of a complaint of harassment from a former employee, and Alex could not wait until he added his own name to the list. 'And when the manager finds out he's been shaggin' his missus,' the employee added, 'I wouldn't like to be in his shoes when he needs to provide a reference for whatever shithole he tries to crawl into next.'

The final revelation that left Alex whirling came from this same nonjobsworthy source. Apparently Alex's workload had been counted as output of the permanent staff, and this designed to increase their bonuses at the expense of the agency stooge's yelled at and strained back. And Badger Valley Farmers had the audacity to label itself as a co-operative.

A co-operative was not what Badger Valley Farmers was at all, for co-operation and sharing and caring values were anything but what was on undeniable in-one's-face display. Cutthroat capitalism, the neglect and abuse of workers' rights, a flagrant denial of basic health and safety, and frankly undisguised managerial corruption were what Badger Valley Farmers represented , and let none be fooled. Alex exited the millyard with a few perfunctory grunts goodbye that final Friday, never ever to return. Steve the grunt grunted what sounded like a fuck off prick, but almost every prick has the possibility to stand proud, and bullies all without exception eventually get a taste of their own.

45

Kingswood Natural Foods sounded like it occupied another pocket of an altogether different universe than Badger Valley, although seeing as Badger Valley had worn the mask of a co-op and behaved as a travesty of such, Alex was nonetheless wary of taking employers at face value, especially where agency jobs were concerned. Upon arriving and reporting to reception, he was shown into the office of the acting manager; a man called Gerald who was either an odd or perfectly apt choice of manager for a natural foods company; being obese, clad in a purple shirt and ruddied cheeks, and looking like an enormous talking plum. After some perfunctory and perfunctorily-pleasantried necessities, Alex was shown into the packing room in which he would work and introduced to Simon the floor manager, who seemed indecisively perched on the cusp of friendliness and seriousness. Alex decided to try pushing him toward the former by, when asked if he had any questions, voicing his customary, 'Is it any fun here?'. Soul-searching, disarming, balance-equalling, and giving no rational cause for offence, for Alex it represented one of the shrewdest job interview questions that could be asked.

Assigned to work alongside Jill, a chain-smoking natural born worrier not quite fifty who looked a hundred and fifty and was skeletal to boot, Alex weighed, bagged, double bagged and sacked dried aduki-, black-, black-eyed-, borlotti-, butter-, cannellini-, flageolet-, haricot-, lima-, mung-, pinto- and red kidney legume after legume in return for beans; poured, scooped and measured barley, bran, oats, rye and wheat until he all but flaked out; sorted through brazils, cashews, macadamias, pecans and pistachios until he thought he would go crazy; and sifted through sticky heat-glued clumps of prunes and plums and apricots and figs and raisins and currants until he could bear it no more. Wishing to draw upon the expertise of one of the more seasoned employees in the packing department, he enquired from a busy female counterpart as to what, exactly, one of the substances he was hitherto unfamiliar with - polenta - was. Presumably on a need to know basis, he was enlightened by an elucidatory 'I dunno. Some yellow shit.'

Alex managed to survive on natural foods and their packing for a couple of weeks, although here too he was rudely awakened as to how unethically a company purporting to represent an ecological cause can operate. From spillages being poured back into stock rather than being disposed of for hygiene reasons, to non-organic produce being passed off as organic when the latter had run dry, to the yet more serious business of arriving grains or flours being condemned, then being un-condemned because sales targets and commission took precedent over product quality. What personally riled Alex the most was the bully boy tactics used to whip staff into working harder and faster than their already hugely unreasonable minimum output for their minimum wage. Emotional blackmail was the tool used here, one department being told that none in the other department would be able to leave at the carrot-dangled earlier than usual Friday finishing time nor collect their shift bonuses if this department did not negate their own breaks and work their already overworked hands even closer to the bone.

There was a simply risible piece of theatre when the second-in-command floor manager stood by watching Alex work up a sweat, then voiced a bemusing, 'Not used to it, are you?'

'I beg your pardon?' was all Alex could think of in return.

'Hard work. Not used to it, are you?'

'*What?*' he thought about saying something else, but was so dumbfounded he could not find the words before the man had walked away. Thereafter, this particular individual in ill-fitting boots, Richard, a man with tattoos all over his arms and repressed sexual ambiguity written all over his face had managed to convince the rest of the employees that Alex was gay and had quite successfully whipped up a lynchmob mentality among many of the staff whom both accepted this at face value and as justifiable cause for ousting him in whatever petty ways they could conceive of.

Alex was removed from Kingswood Natural Foods after a few weeks because, according to what they had reported to the agency, he did not work hard enough and looked miserable. This could be translated as did not jump to the tune some jumped-up wannabee tyrant wanted him to and had a genuine, and therefore unstimulated and ineffective in this environment, sense of humour.

Kingswood Natural Foods could not even be dismissed as a corporate fascists posing as a wholistic cause, for although fascism is liberally peppered with closet homosexuals who choose to express their repressed feelings through sadism, even fascism would oppose the practise of passing off contaminated, soiled and inferior food as something it is not. And companies like Kingswood Natural Foods, like Badger Valley Farmers, and like SharPak, are so blinded by the flippancy with which they flout everyone's basic rights, he was stunned by their gall. He wondered what might happen if, one day, they had, for example, something like an investigative journalist working undercover in their midst. Imagine that.

46

Saturday night's pilgrimage to the Labour Club was thwarted by one of the local anchored traveller families' members – a fourteenth generation gypsy; one part Romany, three parts Irish bitter, seven parts yokel bonehead, 7 stone overweight and 25 lagers in the blood, had turned the lounge of the club into an obesity-cramped, gorging guzzling mouthy sweaty wrestling ring to celebrate sixty years' obnoxiousness on Earth without managing to get killed thus far. Alex and Ian had opted to run the gauntlet of a swift one in the front bar and a nod of solidarity to Simon at the bar before fleeing to the wannabee petit bourgeois gladiators of verbal masturbation arena of the Arts Centre.

Sometime during the straining to hear each other's already strained conversation over the histrionic burly laughter, most of which was aggressive prompting at the end of their own immaterial substitutes for jokes, the one-upmanship overemphasising of pecking order and rank and brawn, the swearing so superfluous its profanity had become inanity, and the jibes and hollers of women unwilling to appear the least inferiority-fearing of their louder and deeper and many times more pathetic for that male counterparts, the Bridgwater version of 'Excuse me, please' jabbed at their eardrums like angry beaks.

'OI!!!'

Both men jumping, they were immediately alerted to the fact a face had just peered through the ajar door into their two-strong company with all the menace and presence of an army drunk on testosterone and sin.

Almost immediately Alex recognized the figure staring straight into his eyes, the interloper's sparkling with the glee a serial killer in the making might display at finding a stray kitten has become trapped in their back yard.

The face of the monster that had attacked Alex on the Cornhill the day he had arrived back in England loomed as large as if it was twice its size and pressed nose to nose with its startled victim of a month or so before.

'You'm that fuckin poofy grass, ain't you?' There was a macabre unsettling collage of emotion in that snarling intrusion of a face; eyes that sparkled with jubilant excitement at the potentiality of violence, mouth and nose hard set with the gravest desire to inflict bodily harm.

Ian, himself an overweight filled out form of a man, suddenly seemed as insignificant an ally to Alex as if he was not even there. Alex wished himself anywhere but here.

'Ain't you, ey?' The interbred interferer loped inter the lounge. 'Fuckin grassed I up to the pigs you did, di'n' you, ey??' Both Alex and Ian were now only too aware of the nearly empty beer glass tightly gripped in his near fist like a drinking receptacle were not its primary function.

Alex found himself raising his hands to show his palms, half in a vain attempt at supplication and appeal, the bigger half in vague defence. Ian remained still out of the corner of his eye he intended to keep functional, though whether or not he were poised for action was something Alex could neither tell or rely upon. 'Man-' he began, wondering how on earth one might possibly try to reason with this guy even if he were restrained, sober and sedated.

'I'll fuckin show you what I think of fuckin grasses.' He further closed the physical and expanded the ethical distance between them. 'And there aint no fuckin pigs around to help you now, are there, EY??!'

47

'LEE!'
The second terrifying-looking character entered the front lounge of the club, this one bigger than Ian, meaner faced than the one that was obviously in possession of the trademark Bridgwater bruiser name Lee, and larger than whatever was left of Alex's life. The odds of his ever winning the lottery had never looked more bleak.

Lee snapped to attention a racing heartbeat before it looked like he would snap Alex's neck.

'Wha's goin on?' was demanded, presumably of the smooth talking eloquent articulator ready to let his beer glass do the negotiating.

'This fuckin cunt grassed I up to the cops,' he orated with elucidatory enviability.

The man who couldn't have looked any less menacing were he a 900 pound gorilla with a swastika tattooed on his brow and AK47 in his clutches sized Alex up like a Shia Moslem a feminist intellectual.

Simon the barman, presumably sixth- and all other five senses sensing the senseless were up to some nonsense, appeared at the serving hatch, a wary but calm concentration on his face. 'Pete, no trouble, please, if you don't mind,' he gently but firmly voiced, grammatically a request, tonally the imperative bottom line.

'I ain't gonna let no trouble happen, Simon,' Pete declared, and Alex prayed the double negative was merely a negation of linguistics and not reason. 'You,' he implored Lee. 'Get back in there.' He jabbed a thumb toward the main lounge. 'You show some respect for the man's club.'

'This fuckin cunt needs to be taught a lesson.'

'You fuckin spoil my party, I'll be teachin you a fuckin lesson alright. Naa move!'

Lee did as he was told, but couldn't overrule his lust to voice a 'Next time I fuckin see you, you're fuckin dead,' at Alex in lieu of farewell.

Pete slapped Lee across the side of the head. Once. Hard.

'Wha' d'you fuckin go and do that for?'

'Get back in there now!' Pete then yelled at someone just inside the main lounge to grab ahold of Lee, sit him down and get him a drink, and make sure he stayed where he was. Lee was removed from the scene he had created.

'Sorry about that, Simon. You know I ain't interested in causing you any trouble. I appreciate the trouble you've gone to for me by letting me have my party here tonight. We'll draw a line under that, yeah?'

'Well, thanks for stepping in, Pete. I would greatly appreciate it if that's the last we hear about that. These lads here are good lads, it can only have been a misunderstanding.'

Pete turned to Alex and Ian. 'Sorry about that, gentlemen,' the man whose birthday was being celebrated in inimical style let ooze out of his mouth, theatrical overcompensation with a thick coating of slime. 'He ain't a bad lad, really, he just gets a bit lairy when he's had a few. I apologise to you all. Allow me to buy you a drink to make up for it.'

No, thank you, no really we insist, we were just going anyway, don't give it another thought, and no we won't let it spoil anyone's evening were along the lines of the lines Alex and Ian spouted through self-preservation before, ensuring the best they possibly could the coast appeared to be clear, they ran like the wind that had just been put up them to the Arts Centre, perhaps the most bonehead-free waterhole in town.

48

The national heritage monument and heirloom that is Bridgwater Arts Centre, first opened in 1946, a fact that the local council seem pathologically predisposed to blatantly ignore, stands in Castle Street, a thoroughfare running parallel to Fore Street (which many locals mistake as the High Street), and this street was committed to filmic display in the 1963 film adaptation of Henry Fielding's Tom Jones, when it was cobbled, another historic feature of the town destroyed by a philistine local government when it became blandly tarmacced and line-marked in the name of progress and the arrogant sacrifice of charm, taste and aestheticism.

This evening the Centre was uncommonly lively, about as occupied and crackling as the Labour Club had been, although here the clientele were less inclined to endanger life with their fists than cause longer-term psychological abrasions with their pompous up-their-own words. It was a members' night party, cabaret entertainment to those in possession of a ticket, fine wines and champers to be quaffed with theatrical aplomb, and a pseuds' buffet complete with vol-au-vents, caviar and quail was being tucked into by fattened bores. At least it seemed psychopathic lunatic free and was the last place in Bridgwater to be visited by the likes of Lee.

The alien feel of the normally largely dormant bar was also a welcome distraction for Alex's stricken mind. Not only had Lee remembered him, born a grudge, and was threatening to continue putting Alex in mortal danger, he was also now aware of the only watering hole in Bridgwater he could call a local. How was he going to return there, or leave the place after closing, or simply walk the streets and feel anywhere near safe for possibly months to come?

'Where've you been hiding then?'

Alex turned to find Daniel standing with a pint of lukewarm ale, presumably his favourite temperature for alcoholic beverages, standing in the only bar a sensible local of the Labour Club would this night. Alex explained his change of address, keeping the subject confrontation-free, and was warmly congratulated on his stroke of luck, to be neutralised with a commiseration at the regaling of the Labour Club ruck.

As well as Alex, Ian and Daniel, Ken, Malcolm, Pavla and Patrick were also doing their best to make the most of the Labour Club's temporary boundlessness and filter the stimuli of the Arts Centre's all microcosmic world being a stage. Drifting from the squeeze of the bar into the gallery, they all made smug self-congratulatory jibes at the fancy dress, unfanciable waistlines and fantasy I-I-I conversations, irritated staff by trying to sneak into the auditorium for a peek at what they would never in a million years buy tickets to see, and stole immodest crumbs from the spread laid out and paid for by what were now unconscious benefactors of those used to living on benefits.

After eavesdropping through –nths of 'Of course, now Margaret and I no longer need to work…', 'Like a ciggie, darling?', 'Well, I've just come back from the Andes and I'm about to spend three months in the Far East…', and 'We were actually in that area last week, because both our daughters had their graduation ceremony…' the group of friendly mates left as one unsated mass, returned to their respective homes due to lack of enthusiasm and optimism paraded as tiredness, and forgot the whole inconsequential wannabee night out for the rest of their lives, all except Alex, whom had not seen the last of the creature called Lee quite yet.

49

Far and away the worst spectacle Alex witnessed at an agency job occurred shortly thereafter, at another enterprises's premises one could be forgiven for thinking were eco- and ethics friendly and promoting due to the official nature of their business. A plastics recycling plant procured the assistance and exploited the circumstances of Alex and a sixteen-year-old boy through a busy period. Whilst loading red plastics onto the conveyor belt of a baling machine, someone in the hierarchy of the trade making a looming tour of the premises, dressed in what is universally recognised as the uniform of respect and universally almost mandatorially worn as a mask for organised crime and cutthroat exploitation – a suit and tie – stopped in horror at the sight of something the semi-involuntary stooges had done.

'Stop the machine! Stop the machine!' Alex and the boy paused and looked dumbfounded, searching for a stop button they had not been shown the location of. In exasperation, the suit stopped it himself, poor thing. 'That piece of plastic up there's the wrong colour!' he declared, pointing up at an area of the conveyor belt close to the top and drop into the baler itself. 'Get it down, please,' he all but barked at Alex.

Alex took one good look at the sloping conveyor belt, the amount of loose plastic piled up on its length, the support wires like anticipatory garrottes awaiting the consequence of unsure footing, and the ultra-powerful hydraulic compressor yawning like a behemoth's mouth. Then he saw the small one foot square piece of pink not red plastic sheeting that was causing such time and money wasting kerfuffle and expense. 'I'm sorry. I'm not prepared to go up there to get it,' he declared, flatly but politer than the question deserved.

'Go on, it's quite safe.' As if reading the obvious in Alex's mind, he said, 'I'm not going up there in this suit.'

That was all Alex needed or wanted to hear. Could such words have had any less impact or injustice were he to have mouthed, 'I am the Ubermensch Gestapo. You are a filthy Jew.'? 'No, I'm not doing it.' Alex turned away, not trusting himself to do anything but.

The younger, more impressionable, of the two agency expendables chirped up with an overenthusiastic 'I'll do it', then began racing up the precarious belt with the desire to score points off of someone who did not even value his life.

Alex heard it happen as much as saw. The machine kicked into life again, its churning rumble drowning out the rest of the sounds in the roofed yard. There were urgent shouts, shuffles of feet, and then the belt was turned off again, having been kicked back into life by someone from around the other side of the machine whom had been puzzled as to why it had stopped and turned it back on without checking the coast had been clear. The boy was safe, having managed to scramble back down the belt before he himself could be baled and shipped home to his mother in a box, and actually seemed largely oblivious of exactly the degree of danger he had been in. The suit and second employee tried to appear casual and as if nothing had occurred, hoping the moment would be swept beneath the carpet and go unnoticed or ignored by nothing more than a few temporary helpouts, a few superfluous sets of limbs, inconsequential disposable lives. Alex later learned that the machine should have had a second stop engaged before the lad (or him, or anyone) had climbed up onto its belt to prevent such a mistake as had happened. A tiny square of pink plastic, ill-gained profits, the uncrumpled garmentry of a bloody-handed, bloody-minded suit, had all been given priority over the life of a child.

Alex phoned Ideal Staff of The Mount, Taunton, explained in carefully articulate, calm and patient detail what he had witnessed that day. 'We'll make a note of it,' and various synonymous platitudes were all he could get out of the highest-ranking employee he was able to talk to.

50

'Hello, stranger.'

In the dark U of Court Street, Alex paused, myopia vying with gloom to obscure the identity of the female addresser.

'Hello?' The intonation was designed as a clear 'Excuse me, but do I know you?' although the woman seemed to take it she had simply been recognised and hailed.

'How are you, then? Haven't seen you for a long time.' There was plenty of localised accent in the voice, although Alex got the impression she were striving to suppress it a little.

'I'm…just about alright, thanks.' This was fun, he thought. This was just the kind of thing he enjoyed – speaking with someone as if you've known them a lifetime when you don't even know who they are. 'And…what about you?'

She giggled. 'You don't know who I am, do you?'

'I must confess I don't, no.'

Alex shifted his position, hoping the light might be better with which to view the woman who had hailed him clearly, and she accommodated by stepping further into a weary streetlamp's sickly glow. In the pale off-coloured illumination she appeared quite attractive.

'I'm Sheryl. We've never actually spoke before, although we've seen each other about a lot.'

Alex remembered her. Indeed they had never spoken before, although he had certainly noticed her before. Like him, she was one of life's natural walkers, wanderers, never to be seen behind the wheel of a car, which Alex believed people occupied 90% of the time out of sheer slobbishness alone. Alex had noticed this woman, Sheryl, as a bit of an eccentric, another Bridgwater weirdo, as no doubt he himself was noted and recognised, harmless and quietly interesting and even more so now she had opened her mouth. She was easily his equal in height, clad in black in shapely fashion, her body slim and neatly curved. Her hair, he remembered more than saw, was the off black of crows, and she normally wore it tied back, her gentle and quite innocent face with its even structure tainted by a few premature-looking wrinkles, as if she had seen hardship in her younger years. The overall effect was nonetheless appealing, and she was anything but unattractive. This was indeed a curious and interesting turn of events.

'What you been doing with yourself then?' was asked of Alex.

'Well, to be perfectly honest, there's been an element of struggle the past several weeks, but I think I'm finding my feet again.'

'Wha've you been strugglin' with then?' she interrupted, Bridgwater claiming back its hold on her voice, restrained impatience in her tone. Alex began to wonder just how eccentric, or how mad even, she might be.

Alex wanted to hesitate, to test how patient she might be, but wanted to maintain her interest as well. 'I came back from working abroad for a couple of months and I-'

'Where you been then?'

'I was in Spain-'

'In Spain! I'd love to go to Spain! What were you doin' there then?'

'Well…teaching English at a summer sch-'

'You're a teacher!' Alex couldn't make out if it was wonder, disappointment, or plain incredulity he was having fired at him now. He found the job title engendered all three in him himself.

'When it suits me to be labelled as one, I guess. Anyway, I'm not doing any teaching here.' He drew a breath. 'Anyway, to be honest, I've had a bit of a battle with getting myself somewhere to live since I came back, and I've been doing various agency jobs. It's been a slow uphill climb. But tell me, what about you, Sheryl?'

She immediately fired into a gabble, although Alex didn't sense her at ease with the question. 'Oh, I keep busy, I do. You know. This and that. I do a lot of visiting people. Loads of people I know, around here. I just come back from me sister's, I go there three or four times a week, she's got a couple of children, I like to see them.' She trailed off, having communicated effectively nothing except that she really was at best not the sharpest card in the deck. But dammit, she was at least being friendly.

'And do you work, Sheryl?'

'No. I used to. I used to have a job in one of the cafes. I wanna be a travel agent, I do. That's my dream.'

'Fair enough. Um…Have you applied to be one?'

'Not yet, no. I need to go back to college first, get my O levels.' Alex kept a quiet counsel. 'Anyway, I better go now, where you off to then?'

'I'm…possibly going to visit a friend.' He had actually been on his way to the Arts Centre, but didn't want to tell her this, and did not quite know why. Had he bargained on the possibility that he could go somewhere with her instead? Had he thought it might be a little shameful to take her to his second choice local? Did he not want to tell her where he often drank? 'And you?'

'Oh, I gotta go home now.' She quickly blurted out a 'But it was nice to see you,' in a way that politely let him know that she would be going there on her own. 'I'll see you around again sometime, yeah?'

'I hope so, yeah.'

'I always see you around from time to time anyway, don' I? Well, you 'ave a nice night with your friend. You take care, stranger.'

He chuckled, unsure if she had said something funny. 'I will, you too.' He wanted to shake her hand, however odd that might seem, but she was already putting distance between them. A moment later, she was out of sight and gone, or over the hill and far away.

Alex shrugged, then continued on his way. He felt almost certain he would indeed see this peculiar character again soon.

'Come on, stranger,' he urged himself, and took himself to another eventless forgetful regular Arts Centre night out.

51

Amberseal was the next ultra-short-lived piece of temporary work he did, and he felt he was fast running through all the available places and agencies that were prepared to allow him to allow them to mistreat him. Aerosol products were the stepping stone evil under production here, although he had been assured the management and staff were gentle-natured and the agency had 'never had a complaint from or about anyone they had sent there yet'. The thin ice was thinning in every direction.

He spent the entire first day propping up cans of windscreen washing solution each time they toppled on their belt, no-one to talk to, nothing to look at, nothing to listen to, slow motion death by interminable tedium. The second day was the last when he spent the first few hours hammering the depressible nozzles onto what he thought were cans of compressed air. He had not even noticed a smell coming from the short spurt of mist that had issued from each in the generally chemically-laden environment, and did not realise how naïve he had been until he discovered the label that was later affixed to said cans read grease removing solvent. His only blessing was that he had sat on this production line one single day, unlike many whom had been working at the plant for years, for the absolute minimum wage; employees who seemed irritated, almost defensive, when he tried to point out the obvious danger in which they were putting their health.

Another two days work, two days more pittance making a transient and fleeting appearance in his threadbare pockets, a few more tens of thousands of toxic accumulants clogging up his undernourished overstrained and already alcohol-poisoned body, he threw himself back onto the streets in the name of staying alive, cursing the gangster-run travesty of employment that the institution of employment agencies has become, learning that anyone can establish such an agency, that one agency in the town was already being managed by someone with a series of criminal convictions, wondering if the communists had it right after all, then asking himself if anarchy was really such a dead end idealism with no particular place to go, then sociological ideals were once more overshadowed with uncertainty as to just how he was going to keep from starving, unable to bear the dole, unable to bear the work he could find, in possession of no financial foothold to hoist himself up to something or somewhere more beneficial, wondering if and how he might ever have a girlfriend again, trying to assure his poisoned depressed self that he still had his health, ha fucking ha fucking hahaha.

As he walked, skulked, back to the empty sanctuary cum hideaway of Alfoxton Road, an office-attired employee and cosmetically weekend thug exited a business premises and spat, as absent-mindedly as needlessly, upon the pavement. Perhaps he owned the place.

Alex felt like doing the same, although clung onto the decorum not to, feeling sure at that moment that no-one else on Earth or in Heaven would appreciate his self-restraint.

52

Two days later there was a piece of street, and river, theatre laid on for the locals, no tickets required and ultimately paid for by the council in lieu of the fact they cannot normally be bothered to spend the people's taxes on cultural entertainment or public services worthy of mention. A woman had tried to commit suicide in broad daylight in the heart of the town and in full view of every potential rescuer. Screaming obscenities at the man who was clearly the bane of the moment in her life she decided to avenge herself on him by ending her own life before he could do the job for her. Wading into the Parrett just by the town bridge (one of several town bridges but, due to its central location, colloquially *the* town bridge) she promptly became stuck in the mud within half an hour of the bore's being due to put in its daily appearance. Responding gallantly and heroically, the man who had been blamed for all the fuss shouted a couple of 'I fucking love you, you bitch' lines at her in lieu of vandal-removed life rings, then charged headlong into the mud and got stuck himself, complicating the situation for the rescue services while seemingly attempting to do the drowning damsel the biggest favour he could. Meanwhile the shoppers, loiterers and unemployed, which totalled around half the population, gathered in force to watch, gossip, joke, gape and ogle; albeit for a handful of children who decided the best contribution they themselves could make to the situation was to throw stones at the stuck targets and shout 'Die, fuckers, die!'. The woman was pulled out first, now hurling obscenities at the fire brigade for their part in her misery, while the man proved a little more tricky. Managing to get dislodged from the entrapping effluent he seemed determined not to haul himself to safety and allow the fire brigade to get themselves out of the oncoming bore's way, causing them to refer to the tactic of luring him with a pint of Stella and a donner kebab on a rope, according to one of the rumours Alex heard. Everyone survived to kill each other another day, just in the nick of time. Alex missed the lot, and this was his patchworked joining together of events based on the eye witness accounts he heard, and all of which widely differed, of course. Alex missed it because he himself was caught in his own new quagmire of soul and body-endangering suffocating ordeal, the first of what would turn out to be an almost personal record length of ten days' worth of character building experience at Exces Logistics, distributors to hospitals a day's work there threatened to put its staff inside.

Alex's job at Exes Logistics involved collecting, washing and stacking totes – plastic trays pickers were ordered to fill with orders. Alex's assistant was a man called Graham, an overweight alcoholic in a permanently despondent mood Alex did his level best to try to get on with and lift the spirits of through non-too-challenging jokes, some of which even succeeded at their task. The work was physically demanding and ergonomically nonsensical, not helped by the regular appearance of Terence Bellringer, a chargehand whom had clearly misread his job title as Demigod, hardly surprising when the man displayed such scant intelligence it would be a wonder were he able to read. The shift manager for the first week was an immigrant Alex rather liked, but whose accent and ethnic background he was unable to place. Upon asking one of the long-time employees for enlightenment, he was promptly informed the man was "an Algerian cunt". Partially the wiser, Alex had to admit the shortcomings of his own knowledge compared to that of the man he had asked. He himself had never heard of that particular Algerian clan before.

The second week the shift manager was Jimmy, a squat thick-set Scot, stereotyping the short and male by struggling to convince everyone around that at least three times the regular amount of testosterone had been crammed inside his vertically-challenged form. Alex entered the toilets a few minutes before one of the twilight shift's two mandatory half hour breaks were due to start, needing to scrub his hands before it was safe to eat, to find Jimmy berating another employee for having come in to do the same "three minutes 'fore yer entitled to yer break". The employee was told he would have to get back to work three minutes before everyone else and that Jimmy the shift manager, incidentally wearing shorts which was against company policy, would be watching to make sure he did.

As Alex picked up the pace and learned the ropes, so Graham

found more and more increasingly inventive excuses to leave him on his own while he "had to attend to a job somewhere else in the building", but Alex found this largely a blessing, as being by himself and away from his team-mate's self-pitying monologues was the closest this job got to being bearable. Clearly relishing the fact he had caught him alone, His Deific Terence Bellringer made a surprise attack visit to demand how many totes Alex had washed so far that shift.

'I haven't got a clue,' was Alex's flat, factual reply.

'Well, there's a counter in there,' he countered, nodding at the tote washing machine, 'that records exactly how many you've done.'

'Is there??' he responded, wondering as he said so why someone would put such a counter *inside* the apparatus, and sniffing as he did so the product other than beef and leather for which the bovine are famed. The chargehand left after his usual intended poisoning of the atmosphere and overstepping his mark, presumably in order to make himself feel less like an own hands stimulator of the organ he had just stirred into life, and giving Alex the pleasure of telling everyone at the next break what everyone's least favourite chargehand had tried to convince Alex, and possibly even believed himself. Mr Bellringer nil, Mr Whistleblower won, game over.

53

Bridgwater Fair came to the town, stopping for its rudimentary four-day visit at the end of September, a magnet for teenagers, truants and sexually frustrated adolescents and a vacuum for pocket money and a cue for the rain. Alex decided to pay a cursory visit to the event at St Matthews Field on his way to the Labour Club, for the adrenaline rush of trying to avoid Lee and his gang members, should they still remember him and have him down as a marked man, for the likes of him are tethered to the town, believing the be all and end all of the universe is the Bridgwater town limits, marked by signs welcoming visitors and passers through and naming the three continental twin towns, one of which is misspelt. He weaved his way through muddied-booted families, across the sodden grass insufficiently covered with sawdust, past the ghost train with teenage girls screaming at the antics of the boy in the carriage beside them, dodged past the bumper cars surrounded by young boys desperate to prove their mettle in case any of them were Lee or his gang, circled the Ferris Wheel, sidestepped the sideshows, hustled his way past the try your luck indeed stalls, and finally settled on the most white-knuckle iron-stomach demanding attraction the showground had to offer – the cheeseburger stall. As the Bridgwater Mercury, a paper he had applied for a journalist position at and been turned down for lack of appropriate literary qualification, had boldly displayed in yesterday's front page headline, it was "All the Fun of the Fair".

A moment later, finding the fast food curiously palatable and too early for the signs of salmonella to rise in his gorge, a further attraction presented itself. Another visitor stood between the hawkers and gawkers, another sentinel observer also dressed head to foot in black.

'Hello. Here on your own?'

'Hi, Sheryl. Uh, yes, I am. I'm only just passing through, on my way…into town.' He suddenly felt awkward with the greasy burger in his grasp, smears of which must surely be plastered on his multi-coloured lights illumined face.

'Told you I'd bump into you again, didn' I?'

Alex was trying to ensure his face was clean as surreptitiously as his spotlit self was able. 'You did indeed.' He swallowed down a half-masticated sliver of questionable identity meat, trying not to choke in the process.

'When you gonna tell me your name then? You know my name. You never told me yours.'

Alex frowned, realising she was probably correct. He was, after all, the stranger. He told her, tried to think of something else to say, settled for an enquiry as to what she had been up to recently, then worried it sounded lame, then consoled himself it was the best he could think of under the circumstances.

'Oh, this and that,' she said, saying nothing. He was still being kept at a tentative arm's length, but with the suggestion of a beckon in the digits. 'I've been out of town a lot recently.'

'Oh? And where have you been?'

'Oh...Taunton...Weston...' His heart sagged a little, although there was still the small mercy that she did not think the map of the world quite ended at Pawlett and Somerset Bridge like too many locals.

Alex gambled the chasecutting obvious. 'Look, I was thinking about getting a drink somewhere. Would you like to join me for one?'

Sheryl's expression seemed momentarily a little taken aback, then quietly albeit carefully pleased. 'I can't at the moment, I'm looking after my son, speaking of which he's being a bit naughty as well...Anthony!' she yelled, and Alex turned to see a boy of surely less than ten turn his head in Sheryl's direction, then run off in another at speed. 'I'd better go and get him actually, but another time we will go for a drink. Well...maybe, OK?'

'OK.'

'Look, I'm not bein' funny or nothin', but I gotta go catch up with my son now. Nice to see you again, anyway.'

'Yeah, yeah. Likewise,' he called after the woman disappearing into the crowd. He stood there for a moment, wondering if he ought not to have gone with her, ought not to have tried to exchange phone numbers, ought to try to catch up with her even now. He felt clumsy with this kind of thing at the best of times, quite out of his league now after the solitude and trauma of recent months.

He immediately replayed all they had exchanged in the minute or so's worth of conversation they had had. She wasn't exactly his natural-born type, but then who in this world was going to come along and fill that particular vacancy, especially with such a surface loser as him?

He decided he would try to forget about it, at least for the time being. He remembered what he had really come into town for – a drink.

54

The fair went and a visitor came to Alex, disturbing his light morning slumber on a living room chair. The doorbell jolted him awake in an instant, being an almost alien sound to him, coupled with the fact next to none knew where he was housed. Instinct told him to be cautious, and he was glad he listened to its advice.

Peering from the landing window after tiptoeing from the living room and ascending the stairs, the man on the doorstep's employer was evident in a flash. The short grey hair, clipped moustache, hi-vis striped jacket, white shirt, black trousers and clipboard in hand could only be an agent of the general public's arch enemy – the council. And Alex was illegally living at the officially empty address.

Three times the doorbell sounded, the civil service foot soldier was certainly persistent. Alex waited five full minutes after the third and final ring, then carefully glanced out of the window again.

The wet worker stood in the faint drizzle, exhaustively filling out a form. Alex retreated from view again, waited a few minutes more. The doorbell rang again, and again Alex jumped at its sound.

Shit. Had he been spotted? Shit, no.

Plentiful possibilities presented themselves for Alex's started mind, primarily the idea that someone who knew he was not meant to be where he was had tipped off Sedgemoor District that some penniless squatting unfortunate (for who else would want or run the gauntlet to live like this?) was not quite being sucked of every last drop of blood they could possibly possess. Each council department's dishwashing machines don't grow on trees, you know.

The daylight vampire – the kind who sleep at night – finally disappeared to ultimately end up back at Castle Living Braindead that is Bridgwater House, leaving Alex a letter on the mat that might as well have been soaked in cyanide and written in blood.

55

S arah put down the phone, and turned to face Alex, sat in a chair in next door's living room, cowering behind a mug of tea.

'Nothing to worry about,' she assured him. 'I told them the reason the lights have been on and water has been used and people have been seen coming and going is because we're moving there shortly from next door and we've been having some people do some maintenance work on the place. They kept on saying "Well, there was a man in the house when our inspector called round"-'

'You mean I was spotted??'

'Oh yes. You were spotted alright.'

'But I was really careful.'

'Well...obviously not careful enough. If you were asleep in the chair when he called round, he probably had a peep through the window before he rang the bell.'

'And they wanted to know why I didn't answer the door.'

'Yep,' she said, flatly, and refusing to be flustered. 'I just told them you were doing some work, heard the doorbell and didn't want to be disturbed, presuming the only person it was likely to be ringing the bell was a salesman, and so just ignored it.'

'And they were happy with that?'

'Not got much choice, have they?'

'I guess not, no.' Alex was pleased with Sarah's calm and quick thinking. Indeed it is the case that perhaps most occasions where the council or DSS try to intimidate someone into confessing some illegal, though motivated through dire straits desperation, behaviour, they are largely calling bluff; playing on fear and misinformation to goad their intended target into a confession when where there is no paperwork involved there is usually no provable misconduct to be had for.

Alex returned to his effective squat, presumably one under a certain amount of scrutiny from a self-righteous or just plain malicious or somehow misguidedly jealous neighbour, a needle of impotent rage pricking at his thoughts. It was the middle-class equivalent of vandalising someone's property then skulking off before you can even get the perverted satisfaction of seeing whatever effect it might achieve.

Alex not only needed to keep a roof over his head, he also wanted to remain as invisible as he could in order to keep away from the clutches of an uncontrollably spiralling credit card debt, unpaid opticians' bill, and to cap it all, a debt to a herbalist who had treated him for skin problems. He hated the idea of being in debt, especially to a complementary therapist. The opticians too were hardly evil, and he may require their services in the future, but the health cuts implemented by Lady Baroness Thatcher and the spineless PMs that had slithered in her wake led him to convince himself that he really could not pay it. The credit card debt he had no qualms about – Halifax bank's own investments were sure to grease the palms of child labour slavers, banana republic arms dealers, and forest devouring construction projects worldwide, as did every High Street bank.

He was sure he was in the right. Wasn't he?

How much money did he have now anyway? Not more than several hundred pounds, and that from a frugal, almost monastic, existence. Except for the drinking, of course.

But he would go mad from solitude and depression were he not to have some kind of social life.

Debts. Building. How much deeper was it all going to get? How much trouble could he get into, hiding from his debtors in this not-so-secret den he had to try to keep secret. How much might he be stitching himself up for in the future?

But what the hell was he really supposed to do anyway?

It wasn't as if he could really afford any luxuries. He certainly didn't have anywhere near the necessary deposits on a flat or something yet, and he was damned if he wanted to anchor himself with that anyway. At least here. He wanted to escape abroad again, but where could he go so far except as far as another country's airport?

Fuck it, the voice inside him cried, surrendering to obscenities that were so much the language of the lazily inarticulate, he cursed himself at the wording of his thoughts.

I'm keeping my money. The little of it there is.

He knew how hard it had proven to be to make. And with the next imminent agency job he had managed to beg or talk himself into, the ride was not about to get any smoother any time soon.

56

Gerba Foods was one of Bridgwater's longest standing employers, providing preserved goods packaged according to supplier but produced in the same way, manufactured and distributed by the provincial underpaid. Alex and his fellow graveyard shift zombies were to work as an ill-matched, uncommunicative, uncooperative team. The megabucks enterprise, at least to its owners, had invested millions upon millions of pounds designing and building a machine that would stack cartons of fruit juice onto pallets without causing breakage and with just the right amount of technical precision to ensure undamaged transit. Employing the services of this revolutionary ergonomic creation, these cartons were loaded onto pallets at the plant at one end of the town, transported to the plant at the other, and then – and wait for it – manually unloaded from the pallets and stacked onto dollies to await further distribution to retail outlets. Ours is not to reason why.

Needless to say, Alex had great fun with the dollies, failing to square the load, forgetting the pattern in which the cartons were meant to be stacked, creating teetering towers of produce waiting to topple on a loader/unloader's feet, managing to turn the final procedure of wrapping the load in cellulose film into a slapstick reel, and unerringly coming the last to finish the job, each and every time, take a bow, Mr Bishop.

The supervisors realised about halfway through the second shift that there was no way Alex was ever going to master the job he had been assigned (£1 per 80 litres stacked, yes, thank you very much, Mr Gerba, you do give people jobs, you're a marvellous contribution to the local economy), and he was taken off to spend the final four hours of what he knew would be his very last shift not to mention the last four hours of his life he would spend inside Gerba Foods Limited sweeping the floor. After having to ask a supervisor where the broom was kept, he was answered with a too-busy-but-I'll-tell-you-anyway 'Beside the machine'. His eyes locating approximately several dozen machines with one quick scan of just the immediate environment, he had to find another member of staff with a job title almost as menial as his own to answer the question the man on three times his own pay had found too taxing.

Alex swept the floor, then swept the floor he had just swept again, then walked up and down, back and forth, with a broom handle extended, pushing the broom, pulling broom, going to the toilet for ten minutes as if it would break up the monotony, walking around in circles with the broom, sweeping with both hands, then the left, then the right, cha cha cha, what the fuck, sweeping faster, sweeping slower, watching the clock stare glibly, motionlessly back, hiding with the broom, standing still until a supervisor walked past, one hour, two hours, two hours and twenty-five minutes, two hours and twenty-nine minutes, this is what it's like, this is what it's like, in hell, he thought, this is what hell is really all about, Gerba Foods Gerba Foods, I'm going off my trolley, got to stack up all those dollies, look at this job I've found, just 80 litres for one whole pound, wonder why this plant is surrounded by a fence, minimum wage plus fifty silver pence, gonna sweep up all that invisible dust, because that's what business sense says that I must.

When the four hours of sweeping were finally through, Alex threw the broom down on the floor and left it there. Gerba Foods could stick it where it belonged.

57

Something had been in the air for a while now, half an idea kicked about by those regulars that represented the closest things to friends such a place got at the Labour Club: a pub crawl, with safety in numbers, around the other watering holes in the town. It had taken a while to get off the ground, especially when the list of likely suspects were, namely, Alex, Daniel, Ian, Ken, Patrick and, as Pavla seemed to have disappeared off the scene for another eternity, this one looking like it might last a little more than a half hour long, Councillor Stoodley too. To get everyone in the frame of mind to agree on such a seemingly simple quest at the same time felt like asking too much from life, and there were plenty of false starts and broken arrangements before about the closest thing you can get to a miracle in Bridgwater town occurred, and they all at least set off on a pub crawl of the town together. That they would pass the evening without any fall-outs or petty dramas would be expecting one miracle too many.

In order to make the mission work, or to give it a fighting chance at all, the rendezvous point had to be somewhere other than the La-bore Club or Fart Centre, for that was what both places inevitably became if you never went anywhere else. And so it was, with calling, coaxing, persuading, goading, patience, prayer and basically shock, the odd-looking troupe of curiously disparate personalities met, just forty some minutes late, at The Carnival Inn, part of the Wetherspoon chain, music-free babbled-filled lounges with cheap by comparison drinks and not a sniff of the atmosphere of tradition or a local feel. It being Friday night, and sometime shortly before eight, the place was packed with regulars pouring cut-price beverages down their weekend welcoming throats, tanking up before launching themselves on the only night club left in the town not yet closed down due to ill-behaviour of punters and owners alike. Alex entered with Daniel, whom he had had to push out of the door of his own home and out of the go-nowhere bubble of his comfort zone after a long battle that had already part-tainted his enthusiasm for the night ahead. Patrick seemed to know everyone in the pub, or at least everyone knew him, which appeared to make him feel popular, though with radar clearly on red danger alert, perhaps having remembered a visitor to his shop he had absent-mindedly short changed. Ken was in amenable form, fortuitously for all having forgotten he was the sole member of the Bridgwater Bolshevik Army, while Malcolm, normally a natural born comic and entertainer, was wearing a grey mood, always ready with a joke at anyone else's expense but not able to see the funny side of life when he chose not to be in the mood. Maybe he would lighten up later. Ian had been collecting jokes a rugby team would hesitate to tell, and was itching to throw them around as if they were balls in the literal sense too. The only thing missing were the girls.

'Where's the girls then, boys, eh? Eh? Where's the girls then, boys?'

All turned to find Greg Fisher was out to spend his carefully calculated drinking allowance, grinning, spitting, standing straight like a camp army commander. And thus it was Greg made the relatively articulate six into the magniloquent seven.

58

The Rose and Crown was under the management of some hard-core lesbians – not the kind that found their way onto mass-marketed pornography but the heavy booted, heavy set, cropped hair uniform types whom, not content with being wide, generally seemed to want to look like they were thick as well. Fortunately this tended to deter the bonehead types which, on this particular Friday night, left it rather empty.

'Well, lads,' Daniel addressed them, having hoped for the moment to justify his lack of hope. 'Looks like this is where it's at then. What we've all been missing.'

'At least they've got an offer on the new beer,' offered Patrick. He took a sip of the stuff, tasted it theatrically, then held it up like a trophy, causing others in the bar to glance over in puzzlement. 'Not bad that for £1.88,' he proclaimed for the benefit of all, including the brewer.

'Why do lesbians tend to look tougher than everyone else?' asked Ian, presumably for the benefit of the tough looking lesbians within earshot at the bar. Everyone held their breath. 'They always resort to using their fists,' he said, and laughed so needlessly, it was all anyone else could do to laugh as well.

Ken put his head in his hands and groaned. 'I think I'm going to go to the club.'

'You'll miss Daniel's round if you do that,' offered Malcolm.

'Eh?' Ken snapped back to attention. It seemed Malcolm's comment had done the trick.

'Where to next then, men?' stirred Greg. 'Where are we going to find the girls?' He rubbed his hands together, then glanced back at the assembled at the bar. 'The ones who don't look like they use a hedge trimmer to shave their faces.'

'In Bridgwater that only leaves the ones with beards,' said Alex, doubtless karmically destroying any chance he might have had of female company that night in the process. 'But let's go and see if there are any exceptions to the rule after all.'

The bachelor party trundled like a dysfunctional family, dragging themselves reluctantly behind each other, none quite prepared to lose the semi-cool of misery and despondency. Look out, girls, luck be a lady tonight. 'If any one of us scores, I'll be a Dutch bloody uncle,' Daniel said, trying to dislodge the scrap of paper litter that had wrapped itself around one foot. 'I mean, look at us. What a sad bloody bunch of losers we are.'

Ken immediately proved him wrong. 'I won a can of corned beef in the club raffle last night,' the vegetarian declared.

'Where the fuck are we going anyway?' moaned Ian, more of a sit-down comedian, the funnyman amiss when he had to stand up and walk.

'Admiral's Landing, I guess,' shrugged Alex, the ensuing silence suggesting the idea had gone down like an anchor. It was a crisp, cold night, with a roguish wind darting around corners to jump out and be in your face just when you went round the bend. Because of this, Bridgwater folk wore the traditional weekend night out attire of the English in such conditions – as little as was possible. Men's bull necks hunkered down into broadened shoulders, T-shirts accentuating their goose-pimpled musculature. Women seemed to welcome the chill on their exposed midriffs with their two-a-penny pierced navels (Ere look oi got moi belly button done oi did) and meaningless motif small-of-the-back tattoos, bar code cattle markings above legs that opened wider than their minds.

'They still got the trivia machines there?' Malcolm asked, itching to exchange his wits for beers.

'Trivia machines!' Greg burst out in excitement, ready to help Malcolm further trade his wits. He rubbed his hands in excitement. 'Trivia machines for you, Mr Bishop?' he practically slobbered.

'It sounds like that's where the party's at,' Alex said, by way of reply.

The Admiral's Landing was set in the docks area of the town, surrounded by a complex of modern flats that aspired to be somewhere to aspire to live in. Long-standing Bridgwater Conservative MP The Right Honourable Tom King had once had an apartment directly above the pub, and while he was posted as, in Alex's opinion, chief representative of colonial oppression and crusades against Catholicism i.e. Northern Ireland Secretary, he had decided to retire to his apartment while the pub below was still open. His bodyguards had immediately entered The Admiral's Landing and ordered the drinkers to abandon their drinks and leave post haste using direct physical aggression and threats of violence on anyone who chose to hesitate; doubtless regular behaviour of which Mr King, long-standing upright servant of the Bridgwater people, would be wholly aware.

The Admiral's was popular this Friday evening, as was peculiarly typical countrywide for establishments who obviously charge inflated prices for the uninspired selection of drinks they serve. It's funny how clearly getting ripped off and taken for a ride becomes the mark of higher status when a piece of tinsel has been tied around the affair. The main bar was thickly surrounded with people, half of which customarily had their drinks already and were simply getting in the way. They decided to get their drinks at the second bar located on a raised seating area, the cocktail bar Parrots (somebody spare us, please), and each ended up with what was for them the lesser of the evils on display, Daniel paying through the nose for what none of them really wanted to drink. A couple of large screens played music videos, currently displaying the lowest common denominator ego tripping commodiousness of Robbie Williams – perhaps the most suited two-dimensional pin-up to be found in such a place; a lager lout with a slick manager.

The sad club marched as nonchalantly as they could pretend to through the largest of the seating areas, also festooned with pool tables around which clustered youths seemingly a century younger than them and the same age they had been what felt like little more than five minutes earlier, like a bunch of patrolling dads en masse, ready to embarrass their curfew-breaking offspring into grounding themselves for the rest of their lives. At last they happened upon what they had been hoping for in lieu of something truly worth hoping for: an electronic general knowledge tester. Shrapnel in the slot, the combined politology graduate and councillor, astronomer and techno geek, communist history buff, walking catalogue of terrible jokes, encyclopedia of popular music, sidekick encyclopedia supplement, and Alex the horror genre addict and punk aficionado in better times, for whatever that was worth, pooled

themselves in a cram around the machine's screen, eagerly awaiting the chance to appear smarter than any of their mates. The coup
de grace, of course, was to correctly answer a question the answer
to which was unknown to the nominal specialist in that field. The
vanity of the male ego coming to the fore, they were beside themselves to read the words as the first Q flashed up onscreen.

What type of dog is Waggy in the Australian soap drama *The
Folk from Roo Hill*?

The Duke of Monmouth had changed its name to The Duke,
largely because any old duke would do when clearly no-one who
visited knew or cared who the DOM was, and because this was
how the pub was referred to by colloquial locals. Maybe it would
lose the article in time too (Goin' daan Duke/Meet 'e up Duke/Up
Duke inner?). The seven prised their way inside, a little wary of
nudging someone and accidentally spilling some of their drink,
and each ended up with a pint of makeshift beer Alex was not even
sure of the name of, no-one having the guts to order a half in here.
Huddling as they only could, keenly watching the throng and trying not to make it obvious, it was only a matter of seconds before
someone approached them and started speaking to Patrick.

''Ere, you'm that bloke woz got that record shop, ain't ee?' the
beer-bellied, carnival club T-shirt wearing individual half-asked,
half-demanded. None could possibly know what this character did
for a living, although each would likely hazard a guess a poet
wasn't his line.

Patrick's guard went up like a portcullis crashing down. 'I have
got a record shop, yes,' he stated as matter-of-factly and dismiss-
ively as he could, blinking hard as if his lashes were trying to shoo
away a fly.

'Ow much would you gurt give oi fur *One Night in Bangkok*? I
got a twelve incher moind.'

'Excuse me, I don't want to seem rude or anything, but I'm not
at work now, I'm in the pub with my friends trying to forget about
work.' Patrick's cohorts could barely contain their smirks and
smiles, so didn't really bother trying.

'Oh…' The silver-tongued salesman took stock of his methods
for a breath. 'Wha' 'bout Joe Dolce?'

'Shadupa yer face?'

'Yer. Oi d' loike that, oi do.'

'Well, mate, why don' you come in on Monday, when the shop's open and I'm working, and maybe we can do something about it then, but not *now* because *now* I'm in the pub, having a drink with my friends, and *definitely not* working.' Patrick took a long swallow of his pint then turned his back on the interloper with the pint-size selling power.

'Oi got ee. Monday you'm open, roit. Cun oi jus' ask ee one more question 'fore oi go back t' me mates?'

'As long as it's got absolutely nothing whatsoever to do with selling or buying records, yes.'

'No, it ain't got nothin' to do with sellin ur boyin records.'

Wanting the agony over at last, Patrick almost spat, 'So what is it?'

'Ow much you reckon you could give oi fer a Koilie in concert DVD?'

The Great Escape, hilariously nicked The Great Mistake, had a DJ bleeding the latest hits from an increasingly meaningless and pointless and blatantly rigged chart one into another, the time signature as uniform as the mandatory absence of musical instruments nulled and voided by programmers of computers and consumers alike. Presently the individual Alex thought of as the textbook embodiment of post-Thatcherite Britain and all it is able to aspire to, Robbie Williams once again, was polluting the intoxicated's ears. Say no more, thought Alex.

Conversation being impossible, the group managed to spray each other's aural chambers with spittle trying in vain to be heard, Alex resigning himself to watching people with nothing to say to each other being unable to say anything to each other, compensating by drinking their too expensive drinks too quickly. Human nature drawing his eyes to the females in the pheromone zone, he was disappointed though unsurprised to find they fell into the two main categories young women tended to in nightlife Britain; ladettes and courtesans. The former were coarse, abrupt, unpolished and unfeminine, believing that by trying to outdo young men at their own game they somehow had the upper hand over them, instead of the simple truth they looked just as much like wilful artless idiots and a bit more besides. The latter seemed to be in a permanent state of pique, pathologically incapable of a belly laugh, available only to bids the sullen faced trophies are ever seeking to be outmatched in the hope that someday someone will buy them a personality. There was always masturbation to fall back on, but even that seemed to have lost its appeal when the traditional celebrity wet dreams, from Jordan to Paris Hilton, never managed to excite Alex or seemed to be worth a toss.

Alex was glad when they left, unable to disguise the downcast look on his face and awkwardness of posture any more. He wanted desperately to cheer up, surely that was the aim of the evening out, but however hard we try, we cannot tell ourselves how to feel, and trying to normally brings us down the more.

'OK, I wanna see everybody gettin' down,' the DJ imposed, and Alex wondered if he was the only one in the pub obliging him. He walked out the door as the punters that remained enjoyed themselves at the count of three.

The Galleries was one of only three possibilities left now the hour had come for the rest of the town pubs to close bar those having lock-ins behind drawn curtains, which was most of them anyway. The design of this place was the thinnest veneer of gloss that had never seemed to dry beyond tacky over the usual hotbed of rip-off prices, bad booze, testosterone, overapplied cheap cologne, thick curtains of smoke, uninhibited envy and resentment, vapidity, predictability, garish décor, the commercial safeness of an inflammable factory of libido and complex that could not take their drink. The music was depressingly safe and standard as well: remastered 60s soul, the *Pulp Fiction* soundtrack, a Dido here, a Kylie there; stereotypical safe anthems preceding unsafe sex.

Remedies proffered a little more drama, although it being a little white knuckle and directly involving the group of don't wannabee lads and would be dads who didn't wanna look old enough that they could be dads but young enough that they could be lads, it failed to make their night. Managing to secure two tables for themselves dangerously close to what had become an only vaguely parametered dancefloor, they were all trying to think of something to say to boost their spirits when one particular reveller's enjoyment permeated the seated gatherings' gathering clouds. A stout man in his early twenties in T-shirt, jeans and a look that wanted to look like it could kill was blundering through some heavy-handed dance moves that suggested he was kickboxing his shadow to death. Good-naturedly shoving Councillor Stoodley's shoulder with the flat of his hand, he all but sent the councillor into the neighbouring district. 'Come on, then,' the Freddie Krueger of Fred Astaires bellowed at the seated, though it was unclear if he was begging for a fight, a dance, or for someone to hold his winkle while he went for a wee. Trying the same tactic with Daniel, the amateur astronomer was rocketed out of the sucky atmosphere with a professional boxer's force. The redcoat blackshirt was determined that the men gyrate their hips in rhythm with his own while the bouncers looked on smugly, until he finally left to dance to his own tune like he probably did every night.

The Palace was the final curtain for the night, in Alex's youth a fleapit cinema before multiplexes infested the country, now a night club in the vein of any other; a tasteless philistine theatre of urban obscenity and moral decay, that can't even manage an element of morbid curiosity in lieu of an ounce of charm.

The first stop was the bar, through which it was necessary to negotiate a path through the jostling elbowing crowbarring abhorrers of queues, demanding self-assertion and risking a fight just to get a third-rate beer. The long downstairs bar and its several staff on minimum wage stood behind chilled cabinets full of repetition after repetition of repetition of the same overpriced cheap quality bottled lagers and alcopops. Alex remembered having once gone to The Rock Garden, another late opening venue that had since turned into the kind of place where men stimulate their collective sexual ambiguity - a pole dancing club - and asked for a bitter, before the bar attendant informed him he hadn't a clue what a bitter was. Thug petrol lagers in hand, full of chemical aftertaste and the promise of the loss of tomorrow, they made their way back across the carpet that couldn't have been stickier had it been coated in jam to the railed periphery of the dancefloor, where they joined the other men dribbling at the sight of women finding rhythm in rhythmless uniform tempo. One reason Alex detested such places was that he felt himself unable to dance, especially to pop – although it sounds like it is at least technically possible, you can find yourself in trouble once you're expected to move your body to it, or perhaps he was just too sensitive to how soulless such faux music was.

Closeby, a fight had broken out in a blink, a group of people Alex had noticed as seemingly just chatting amiably were now animatedly and fervently trying to commit as much physical harm as they could before security continued the job for them. Four men and four women were tearing at each other in a fever of outburst, leaving the seven recently arrived onlookers to wonder how so much venom could be accessed by such a large number of people simultaneously. Drinks and glasses and curses and fists became a sense-blurring aviation display of missiles launched in aimless shots of anger, resulting in collateral damage and threatening a barroom brawl. Eventually the black-clad bouncers arrived, elbowing people out of the way and seeming to froth at the mouth their moment had come.

Just when it looked like all was about to get calm again, another black shadow fell across the group, no less threatening and with the word INSECURITY emblazoned upon their persona.

59

Marcus Plenty was one of life's self-appointed deities the likes of which form the target for the Anti-Nowhere League song, *So What?* Unfortunately he is walking proof of one of life's less reassuring laws; take yourself deadly seriously for years upon years, eventually the more malleable of society do as well, and grant you the access and authority and subservience you have so lusted after. Give him just slightly different circumstances, social factors and intelligence and he would be another Caligula or Jong-Il, intoxicated and blinded by the need to be revered, inured to the poison of his own arrogance, unheeding of the world beyond the tiny sphere of self-justification. Such characters have three prinicipal characteristics: firstly, the lack of a sense of humour. Due to their strenuously self-serious nature, they see jokes as largely superfluous to their desires, and although they are capable of appreciating one, a joke about them is something they are immediately and obviously uncomfortable with. Caustic smug mockery eroding the dignity of others is a common currency, but try to think of the number of times such characters enjoy a real belly laugh, or a straightforward piece of harmless silliness, and your memory will likely be taxed indeed. The second characteristic is a tendency to anger, violence and physical insinuation. Anyone threatening their idealised self-perception runs the risk of being attacked for their ego is so fragile they are not able to dismiss or keep their cool when faced with such like a genuinely confident person can. Roughhousing is another sly tactic whereby they gain licence to touch and inflict pain upon the unwilling with the same base motives that underlie rape. The third, but by no means least mentionable, commonality of the ego-merchant megalomaniac is their obliviousness to what the majority of people around them really think about them. Certainly they will have their cohorts, for their bullishness is often mistaken for strength of personality, and to be associated with them is something of a trophy friendship, but for all those who might speak up in their favour, there are two who would denounce their tyrannical manner, though are inhibited from doing so through the sheer fact of the intimidatory manner of the unfairly playing gatecrashing uninvited guest upon life's party. So gutted would they be, so thoroughly fighting denial, so overwhelmed by the knowledge of just exactly what most people who know them really entertain as their opinion of them, to truly enlighten them is almost impossible given their degree of denial, and the knowledge of which could threaten their delusory universe to the degree of causing them a traumatic breakdown or worse.

The most unfortunate thing for the town of Bridgwater regarding Marcus Plenty was that through sheer dogged persistence in his life and death mission to be looked up to in some way, shape or form, he now had his own promotions company which, like it or not, successfully brought name bands and artists to the town for rock concerts, and had a big hand in just about every smaller scale local rock gig as well, meaning that in order to get anything done musically in Bridgwater it was just about inevitable you would have to go through Marcus Plenty in order to achieve it. He was the don of the local music scene and he knew it. So did everyone else, which Alex knew well meant that an enormous lot of local musicianship was as stifled as promoted due to many simply not wanting to get involved with the knowledge that Marcus Plenty was a character they would have to get their hands dirty with if they wanted to play a local stage.

'Alright, you sad bunch of fucks,' he sneered, then chortled like a pubescent schoolgirl at his own brand of mirth, a sound he made nearly every time he spoke. 'What you doing? Trying to find some slags as desperate as you lot?' Customary whinnying titter.

'Well, we've found one, at least,' said Daniel. 'What you doing here so different to us?'

'Been arranging some gigs with the management, ain't I? Some of us have had some success tonight.' Public schoolgirl snigger. 'Fuckin' 'ell,' he subtly exclaimed seeming to notice Alex was among the group for the first time. 'Didn't know they were letting *gays* in here these days.'

'Even the semi-closet ones get in,' Alex remarked, without much gusto, simultaneously weary and wary of the stuck-record newcomer. Another oddity about Marcus Plenty was the fact he had a local band himself, Daniel and Malcolm being partially-witting members neither of which quite had the heart or mettle to throw in the towel like they forever lamented not doing. Whilst the lyrics he wrote (he was the band, by the way, the other two were just a bassist and drummer) were self-indulgent to the point of containing the words I, me and myself ad nauseam and pretentious to the convenience of pseudo-intellectualism and rhyming schemes, the man was nevertheless capable of penning crisp, delicious genuinely poetic verse when the muse took him, and yet to hear him engage in conversation was a frankly sickening experience. Drunk or sober, angry, lively, whatever dimensions the chip on his shoulder had swollen or shrivelled to, the patter he delivered in a group gathering was for the bulk sexism, homophobia and put-down, served through a smug sneer and jarringly laced with base-level invective. One of Marcus' songs was apparently inspired by and an ode to cunnilingus, a song that strives to make romantic and seductive use of wordplay and inventive reference and metaphor. He had then heard Marcus say out loud in a bar that the song was about "biting cunt". How could someone listen to the song after that, how could anyone be taken in by his lyrics, how could, why would, anyone who did not have a bitterly twisted and highly misogynistic mind come up with, let alone come out with, an expression like that at all?? If he was drunk, he was an obnoxious terror, for he had a reputation as someone who could never hold their liquor without the seemingly irrepressible desire to spoil everyone else's mood in order to massage his own ego in the cheapest and laziest way possible popping its ever-straining cork. He always made a beeline for Alex, probably because Alex tried his best in life to be the antithesis of the Marcus Plentys of the world. He always had to touch Alex too, a sly poke here, a 'roguish' slap across the back of the head there, roughhousing and space invading, some of it drunken bravado to win the applause of the imps of the perverse, all of it sneaky excuse to send a frisson down his ill-intending lack of spine.

'You ain't gonna get any bunnies standing there, you gotta wade in and grab 'em by the tit.' He spat the last word out as if it represented an object of antipathy.

'Yeah, there's certainly some tits in here tonight,' Ian couldn't resist, its tonality just subtle enough that Marcus missed it his completely unsubtle self.

'Well, fuck me, I ain't gonna stand around with you bores all night, I'm gonna go and grab some tart's asses.'

'We wouldn't want to stop you from feeling an ass,' said Ken.

A comradely sneer and a 'Fuck you, ya old codger,' was the razor bladed reply. 'See you later, queerboy,' he said as he breezed past Alex, pushing him in the chest, his hand at breast level, as he passed, and then the groper was lost in the crowd, doing what he did in an arena where it needn't be so inexpertly hidden.

Shortly, they all went home, or back to their beds and a fidgety unrelaxing sleep. Bridgwater town, Saturday night.

60

Work dried up, employment agencies became wary of Alex's name, the weather closed the door on any lingering trace of summer, the dole became the only source of income, and a tight-belted budget became the only access to bread and, occasionally, butter. He visited the job centre, which was now called Job Centre Plus (plus incompetency/unnecessary complications/needless humiliation/unworkable legislation?), became boxed-in by security staff who seemed undecided as to whether or not they should be taking their own employment role in society seriously who asked him what he was doing as soon as he entered the door and he wondered for a moment if he were gatecrashing. After explaining he wanted to register a claim for Jobseeker's Allowance, all the while praying that too hadn't changed its name to something even more inscrutable, he was told that he would have to phone a call centre instead of speaking with someone in the job centre itself, and was directed to a line of desks with handsets bolted to the walls where the desperate and hungry could beg for help with zero discretion. An automated female voice welcomed him with comic gusto to something called the "One Service" – presumably yet another leg of the government claims system that did not bother to introduce itself presumably due to the frayed-nerved listeners generally not being in the slightest bit interested anyway. Alex pressed buttons on the keypad in answer to multiple choice questions that were not likely to win him a million, then waited nearly twenty minutes with the phone to his ear, being constantly reminded that he was in a queueing system with persistence enough possibly designed to make one slam down the phone in disgust, and being entertained by the stream of wannabee delinquents, actual delinquents, parents under the thumbs of their uncontrollable kids, the seemingly mentally ill, the plain unfathomable, men resorting to invective because they were not entitled to their cheque until tomorrow or had failed to bring the appropriate document, crushed and battered looking middle-aged women, and characterless middle-aged men laid off after decades in a factory and out of their depth now they had to think what to do, until a man's voice suddenly informed him he was through and speaking to Richard, as if Richard were an old friend. Alex didn't know why he didn't call himself Dick. The Dick then took Alex's NI number, asked him for a phone number where he could be contacted to which he gave them Sarah and Roy's number, and was told someone from the One Service would call him on that number in two days' time. He had spent half an hour waiting to divulge what could have been divulged in thirty seconds. He wanted to vent his anger but what would be the use of doing so to a disembodied voice on the phone he had never met and would never meet? He might as well berate the automated one telling him which buttons to press.

He replaced the phone calmly, stood up and made for the door, finding one of the cheap white shirted security men in his path. 'Care to browse the job points now you're here, sir?' he suggested, helpfully or threateningly, Alex couldn't be sure.

'No thanks,' he said, brushing past and desperate to escape the cacophonous impersonal institutionalised building of lost souls. 'I'm too busy,' he called after him. 'I haven't got the time.'

61

In the officially unoccupied Alfoxton Road house, things had started to turn mighty busy. Roy had taken a fortnight off work, though not to relax or go on holiday or busy himself with something interesting; instead, as Sarah and he had a plan to eventually move out of their rented house next door and into this one, which was bought and paid for, he had decided to devote the two weeks to renovations, and he really threw himself into his work. For Alex, it was the most inappropriate time to be out of work, meaning he was often hanging about while repairs and repainting and replacing were seen to with focus and determination. Knowing well Alex's practical ineptitude and walking disaster zone self, he was politely refused upon his offers of help, except for the very occasional request to help shift something particularly bulky or heavy, which thankfully thus far wasn't himself. Roy's retired father came over more days than he didn't, too, a no nonsense man economical to a fault, especially where a sense of humour was concerned. The two believed in an early start and a thorough day's shift, and Alex became very self-conscious about his own lack of work, the times he got up, what he occupied himself with, and the rooms currently undergoing in detail transformation which he attempted to skilfully avoid. Regardless of assurances to the contrary, the whole process seemed symbolic somehow as well, and Alex couldn't stop himself from feeling he was being reminded his time under this roof was impermanent, that he himself would soon have to seriously consider his next move.

Needing a break from civilisation, needing to get out of Bridgwater town for a beat, and needing to do it on the ultra-cheap, he asked to borrow Roy's bike so he could take himself off and out the way of the regrouting of the bathroom tiles that nobody who visited would have noticed were ever there. Roy was suspiciously enthusiastic to let him disappear with his two-wheeler, once he himself had ensured it was in sturdy condition, and so Alex left the ever-mounting pile of DIY for the gentle hills of the Quantocks.

Alex's cycling was symbolic of how he lived his life; in fact, the way anyone approaches any kind of physical task provides the perfect material for a character analysis. Alex liked to travel at a comfortable pace, feeling no great need to rush, and certainly not needing to compete with those around him; after all, there are always those who are better and worse than you at everything – who with an ounce of depth cares whether they're regarded as a winner or loser? Similarly, Alex didn't need to know exactly and precisely where he was all the time. He remembered another cyclist and hiker once proudly showing him his GPS tracking device; a toy designed almost exclusively for men for only men are ever reluctant to simply ask for directions from a local. He also remembered an American whining about how illogical European urban geography is in comparison to their monotonous grid layout of cities and labelling of streets in numerical order. For Alex, it all came back down to the idea that it is mystery that gives to life its beauty, and that discovering is the most fun we can have. Those with the most carefully mapped out existence have the most faithless, dull and ultimately directionless paths in life, whilst being temporarily lost is an adventure and we always ultimately find our way back to where we want to be or something else interesting or richly experiential for us. In one year he had learned the geography of Prague better than countless others whom had lived there all their lives simply because he was not afraid of putting in a little legwork and going places with no particular place to go, just to see where he wound up. And thus it was Alex was attracted to roads and paths that did not seem immediately familiar, although this was oft tempered by the lack of unfamiliarity in the county he had spent most of his life in and the occasional threat posed by farm dogs owned by Tory-voting yokels for whom a passing townie cyclist might as well not exist anyway.

After a couple of hours of cruising past curiosities; pedestrians strayed from any visible habitation, horses backed by teenage girls, dilapidated cottages with gothic appeal, a few fellow cyclists with a greeting to yell in exchange, Alex decided to stop and sit for a while, somewhere with a hideaway appeal, to contemplate and meditate and do nothing at all while he picnicked on the few rations he had stuffed into the shopper-sized saddlebag. Choosing a gently sloping field with twisted trees like tortured souls, out of sight of anything but satellite surveillance, he planted himself in a spot where flowers didn't grow.

Almost immediately he spotted them, yet he could have sworn they hadn't been there a moment earlier. First it was just a couple, then a group, then a whole gathering, standing together in concentrations, waiting silently as if in a vigil for the arrival of such as Alex. He couldn't be sure of what they were at first, but as they got closer, their identity became all but unmistakeable. A sudden turn of the head and he realised they had him surrounded.

62

That night, when the day's DIYing had extended itself far into the evening, until Sarah had come in to practically drag Roy back next door and shoo his father away, Alex found himself in a mood that mixed melancholy with nostalgia. He was also tired of feeling depressed and unlucky, tired of going nowhere with no tangible signs of assistance from friends, family, society or god to really get him pulled up out of his rut. He had made up his mind to try something, not that it was anything really new to him, but this time his circumstances were significantly different and his needs significantly more.

It was gone midnight, and the rest of the world had gone to bed. One of the things he hated most about his mother country in comparison to its European neighbours was the fact it spent half its existence shut down for the night. A wartime law, which couldn't have been any more outdated and restrictive were it to have been imposed by Draco, closed the pubs when the rest of the continent was just going out for the night, and the relaxing of this law was going to be what change always is for the English – painfully slow and overly cautious. When you have 24 hour drinking laws, so many other businesses thrive as a result of this as well, and the problems associated with drinking are significantly reduced. Such was the English fixation with a civilised bedtime, to not be in bed when it seemed like everyone else was invoked a strange pang of guilt. Small hour conversations and the creation of art were always more colourful and libertarian but you couldn't help having a nagging feeling of naughtiness you weren't tucked up and incarcerated in your pyjamas with the lights off and the curtains tightly closed. Alex was a creature of the night, for the dark was the ally of the poet, dreamer and conversationalist, and anyone who isn't at least one of those things is probably, even in the middle of the day, a character rather dull.

Alex fetched one of the kitchen chairs and carried it through to the living room, positioning it so it faced the largest area of blank wall. Then he went upstairs, urinated, and walked into the box room, opening the drawer beneath his borrowed bed. He stared at its contents for a full minute, intrigued by what he saw, then returned empty handed downstairs.

Tonight, in the illegally inhabited Alfoxton Road house, with the black of night providing the town with an unconvincing calm, he prepared himself for the experiment ahead.

63

The following morning Alex received the appointed call from the job centre where he volunteered further information they already had on record from past claims, then was told to return to the job centre on a future date where he would have appointments with two further people while he waited for his fifty quid a week to be ultimately approved by people whose job it was to get him back into work but who were the worst advert for employment themselves.

Alex made a further check on the secret contents of the drawer beneath his temporary bed he had not made but nonetheless lied in. A few days more and he would be able to put what he had there into operation.

Alex took full advantage of the fact Roy and his father were not planning to start work in the house until the afternoon today, devoting their morning to hunting through DIY shops the elusive exact fittings, joinings and trimmings of decadence in permanent discontent. Repeating what he had begun the night before, he was pleasantly surprised at how much easier and smoother it felt, and how the time he wished to devote to it slipped past so much swifter on day two.

His fighting spirit was not dead yet.

Just before the return of the screw-drill-paint-scrape ravers, Sarah came to fetch him from next door to speak to the caller on the phone.

64

In Penel Orlieu, the cops were escorting a convict in the direction of the town centre. They threatened passersby with their truncheons while they searched in vain for the Keystone precinct, their prisoner rattling his chains and tossing a lead ball from hand to hand. Hungry cannibals queued at the chip shop, their primitive minds perhaps mistaking the word for chaps. A bunch of clowns attempted to entertain themselves, maybe waiting for the rest of their group to finish applying their make-up and join their gathering circus at the town hall carnival concert rehearsal. On the Cornhill, cowboys and Indians were engaged in an uneasy stand-off to either side of the street. A sheriff was yelling copycat accusations while a good time girl from a local saloon was catfighting with what could be her clone. In Fore Street and across the town bridge, Alex passed robots, some cheap and cheerful versions of presumably whatever this year's blockbuster Disney cartoon characters were, what could have been wizards or perhaps galactic warriors, Charleston dancers and Tommy gun gangsters and what might have been magicians about to play with their wands. Sometimes it was hard to tell one from the other; costume, float, and year.

At the corner of West Quay, a white male resident of Bridgwater covered in black body paint, dressed in a mock loincloth, and wearing an Afro wig and plastic bone through the nose, threatened him with a spear. Fortunately, the weapon being about as sharp as its brandisher's sense of humour and blunt as his sensibilities, Alex survived to beat a path through the concrete jungle to the flat of Councillor Stoodley.

'So, you thought about what I said?' Malcolm asked, referring to their earlier phone conversation.

'I have, yeah. I think I can manage it. Can you just run the details past me one more time?'

'That's four boys, late teens, here in Bridgwater for two weeks, they want four hours of English lessons a day.'

'Whatever. I'm a bit rusty, and I can't for the moment think of quite what I'll come up with, but I'll teach something somehow anyway.'

'Excellent. They're here for the carnival as well, by the way, so that could be one lesson idea sorted.'

'Certainly could. OK, I need the money, I'll do whatever I can to keep them happy. Are they old enough to drink?'

'Not quite, it seems.'

'Do they look old enough?'

'Probably.'

'OK, so that's another lesson, English pubs and ordering and drinking beers.'

Alex swerved around the fancy dresses, hoodlum uniforms, and formally dressed nightclubbers with open gutter mouths, back in the direction of Alfoxton Road. A group of adolescents zoomed past in a customised wheel-rimmed car, shouting 'Wanker!' at anyone on foot. He could not stay here forever, that much he knew for sure. And the faster he could escape again, the better.

In North Street a woman appeared to be arguing with her boyfriend. 'I din fuckin want you to pull me off her!' she screamed, looking like she wanted to do to her boyfriend what he had prevented her from doing to her intended victim. A few steps further along, a couple of men wearing England shirts with pride finished their takeaways then stood up and dropped their food wrappings nonchalantly on the ground, desecrating their motherland with the hypocrisy that has always festered in England's history and heart.

Alex looked forward to pocketing the pocket money he would receive for his forthcoming teaching, money that would go undeclared as he claimed the pittance of the dole. Who could blame him for doing that? Just exactly who??

65

Alex woke early and got up early; though whether the cause was depression, which tends to deny the refuge of sleep, or a growing enthusiasm to meet the new day he could not quite be sure. He was feeling better, though – not as significantly as he would have liked but enough to notice. Maybe his experiment was working. As he was up in time to beat the arrival of the carpet repainters or window frame shampooers or whatever on earth they would be up to today, he had time and opportunity to further indulge in his increasingly determined – however desperate – plan.

Fetching the chair from the kitchen that was spending more and more time in the living room, he positioned it so that it was facing the blank wall, sat himself down, made himself comfortable, and began.

A few days ago he had felt silly doing what he was doing, even though alone. Now he just settled straight into the exercise.

He began the meditation.

Years ago, when he had first discovered this technique of meditation, along with what was basically the cult of Soka Gakkai, he had felt the effects it had upon him almost immediately. He had felt it stir him inside, shift the world about him, and kick him out of the rut he had found himself in. Later, his initial euphoria at what he had discovered had been diluted by the politics and institutional trappings of the Soka Gakkai organisation; an organisation that, with the rights and wrongs of its philosophy immaterial, harbours all the trappings of every classical cult, and therefore refuses to see itself as a cult at all. No, Alex was not a fan or devotee of Soka Gakkai, but he had incredible faith in the meditation technique they adopted. To him, it was no surprise that so many people whom had got involved with this organisation had divorced themselves from the organisation itself whilst privately continuing with the meditation practise. There was magic to be discovered here, and maybe it is the attempt to dictate and institutionalise that incomprehensible beautiful power that makes

Soka Gakkai such an internationally dysfunctional body, dogged by a history of infrastructure crises. Alex had rather a love/ hate relationship with the meetings he had attended, which was probably a reflection of his relationship with life at large. Whereas he had enjoyed the sense of community that had essentially pervaded the gatherings, he had always found them plagued by inflated egos and people who liked the sound of their own voices too much striving for dominance. 'Open' meetings, designed to stimulate the interest of people who had discovered Mahayana Buddhism for the first time (in Alex's opinion, every meeting must be such, or it cannot be 'Buddhist'), that he had attended were often painfully embarrassing for him. The introductory speech tended to be patronising and intelligence insulting, treating adults with histories as people whom had just come down with the last shower. It all seemed to be a bit psychologically inept, clumsy to Alex; not employing the reading of body language or faces – an elementary skill essential in teaching and therefore in suchlike a meeting as well. How much Alex had been angered when he heard such absent-mindedly delivered statements as 'If the person is ill and suffering, it is probably because they have slandered the Gohonzon [the mandala focused on in meditation] in a previous life' or 'If you abandon the practise, your life starts to fall apart'. Statements like these are frankly criminal. They are also empty philosophising, substanceless commentary. To Alex, it sounded – at least in part – like a way of scaring people out of voicing any criticisms of it, and if a concept apparently so peaceful and gentle and forgiving as Buddhism would punish people so harshly as to, in the cases Alex had firsthand experience of, make them terminally ill or cause their life to collapse, then it is a concept based on bullying and not a faith at all but a fear-fuelled form of blackmail. The other main beef Alex had with Soka Gakkai was the second-, and often third-rate, quality of their literature. *The Writings of Nichiren Daishonin*, one of the Soka Gakkai 'bibles' contains passages like "When it comes to kings, there are great kings and petty kings, and in any matter whatsoever, there are parts and there is the whole. We have talked about the simile of the five flavours of milk, but we must understand when this simile is being applied to Buddhist teachings as a whole and when it is being applied to one part of those teachings." And "I, Nichiren, am the richest man in all of present day Japan. I have dedicated my life to the Lotus Sutra, and my name will be handed down in ages to come." *The Human Revolution* by Daisaku Ikeda also contains some priceless extracts, such as "He looked up into the endless expanse of the sky, through the tops of the cedars. He was quite unaware that he was pondering on a meaning of a part of the Gosho, *Remonstration with the Bodhisattva Hachiman*, in his heart.". Questionable translations of questionable Japanese texts aside, one need look no further than the Soka Gakkai monthly magazine, *The Art of Living* to find that never has so much column space been devoted to stating the perfectly obvious or saying nothing at all, e.g. "Youth is power. I would like to foster an uninterrupted stream of fresh, young talent. It's important to cherish our younger members. Groups or organisations where young people gather together and inspire other young people demonstrate tremendous energy and development. It is vital for young people to have the revolutionary spirit to stir up a groundswell of change and build a new world through their own efforts.". But the most alienating aspect for Alex was the way it was expressed orally by devotees. First there was the interminable pretentious code language. From beings of the two worlds and the eight groups to the devil king of the sixth heaven to the numberless major world, system dust particle kalpas to the thousand armed perceiver of the world's sounds. And beyond this was the inability to discuss and argue Buddhism conceptually, the very same problem that plagues born-again Christianity and all other cults; members instead resorting to hiding behind coded language and quotation in lieu of having the ability to make the points with their own passion and words, which is the very antithesis of faith and conviction.

And yet the better examples of those who attended such meetings i.e. those who did not display arrogance over faith and take the practise or themselves too seriously, had the potential to make such people and gatherings hugely worthwhile. And the practise itself had once proved to be dynamic for Alex, and thus it was that, with nothing left to lose, he decided to call upon its power, with its innate qualities or rightness and divinity and incomprehensibility, once again.

He opened his mouth to voice the mantra once again. 'Nam…
myoho…renge…kyo…' He glanced at the clock. 'Nam-myoho…
renge-kyo…' 09:13. 'Nam-myoho-renge-kyo.'

It was nearly half past ten when he finished the repetition of the
four-worded chant, but he was hardly aware the time had passed.

66

The Czechs arrived and Alex's pockets were gratefully filled with cash. The four, all from Bridgwater's twin town of Uherske Hradiste, were basically everything he could have expected from a group of Moravian teenage boys: good humoured, curious, lazy, intelligent, polite, playful, and keen on getting drunk. The first bungled attempt at a lesson, in an upper floor of Unity House, above the Labour Club, was thwarted by the building's book-wielding caretaker sticking his nose around the door he had just opened without knocking, quizzing, frowning, disapproving and stubbornly lingering until he had succeeded in proving he was the socialist establishment's resident Fuhrer. Exasperated, the barely introduced students sought refuge in the front bar, Alex having persuaded Simon the landlord to grant them sole access to this public space while they were prevented from utilising one of the many spacious upstairs out of the way rooms.

The ad-libbed ad hoc couple of hours in the morning appeared to go down well. Set to begin again in another couple of hours, Alex opted to return to Alfoxton Road and put in a little meditation over lunch to help him smoothly through the rest of today. Even if the lampshades were being filigreed by Roy and his father, he had already prepared a couple of bites to eat that could simply be snatched from the fridge, and he could shut himself away in the box room and whisper his way through mantra if that was what it took to find and make peace.

The day was uncommonly sunny and the mood too for Bridgwater and Alex. He was riding on the sense of achievement a reasonably pleasant job fairly well executed provides, and the meditation was helping him keep emotions on a gaily upbeat and well-balanced keel. The town too seemed friendlier, more open and alive than it normally seemed to present itself. The carnival was by now just two days away, the preceding concerts having received their obligatorily favourable acclaim, and the date on the calendar that appeared to give the most meaning to the lives of more people than it did not in the burg, was imminent. The effect, though nowhere near as powerful as that of Christmas, was nonetheless unifying and it would have been needlessly cynical to find fault in that moment of upbeat anticipation because, whatever it was looking forward to and whatever the quality of what it was looking forward to might be, it certainly beat the hell out of the gloom that generally accompanied the working day, with or without the sun to shine its rays.

Even West Street with its godawful terraces and tenements seemed almost to have a strangely benevolent charm as he drew level with the grocery store and few chatting pensioners with tatty tasteless bags their only shopping companions. He was just contemplating squandering a pound or two on something junky to supplement his lunch with when Sheryl, surname still unknown, came out of the nearby phone box like a Marvel Comics superheroine.

67

'Hello,' they both said awkwardly, at the same time. They attempted to say something else simultaneously, then both backed down mid-syllable, leaving them wondering if the noises they made were any less intelligible than whatever it was they might have been about to say. 'Where you off to then? Home?' was asked of Alex, and he wondered if she had either ever listened to a word he had said before, or whether he had ever really told her anything at all.

'Well...' He spotdanced through a series of options, '...it's possible I'm going in that direction. I'm not entirely certain where I'm going though, to be quite honest with you.'

Sheryl raised an eyebrow. 'Oh, well, you look like you know where you're going.'

'So...what are you up to today?'

'Oh, I'm going up my sister's, I am. I just come off the phone to her.'

'I see. Sounds good. Well, I'm doing some semi-make believe teaching this afternoon, and then I think I'm going to simply let myself do some guilt-free unwinding.'

'I forgot you were a teacher. Where you teaching, then? In a school?'

'No, just privately, fairly low key. It's a necessary evil, but it's actually proved quite fun so far.'

'Oh, right. You looking forward to the carnival then?'

'To be quite honest, not really, no. It's not quite my thing.'

'No, don't blame you. Same thing every year, innit?'

Alex almost found his head whipping back and forth, hurriedly glancing up and down the street to see if anyone had overheard such local faux pas. Suddenly feeling like they were criticising God at an evangelists' convention, preaching pacifism at a celebration of the Second Amendment, or risking an innocuously liberal comment in the company of the overtly left-wing, he replied in an almost conspiratorial whisper. 'It is to me too, but it feels like taking your life in your hands to say such a thing in the street.'

Sheryl laughed, without discretion, and it looked like she had not done such a thing in a while. 'I wouldn't worry about it if I were you. I'll go, my son d' like it, but I could take it or leave it myself.'

'The dedication, planning and engineering that goes into it are breathtaking. I mean, just getting those lightbulbs in place and wired and working alone is a phenomenal feat. It's just that...I don't see any ideas, nothing bold, no-one stretching their imagination...'

Sheryl seemed to be frowning. 'You think a lot, don't you?'

'Do I?' Alex thought that he did think a lot, but did not think that he had given Sheryl any reason to entertain such a thought.

'Yeah, you do. I never know what's gonna come out of your mouth, I don't. A strange one, aren't you?'

Alex could only shrug. *You ought to hear Nam-myoho-renge-kyo come out of my mouth several hundred times in succession, then you'd think me strange.*

'Anyway, I'd better go, I don't wanna keep my sister waiting. Where do you live again, Alfoxton Road, isn't it?'

'That's right. Are you ever going to tell me where you live?'

Sheryl paused. 'I might, sometime. What number do you live at then?'

Alex wondered how they must sound to an eavesdropper. Like a couple of teenagers? A couple of weirdos? A man having a conversation with a comparatively very localised woman of lesser intelligence? A normal (for Bridgwater?) woman talking with a subnormal (or NFB?) man? 'Why do you want to know?'

'Well, I was thinking about coming to visit you later. When I've finished up my sister's. I mean, unless you've got other plans.'

'No, no I haven't,' he spluttered, a little too keenly. 'Uh...What sort of time were you thinking of visiting?'

'I dunno, really, but it'll probably not be 'til about nine or something. A bit late that, is it?'

'Absolutely not at all.' Roy and his father should have finished friezing the hanging baskets or whatever it was they were up to by then, he mused. 'It would be great to have a visitor, at any time.' He realised how pathetic this must sound, then blurted out the house number before she had time to reflect on his comment.

'There definitely won't be anyone else there, will there?'

This is going great guns, he thought. 'No, there definitely won't be anyone else there then.' He would definitely see to that.

'OK.' She adjusted her stance, her weight on one leg, her head aslant, and gave him a look that could have been interpreted a dozen or so agreeable ways. 'I'll see you about nine then,' she concluded, emphasising the word 'you' in an interesting way.

'You will indeed,' he replied, and then they said their byes, and caught each other glancing back at each other as they disappeared in their opposite directions.

He completed the journey back to the house, unable to remember the last time he had worn a genuine smile upon his face at such length.

68

The afternoon's teaching went fine, and the Czechs persuaded Alex to go for one beer with them before he got back to the house and eagerly cleaned his mess and body. He put on the least skanky clothes he could find, arranged the radio in the living room, and went to the corner shop to buy a couple bottles of affordable wine which he hoped to employ the services of. He prepared, scantly and economically, the lessons for the following day, then meditated for three quarters of an hour, trying not to let his mind and imagination focus too intently on whatever might happen between Sheryl and him after her arrival. *If* she arrived, that was, of course; he had been on this earth long enough to learn not to rely too strongly on what a woman might declare – at least the ones he had ever been involved with, anyway.

Having forced himself to eat something vaguely healthy – a ready meal lasagne with a pre-packed salad and chips in lieu of the rudimentary garlic bread for the obvious, he fiddled with the radio for an eternity until he found a station that didn't turn to static once you stood to either side of the set – unfortunately Orchard FM, with its insufferably jollified presenters, tiny playlist and ham-fisted ad after ad, then sat down on the sofa with Ramsey Campbell for foreplay.

Alex couldn't help but watch the clock. When 20:45 arrived he had somehow already half-convinced himself that Sheryl would not show. He was no longer able to take in the words on the page, really wanted a glass of wine, but forced himself to settle for a strong tea instead. *Everybody Hurts* was on the airplay. True, but every dog has his day went through his head.

Somehow, 21:00 came, according to the clock in the living room, though it brought with it no Sheryl. Alex checked to see if the hall's chimer was in agreement. It was. Alex looked out the windows while not wanting to be caught in the act by his approaching expected visitor. The green across the street was black, Alfoxton Road seemed empty. Cars were heard droning past as if bored of their routine.

Alex urinated, washed his hands, checked his appearance in the mirror yet again. He returned downstairs, hoping that just one song he might like would be played on the radio. *It's Raining Men* flooded the living room, Geri Halliwell's version at that. Swell.

21:15. *Against All Odds*. 21:20. *It's A Hard Life*. 21:25. *Ghostbusters*. Who the fuck was Alex gonna call?

21:30. Robbie Williams was the only, uninvited, guest.

21:33. A knock at the door.

69

There was nobody at the front door. For an instant Alex wondered if he had imagined it, or if the sound had come from the adjoining house and been misinterpreted by his too hopeful mind. Maybe Sheryl had turned up after all, knocked, then had a whirlwind change of attitude and was now hiding somewhere behind the front hedge.

And then the knocking came again.

Visitors to the place had been almost non-existent, save for the council mercenary, so the acoustics of anyone announcing their presence without the use of the doorbell were an alien sound to Alex. Almost instantly he realised the visitor must be tucked around the side of the building, at what was effectively the back door. He investigated to find Sheryl, black clad and shadow enveloped enough to be a cat burglar, stood there with a generous collection of well stuffed plastic shopping bags. *Oh my god, I hope she doesn't think she's come to move in or something.*

Alex cleared his throat. 'Hello, Sheryl.'

She screamed in shock, a sound that would easily carry to Sarah and Roy next door. Then she theatrically caught her breath, looking as ham as an actress in a WI drama. 'My god, you scared me, you did,' she stated for the benefit of the deaf and blind, her accent in her abandon abandoning all dilution of localness.

'The front door's around here,' Alex indicated. 'Can I help you with that?' he indicated her baggage.

'No, no,' she said, almost abruptly. 'I cun manage with what I got.'

'Are you sure?'

'Yeah, yeah. Coo, big house you got, innit?' She seemed to marvel at the exterior of the boxy semi-detached two-a-penny building.

This woman's mad. If it's not clear now, if never will be.

'It's not actually my house, if you remember.' He was suddenly aware whoever must have shopped him to the council might well have heard Sheryl's scream and be scrutinising them now. An opportunity to call the police with a report of a woman screaming from a supposedly empty property could be all the ammunition they had been praying for. 'Shall we go inside?'

Sheryl looked about her, almost as if she were checking she had not been followed. 'There definitely ain't anyone else in there, is there?'

'No-one at all. I live alone, and I am alone.'

She seemed to be straining with her thoughts. 'Well, alright then. I suppose I've come all the way up here, I might as well come in now, 'ey?'

Alex shrugged. 'Why not?'

Slowly, very deliberately, all the while looking like she might turn tail and flee, Sheryl eventually crossed the threshold, five well laden Sainsburys and Asda bags crackling their plastic selves in her hands. At last in the home with her, Alex felt a momentary bout of extraordinary doubt, as if this wasn't a good idea at all. But now she was here, and that could not be changed. Maybe they could just have a cup of tea and then he could get rid of her, if that was what seemed the wisest plan. He led her into the living room, where she insisted on taking her collection of possessions with her, arranging them on the floor beside the armchair she had chosen to tentatively sit herself down upon, choosing this over the half of the sofa Alex had gestured towards.

'Coo, nice 'ere, innit? Spoilt, you are, aren't you?' She was staring at the spartan room with its musty smell, dusty furniture, and tinny radio the only non-necessity item. Her face could have belonged to a visitor to a museum displaying their favourite works of art.

'I don't think it's anything particularly special, but it's certainly preferable to living on the street. But it's not my place, remember? I'm just sort of borrowing it.' He wondered if his words would at last sink in. 'What about something to drink?'

Sheryl wore a waist length black leather coat, a black sweater and black jeans, finished with black pointy shiny shoes that looked like part of a dinner suit, not quite in keeping with the rest of her attire. She was sat tensed, slightly huddled, certainly not as relaxed as a social animal would be. 'Ooh, I don't know,' she said, as if she had just been asked if she wanted to take a bath in champagne.

'Would you like me to hang your coat up for you?'

'Ooh, steady on. You ask a lot of questions, don't you?'

My god, what kind of person have I let into this place? 'Certainly nothing personal, I don't think. Well, anyway, I'm going to have a drink, I might as well get you one too while I'm at it. You can have a glass of wine, or you can have some tea or coffee if you'd prefer?' *Or straitjacket? Or hockey mask? Or role in an Alfred Hitchcock film?*

'Ummm…' She was one of those people who was clearly going to test the patience when faced with a simple choice, so Alex tried to save the moment with 'I tell you what, I'll bring the wine and a couple of glasses. You can decide in your own time.'

'Yeah, alright.' She was beginning to sound like a child, not just in choice of vocabulary but in the sound of her voice as well. 'Sorry I'm not very decisive. It's not every day I get invited into a strange man's house and then offered wine when I've only just sat down.'

Alex was starting to get irritated. He wanted to emphasise ten times in succession that this was *not his house* but thought even that would fail to drive the point home anyway. 'Surely it's not that unusual to get offered wine at someone's place when you visit them?'

'Well…' She shifted about in her seat, looking more like she was deciding whether or not she wanted to get comfortable than trying to achieve such. 'Not for you, maybe.' She continued to appraise the living room's bland interior as if it were an alien artefact, and Alex excused himself firmly while he went to uncork some much needed wine, as well as wrestle with his thoughts alone for a beat.

She was in the kitchen with him almost immediately.

'Coo, this the kitchen then, is it?'

Alex kept his counsel, as was his increasingly habitual wont.

'I mean, of course it's the kitchen. Any fool can see that. Bit daft sometimes, i'n' I?' Now she was babbling, and snorted at how she thought she must sound. 'Anyway, what I was gonna ask you is, have you got a bathroom?'

Alex shook his head gravely. 'This house was built in 1967, one year before the law made it compulsory for houses to be equipped with washing and toilet facilities. There's a portacabin at the end of the garden. The builders are coming to build an extension that will house a bathroom next month, but I'm afraid there's not much luxury until then. Here, I'll hand you the torch, I think you'll be able to see what you're doing alright.' He opened a cupboard and began rummaging through its contents.

'I ain't that daft!' she noisily proclaimed, relieving him a little in the process. 'I know you got a bathroom in here somewhere.'

'Go up the stairs, it's the door at the far end,' he said, information Sheryl repeated to herself in a whisper before attempting to follow it.

Alex took the wine through to the living room and drank a full glass before Sheryl returned. Then, before she managed to get back downstairs, he managed to consume a second.

70

Sheryl walked back into the room as if she had gathered both her thoughts and confidence while she had been upstairs. Even her manner of returning to the armchair had a certain slink to it that had definitely not been there earlier. She crossed her long shapely legs then tucked her off-black hair behind rather a cute-looking ear, slowly rolling her eyes to waveringly look at her host who was also a guest. Alex patiently waited for her to break the silence, save for the man who had made his living professionally killing people before becoming a manufacturedly-offbeat crooner, James Blunt.

'Right, where were we?' She was struggling to neutralise her accent a little again.

'We were just about to toast.' Alex raised his third glass of wine and gestured at Sheryl's first, beside her chair.

'Oh.' She looked dumbfoundedly at the drink, seemed dangerously on the brink of out-of-depthness again, then quickly picked it up. 'Alright then.' She moved the glass to her lips, keeping her eyes on Alex.

'Cheers.'

'Cheers.' She took a measured swallow, tasted it indecisively, then – to Alex's relief – took a longer second swallow.

'You are carrying your worldly possessions around with you?' He indicated the family of bags.

'Oh, this?' She searched amid them, then stooped toward one of Sir John's unflattering adverts. 'This is mainly clothes. My sister's been having a clear out, and I thought I'd take some of it off 'er hands. Got some good stuff here, mind.' She pulled out a black cardigan, holding it against herself. 'I got this, look...' She searched the bags again for something in vain. 'I got a new pair o' slacks. Somewhere...'

'So all that is clothes?' Alex wanted to close this particular subject, not wanting to be subjected to an interminable use-your-imagination fashion show.

'Yeah, yeah. Got some stuff for Anthony somewhere too.

Somewhere...'

'Anthony is your son?'

'Yeah, that's right,' she said, looking up. He had succeeded in diverting her attention from the hand-me-downs, and intended to capitalise on it.

'And how old is he?'

'Oh, he'll be nine in December,' she informed him, in that peculiar way people have of always referring to the next birthday.

'And where is Anthony now?'

'Oh, 'e lives with his father most of the time. In Taunton.'

'Uh huh.' He sipped some more wine, seeking inspiration.

'So how long you been on your own then?' At last, a question, however vague.

'Do you mean living alone, not having a partner, or being a bit of a sad case?' He hoped she might find this mildly funny, however tragically. She didn't.

'Oh, I don't mean nothin' personal. I don' wanna ask you anythin' you're not comfortable with answering, mind.'

'My friend, don't worry, I don't take anything seriously and there are no taboo subjects where conversation with me is concerned.' He hoped she caught his drift.

'Oh. Well, I'm not really sure what I meant. Living alone, I guess.'

'On and off about five years, I guess. How long have you lived alone?'

'Oh...longer than that.' She took another sip of drink. 'Nice wine, innit?'

Alex's was already going to his head, likely helped by the oddness of his guest. 'I've had better, but it's certainly not bad.' He felt caught between trying to lead the conversation into interesting territory, wondering about the gamble of taking it somewhere suggestive, and puzzling over whether or not that wouldn't be a grave mistake.

'Gets lonely living on your own, dunnit?' *Oh my word, looks like we're going there anyway.*

'You're telling me.' *God, that sounded pathetic. Oh well, who cares anyway?*

'D'you mind if I have a bit more of that?' She pointed at the bottle of fast disappearing wine.

'Please do.' He topped up her glass, then his own, and then their glasses, like the night that lay ahead, went bottoms up.

71

'Is'pose I'd better move over there with you.' She indicated the two-seater sofa on which Alex still sat alone. He had just uncorked the second bottle and found, to both his delight and disgust, Sheryl was giving him a run for his money at the speed with which she drank it.

'Feel free.' Alex shuffled over to one side of it, a little.

'Well, I will in a minute.' She quaffed more *vino* as if she believed British licensing hours applied to private homes the same as pubs. 'Alright, I'm coming.'

At last she removed her leather jacket, folding it neatly in a way that most men would never bother to do when drunk and with the seeming imminence of a carnal episode, let alone at most any other time. The black sweater she wore fit her slim and shapely frame with snugness, a leather belt snaked around her slim waist, her hips were gentle curves with as much aesthetic as erotic appeal. Her beauty was either the product of regular exercise and sensible eating or, as Alex rather suspected, genetic good fortune. All she needed now was a voice coach and injection of intelligence to make her drop-dead gorgeous. The alcohol, needless to say, was successfully bridging that gap.

'I can see where this is going to end up,' she said, when she was comfortably beside him, her legs tucked up under her.

'You can?' was all he could say.

'Yeah.' She interpreted his subtlety as naivety. 'We're gonna end up having sex, aren't we?'

72

This close, the telltale wrinkles that cornered her eyes, feet of crows previously all but flown from view in general social contact, pecked away at her former perfection now they were so close. Her eyes, wide and shiny, revealed the depths of a soul remarkably shallow, now she was this drunk. In them, he read the best part of a lifetime's shrinking from thinking, a hiding behind alacrity and concealing of whatever filled the back of her mind. Like so many of us, this was a person whom had been hurt and hurt badly at an early stage of her life, to react by distracting their hearts and minds with distractions of the mindless and the lacking in soul. She was fragile, more secure by circumstance and evidently by her sister's care far more nurtured than Alex perceived himself to be, but far more at the mercy of the mercilessness of life in her unphilosophical universe. And now she was at the mercy of Alex, fuelled by drink and libido and lust, by self-justification as a reaction to the barrenness of human contact in his life, by that altering of the focus, the human selectiveness with which we view this daunting world.

'Are you alright?' She was frowning now, the lines on her face a map to a world from which she herself steered clear.

'Uh, yeah.' What the hell was the answer to that anyway?

'So are you going to kiss me?'

For better, for worse, for all of the reasons and all of the excuses, kiss they did.

73

*O*h *my god*, he thought as their mouths met. *This isn't what I expected at all.*

Her lips were so soft, her method so patient, her tongue so gentle. She was certainly an expert kisser.

But her breath was bloody awful.

He had almost recoiled when she brought her mouth to his, but he didn't want to just let his olfactory glands throw in the towel after so many months' anticipation and social foreplay. He tried to convince himself he was mistaken, but the foul odour was definitely proven to be issuing from her cosmetically extremely kissable mouth. Then he tried to tell himself it was only a momentary accustomisation, that it was probably more in his mind than not, would pass in a matter of seconds.

It didn't.

The taste was sour and sulphurous. It was gone off eggs and mothballs. It wasn't just unpleasant, it was frankly repugnant; a stink that exploded like a bomb to every sense.

And, somehow, though he was certainly trying not to breathe, he was *still* kissing her.

And God the cosmic jester plays the joker card again.

What the fuck was he supposed to do? Just exactly what? Tell her her breath stank, suggest she came back when she'd Macleaned her teeth, eaten a packet of mints, and successfully been cured of halitosis??

The tongue was probing deep into his mouth. Somehow he was still locked in the prison of her kiss. He felt utterly frozen and privately sick, yet she didn't seem to have noticed at all.

What does one do *in this situation??*

Finally released from the iron grip of her less than magnetic kiss, he discovered she had managed to position herself dominantly atop him. And then, as if capitalising on surprise, maybe sensing the moment was now or never in a million years, her hand was inside his jeans, gripping his member painfully hard, stealing the chance it had to shrink to a flaccid escape.

The most peculiar cocktail; lust, sympathy, drunkenness, shock, took him like a sacrificial lamb into the fold. Resistance and resolve and sense and opportunity were swallowed within her desire.

74

He woke to find they were still on the sofa, the radio still crooning, the lights still on. He felt half-crushed beneath his guest, one arm was still sleep. They were still largely dressed, apart from their crudely exposed midriffs with a sticky scale of sperm spent in anything but orgasmic joy.

Sheryl was snoring, a sound so unfeminine and base, and in that moment he knew that all the appeal she had had for him had gone. It was the archetypal stereotypical male bastard wham bam drama to any and all who were on the outside. But Alex did not perceive himself as any such creature; he was simply a highly-sensitive individual who had little choice but to listen to his intuition and accept the weight of the feelings he had. Wasn't that what every using hit-and-run predatory chauvinist told himself?

She stirred above him and her breath invaded his nostrils, even more repellent after drinking and sleep. He prised himself out from beneath her, her deeply unconscious in her unaccustomed reaction to the drink, and practically threw her limbs off him and on to the sofa in disgrace. He took one look at her face, slack and moronic, the cheeks and mouth twisted by the cushion on which she lay.

He was looking forward to her leaving now, that much he knew for sure. He couldn't wait to get rid of her, and he knew he would never ever sleep with her again.

She knew where he lived. He hoped like hell she would just leave him alone. He couldn't introduce a woman like this to his friends, what would they think the moment she opened her mouth?

What fucking way of thinking about someone is that? How plastic are your fucking emotions?

But she was not the one for him, and he had known all along she never could be. The one for him was currently hiding in the same place as his security, as his money, as his health and his harmony, his worth and his life.

In an invisible otherworld.

75

He woke again, early and anything but refreshed, with an eye on the time and today's – only the second – bout of teaching with the Czechs. He was in, or rather on, his makeshift bed in the box room, still clothed, a little afraid of getting into it naked lest Sheryl should find him there. And, with as much self-loathing as it takes to form such a thought, and as little as to enable him to think in such a way, he wished she had been a dream, but his dream she had turned out to be anything but.

He wandered into the bathroom, hating having to look in the mirror but having little choice. The man who felt anything but proud of his non-conquest looked at the aging reflection, the one-dimensional version of the man he used to be. His sullen face was red and puffy from drinking, and not just from the night before. Grey circles accentuated the starkness of his bloodshot eyes. Zombie make-up need not be applied.

He started to tiptoe down the stairs, then decided to tread heavy-footed instead. Sheryl, whom had not conveniently disappeared in the night, stirred in her continuing drunken slumber, looking like she hadn't changed position at all. To the rest of the world she wouldn't look as rough as Alex, but to Alex she looked rougher than his own reflection now the morning after had come.

'Uh, Sheryl.' He prodded her with a finger, neither feeling nor acting like a gentleman at all. Even though there was no-one else in the house to hear, he felt strangely ashamed to raise his voice as he spoke her name.

She groaned, smacked her lips inelegantly, and her eyes flickered open though but for a second. She seemed to be asleep again immediately.

He tried again to rouse her, a little more aggressively. The reaction was much the same.

'Shit.'

76

Alex was ten minutes late for the lesson; fortunately, the Czechs were as well. He had eventually managed to drag a groggy Sheryl out of her slumber, persuaded her to stumble out of the house with him, himself carrying her wretched shopping bags full of used clothes, feeling like a porter to a bag lady. Conversation had been blessedly little as they had got as far as West Street, then Alex had pretended to be needing a different direction, part because he wanted to be shot of her, part because he was late already and could not continue at her laboured irritating pace. There was a brief farewell, and Alex deftly used his monopoly on articulation (and likely manipulation) to sugar the non-commitment of his words just enough to speed him on his separate way. The unshowered man, liberally coated in an alcoholic sweat, the residues of sex clinging to his body, made as clean a getaway as he could manage, feeling disgustingly filthy inside.

He arrived at the Labour Club's front bar to improvise his way through two hours of a routine tired from repetitions at the Spanish summer school, though pedestrian enough for him to handle it with a hangover and jaded conscience. To his delight, shock, and almost certainly ill-deserved surprise, the students presented him with a gift, having decided amongst themselves the previous day they liked him enough to shower said token upon him.

Alex had acquired a full bottle of absinthe, quality absinthe at that. The liquor erroneously thought to have been illegalised throughout Western Europe for decades before someone discovered a technicality that deemed this was not so, was a substance Alex had experimented with a couple of times before. The extremely potent concoction, as well as being extremely alcoholic, contains wormwood, a shrub with psychotropic properties with an interesting variation on the effects of psilocybin. With fewer visual aspects but the seeming ability to pull abstract ideas out of the imagination and manifest them as physical reality moments later, as well as amplifying the tendency toward mischievousness, rocketing pheromone production and profoundly inflaming the libido, it was an experience the curious would want to partake of, but with a cautious approach. It was also highly toxic, an open invitation for alcohol poisoning, could induce flashbacks and, when used habitually, could result in a form of madness called absinthism. It was Alex's kind of drink.

77

Today was the day Alex had to report to the job centre, now ingeniously, or ingenuously, reinvented as Job Centre Plus. He had arranged the time of his interview to secure the finalities of his Jobseeker's Allowance claim with his two hour lunch break from his temporary job. He announced his name to security, who also seemed to double as reception, and was asked for his completed forms.

'Forms?' he asked, racking his brain.

'You were required to fill out some forms that were either posted to you or you were supposed to collect from us prior to the interview, sir.'

'Nobody told me anything about filling out forms before today,' he quite truthfully declared, reading disbelief on the public servant's face.

'Well, I'll give you the forms now, sir. You can fill them out while you're waiting.'

He was handed an unecological pile of colour-coded questionnaires, then was directed to a seat opposite another waiting for an appointment; a man who stared incessantly at and appeared to mentally undress Alex while he tried to summon up the will to put pen to paper. Five minutes later the skincrawler was summoned by an employee so brusque and fat she looked like she might consume human flesh. Avoiding the trap doors, glossing over superfluity, fictionalising the legally binding, Alex made it to the end of the paperchase just as his own appointed advisor arrived to lead him to his fate. The disabled woman, with perhaps the greatest power in the building to disarm, guided him to her desk where she announced she was the first of two people he would be introduced to today. Her business was to check his forms and ensure they appeared error-free and tested positive for eligibility. With a few tweaks, thanks to her nonjobsworthy advice, they had the papers ready to be traded for the folding variety quicker than any black person would have money thrown at them at the DSS by far.

After another five minutes, he was fetched by his claims advisor, unfortunately the ruddy-cheeked no-nonsense likely candidate for cannibalism. Going through his details with the minimum of overture and maximum economy, they got to the end of the grilling and Alex signed his name for his first instalment of by now hard earned cash. 'You won't be paid for the first three days of your claim,' she told him. 'We don't know why. So you'll come again on Monday the-'

'Why don't you know why?' Alex asked, stopping her in her tracks as if she had been slapped.

She blinked hard, as if amazed at his cheek. 'It's government policy that the first three days of the claim go unpaid. We don't make the rules.'

'But you could know why.'

She paused, looking him over, as if contemplating how he would look on her dinner plate. 'We don't get told why. Those are the rules, we have to bide by them as well as you.'

'But surely you must be curious as to why?'

She seemed to be considering the concept for the first time, as if she had just discovered the capacity to question in her brain. 'What difference would it make? We're not going to change it.'

'But you must have been asked the question by a multitude of claimants. Surely you could have a better answer than "We don't know why" prepared.' Alex realised he had started to raise his voice, and noticed a couple of the woman's colleagues were listening with measured interest.

'Mr Bishop, check your attitude, please. I don't have the answer to your question any more than you do. There's no point in getting upset about it.'

'I'm not upset, I'm just plain curious. You deal directly with a law you claim you cannot see the logic of. If I was in your shoes, I can assure you I would have asked my superiors until I had the reason explained to me.'

'Well, you are not in my shoes, and now I have another client to see to, so I'm asking you kindly to leave.'

Noticing movement from the corner of his eye, Alex turned his head to find a member of security hovering closeby, a blank expression fronting the blankness of his being and mind.

Alex laughed. 'I'm curious to know how you deal with real troublemakers.'

The advisor, having advised him of little but his need to numbly comply, was busying herself with pen, paper and frown. She was exercising ignorance, and Alex imagined few could do it better than she.

'Care to look at the jobpoints, sir?' the security man asked, pointing the way away from the non drama.

'Thanks, but I need some fresh air. Frankly I find it too stuffy in here.'

78

Alex made it through the rest of the day, kept the Czechs happier than he had expected to, and returned to the house and the aftermath of the night before, being reminded of what he had almost succeeded in erasing from his mind with no less subtlety than if Sheryl (surname still unknown) had slapped him across the face, which maybe she ought to have done. He took a long relaxing bath, feeling he needed it more than ever before.

It would prove to be the lull before the storm.

Tomorrow was Friday, the night of the Guy Fawkes' Carnival. He didn't really want to see it, but had already promised the Czechs that he would with them.

He had always found the carnival instantly forgettable whenever he had seen it before. Not this year.

This year's carnival, and not necessarily for all the right reasons, would mark a day and night he would remember for the rest of his thereafter dramatically changed life.

79

Alex awoke with a start, the alarm clock ordering him to get the fuck out of bed. He had succumbed to the charms of the bottle of whiskey that had seduced him into its warm embrace after the chill of getting out of the bath. Its lingering presence betrayed its promise like Alex had done the morning before. He had a hangover that was far from slight. He felt like he had had one for most of his life.

The mirror held no surprise. His appearance had been transformed into that of a movie star, unfortunately an extra in a George Romero flick.

Ho hum.

He took his lesson plans, headache, sour stomach and cold sweat with him to meet the Czechs. Today would see the class they attended was that on Bridgwater's streets. Alex had devised a quiz for them to work on together, a voyage of discovery that would take them on a tour of the town. The teenagers were restless and curious with the imminence of the carnival, therefore he had seen little sense in them sitting in the front bar of the club with little or no concentration. The quiz would have them noting such largely unnoticed curiosities by locals as the pavement submerged grindstone in Castle Street and the terracotta dragon on a Fore Street roof. It would also give the Czechs an opportunity to breathe in the atmosphere of the never busier town, and Alex an excuse to have an effective day off.

But his plans to relax were to go seriously awry.

80

He was spending the money he had been given for teaching the Czechs dangerously fast. He needed to save, and he needed to put temptation out of sight. He needed to bank his cash.

He handed over the notes to the Halifax teller, all but twenty pounds which he had promised to limit himself to for the day and night ahead. Aware that the last payment from an agency had since been deposited in his account, and unsure as to how much else had gradually collected itself there, he dared to stick his card in the wall to check his total so far. At a push, he hoped for a monkey. But the monkey he would reveal would be the one upon his back.

He entered his PIN, then held his breath as he waited for his balance to show. The amount displayed was a hell of a surprise indeed.

Zero pounds supplemented by a fat zero pence.

He blinked, wondering what kind of glitch could have occurred.

He looked again, distrusting his hungover eyes.

£00.00.

Impossible.

How could it be?

What the fuck??

A mistake. A technical error. The bank's computer must be on the blink.

It was surely the only reason there could be.

He walked back into the bank, with its long line of customers waiting to be served. A woman was working at a help desk, helping someone in a suit while Alex looked on helpless. He positioned himself behind the suit, with rudely close proximity, and waited ten minutes and half an aeon for the uniform Alex could never respect to get the fuck out of the way.

It was Alex's turn at the help desk. There could have been a queue of a dozen behind him, but he was not aware of anyone else in the world right then except himself.

'Yes, sir,' the bespectacled employee asked, discreetly appraising his scruffy pungent self.

'I think there is a problem with my card.' He held it before her as if she wouldn't know what it was otherwise. 'It tells me I haven't got any money.'

The advisor bit her tongue. 'And you're sure there should be money in your account, sir?' To Alex, her intonation sounded ambiguous.

'Most definitely. For one, I just put some money in my account seconds before I checked the balance.'

The advisor took the card off him and frowned at it. She turned it over as if checking its authenticity. 'OK, I'll check what's happened for you.' She picked up the phone on her desk, got through to someone in the know, then spent a couple of minutes jotting down information and hmming in either concern or delight. She finished on the phone, folded her hands together, then took a long deliberate breath as if to prolong Alex's agony more. 'Mr Bishop, it seems you have an outstanding debt on a Halifax One credit card account you took out with us last year.'

The room had started to spin.

'Unfortunately you didn't meet the terms of the agreement and your overdue payments total...' she picked up her notepad as if she were fondling the thing '...two thousand, four hundred and sixty-one pounds...' and then she dealt her ace with '...and seventy two pence. The debt is overdue for repayment as it should have been settled within twelve months. The last repayment you made on this account was...over four months ago...for twenty pounds. Because of this the bank is legally entitled to confiscate funds from any other accounts you might have with us in order to help make up for the balance due. I'm very sorry to have to tell you this, Mr Bishop.'

Alex gripped the desk he stood before. 'But the teller didn't tell me that before I put my money into the account.'

'The teller wouldn't know, Mr Bishop, nor would they be bound to tell you anyway, I'm afraid.'

Alex noticed the poster in the window behind the help desk. Howard was flashing his corporate smile. Halifax, the wording on the poster read. Always giving you extra.

Alex was aware he had begun to tremble.

'Is there anything I can do? Is there any way I can appeal against this?'

The look on the woman's face answered his question plainly enough. He did not need to hear her voice her mind.

'I haven't got any more money,' he beseeched. 'I've lost all that I had.'

He was speaking in volumes, and telling her what her eyes already had.

She made some practiced consolatory remark, one that he did not even hear.

Someone cleared their throat behind him. It was the suit. He had returned.

Alex threw himself out of the bank before anyone else could do the same, or before he got himself arrested.

81

Christ on ffffucking acid.

Alex half walked, half fell toward the nearest Fore Street bench. He sat down with all the grace of an obese geriatric. He tried to think. He dared to think.

Foot traffic was plentiful, busied and buzzing, everyone was talking, no-one else appeared to be on their own. Anticipation. That was the flavour of the day. The tension was mounting, the temperature rising, the mercury was on the climb.

Carnival day, the most eagerly awaited on the calendar, was here at long, long last.

And Alex felt like it was the worst day in his entire life.

Surely this was all one long bad dream?

Yes. One from which he feared he would never wake.

The clock hanging outside the jeweller's was still stuck in the forgotten past, its face frozen in a neverending expression, reliable only for two minutes a day.

The voices in the street were a babble, a mixture of locally accented non sequitirs. The cacophony made him dizzy, the obliviousness of the rest of the world made him thoroughly sick.

Three months work, grafting, scrimping, saving, scratching out a living, forcing himself through day after day of nerve jangling grind. For absolutely nothing at all.

He was as broke as he had been at the start, no, worse, now he really had nothing, now he was truthfully right on the skids.

A waste, a criminal unbelievable waste.

Forget cheap labour, his was given for free.

He had so seriously wanted to kick his karma into territory anew. He hadn't thought things could get much worse.

Well, life is full of surprises. Isn't it fucking just?

Something was nagging at his mind, he couldn't quite be sure of what. Something he ought to do, right away.

What, what, what?

How was he supposed to have a clear and reasoning thought right now?

What was he going to do now?

What am I going to do now?

Everyone's voices in his ears. In his head. In his face.

Fuck.

Fuck, no.

He had twenty pounds in his pocket, twenty pounds on the whole planet Earth.

It was like the price tag on his life.

You think you're worth twenty quid? In your dreams, mate. In your dreams.

The whole world was walking past, half of them thoroughly excited.

He wondered if any had worse luck than him.

A chuckle escaped him, took him by surprise. He couldn't even dare buy a drink to commiserate. It was almost funny. Maybe it even was.

What about a shoulder to cry on? Not much gold to be found in that department either.

Alex stood, his body doing the thinking for him. He wondered what it might do next.

In his pocket was twenty pounds. His head felt emptier than his pockets.

He turned toward the Cornhill. He took a couple of steps.

Then he stopped.

He turned tail.

All at once he knew what he had to do.

82

The job centre was unhelpfully busy, perhaps filled with people in a similar predicament to Alex, waiting to watch the carnival's free show but wanting a chance to get drunk in the process and needing a handout to make that happen. Alex was under no illusion that he was going to get any credit from under this roof, but he had to save his dole from the same fate as his wages.

He tried to explain his situation, all dignity as much a part of history as the money that had just been stolen from him that he had squeezed out of the thieves of his time. The security/reception man seemed to struggle with the information, possibly because, through sheer necessity alone, Alex explained himself articulately and concisely, avoiding invective or subjective remark. It was a language the employee appeared never himself to have grasped. He asked Alex who his claims advisor was and Alex, the floor beneath him dropping further by the second, told him the half-remembered name and euphemistic description of the woman he had upset the day before. He waited in the JCP five plus minutes for the security plus reception man to tell him that the sixteen-plus stone advisor minus empathy was prepared to see the freshly nonplussed rag of a man in ten to twenty minutes non plus.

Thirty-five minutes later he was summoned to her desk, her face red and harassed as if she hadn't calmed down from the day before. 'How can we help you, Mr Bishop?' she curtly puffed.

'I've got a problem with my bank account into which my JSA payments are due to be paid.' He swallowed, ready to spit it all out, ready to see the impact on the look on her face. 'I have a credit card account with the same bank, and due to overdue payments on that, the funds in my deposit account have been and will be seized. I need to halt the payments going into my bank and change the arrangement so I get a girocheque instead.'

The advisor licked her lips, as if savouring the residue of the words just spoken suspended in the air. 'It's possible to arrange for a girocheque payment, although very few people have those these days, and we prefer to make payments into an account. You don't have another account into which we can make the payments?'

'I haven't got any other accounts, no.' And he would be on a credit blacklist for the next eight years, he quietly mused. Should he live that long, that was.

'And you're not planning on opening another account with another bank?'

'I think I would prefer a giro payment if I am entitled to that possibility, please.'

'OK. First I'll need to make a phone call to stop the payments going into your bank account.' She did so, being put through to first one then the other nameless faceless other on the phone, before her face registered something akin to discovering a new taste she couldn't quite work out if she liked. She replaced the phone down on her desk, then sighed in a fashion not dissimilar to the bank clerk an hour before. 'Mr Bishop, I've stopped any more payments going into your account, although I'm afraid the first instalment of your JSA, which you signed for yesterday, has already been processed and transferred to your account.'

'Oh *what*?'

She shrugged. 'I'm sorry, but there's no changing it now.'

Alex sat there with numb detachment affixing itself back onto his world.

'Did you lose a lot of money when your funds were confiscated?' she could not resist to ask after however long Alex had been sat staring into the growing void.

Alex stared at the woman sat staring back at him. If he burst into tears it would really round off her day.

'I'll make another appointment to come back and set up the giro payments,' he told her, already rising from his seat.

'I can just get a form and all you need to do is sign-'

'Thanks, but I need to go somewhere else,' he finalised, and swiftly left the building and was back on Bridgwater's streets, to go somewhere, to go nowhere, to go anywhere *anywhere* else.

83

Virtually opposite the job centre, the four teenage Czechs were making observations and scribbling notes about the Chandos glass cone, and Alex hurried himself into the centre's car park and out of potential site of his students. He wasn't in the mood for seeing anyone he knew right now, at least not them. Sometime in the past hour he had developed a headache which seemed to be intensifying at a frightening rate. His eyes felt sore and teary in the wind, which had whipped itself up into a biting rage. His mouth was dry, and he licked his lips, feeling like his tongue were tracing the contours of some chitinous desiccated husks. His gloveless hands were cold and turning red, save for the places where some sweatshop's grime still stubbornly clung to the cuticles and resided beneath the nails. He felt thin and undernourished. He shuddered the length of his spine. Perhaps he was going down with something. Going down with something, ha bloody ha. Perhaps he could fall even lower than the mo.

A woman, reversing her car out of a parking space, did not see him as he tried to walk past, then braked sharply as at last he came into her blinkered view.

Perhaps I'm invisible. Perhaps I really do not officially exist anymore, perhaps I'm just a ghost.

The woman's face registered the sternness of one who secretly knows they were in the wrong. She glared at him as he stubbornly slowly trudged past. He felt like kicking her car, he felt like kicking the world.

At West Quay he sat himself down on the cold riverside wall, stuffing his hands in his pockets for warmth, but the pockets contained as much of that as they did money. He felt giddy, unsure on his feet, his mind was juggling thoughts like a plate spinner plates.

It was as fruitless the search for questions as it was answers.

He was going nowhere sitting freezing on the wall, he might as well be at least geographically locationally be going somewhere, like home. Oh. Well, like Alfoxton Road.

He got up off the wall, minus nimbleness and plus the feeling of getting old. From a lost wasted youth and onward into lost within a waste of middle age. And along West Quay, past the CAB into which he could drop and ask if they could tell him whatever it was he needed to ask them in order they could tell him he was fucked, past the Lions Club with its grizzled old drinkers seniorising those of the Labour Club and forecasting the latter's future, to the junction of Castle Street. Alex noticed Patrick stood at the doorway of his shop, glancing up and down the street for elusive customers. Knowing he was spotted, Alex raised a hand in return salutation before hurrying into Castle Street and out of sight of the shopkeeper, not wishing to be drawn into a shop or conversation of any kind. He trudged his way up Castle Street toward King Square, the slight incline feeling like a right royal climb. From somewhere a carnival cart could be heard testing its sound system, the strains of some singalong party anthem straining his ears. He passed the Arts Centre, stooped, face turned away, praying none he knew caught him in the act of passing and forced him into social contact and putting on some kind of show. He made it to King Square, marched towards its centre; a lone survivor making it to the war memorial, an unsung nobody before men's conflicts' winners of token mention, of worthless posthumous fame.

The heavens above rumbled, as if admonishing him for dishonourably forgetting to salute the freedom paid for by the soldiers gone to the skies.

The wind whipped more cruelly, as if punishing him for his punishing thoughts.

Carnival day. The first Friday of November. Late autumn in the west of a country famed for its rain.

The light was fading. There was a storm on the way.

The day was turning darker.

And it was going to be one *hell* of a storm.

84

Roy and his father were busy, busy, busy, and looked like they would continue entertaining themselves with chores while the rest of the town consoled themselves with the lesser thrill of the carnival. Pretending to be in a hurry, Alex made it upstairs without being drawn into social contact, while father and son absorbed themselves in oiling doorknobs or sexwaxing windowpanes or ensuring all carpet fibres leaned exactly the same way.

Alex couldn't possibly remain inside the house. He had to get out again quick, without a word exchanged or a token glance in his direction if he could.

But he was damned if he would leave without a couple of preparatory measures first.

Opening drawers, Alex searched under clothes, between sheaths of papers, inside boxes, and underneath the bed. At last he found it, or at least the main part of it. A few cursed-breathed minutes later he had the other two components in his hand.

Alex unscrewed the cap from his previously unopened bottle of absinthe and poured it through the miniature funnel into the metallic hipflask he had almost never used. As he carefully ensured - as much as impatience and shaking hands would allow - he filled the receptacle to capacity, he thought of the Czechs that had given him the liquor as a gift, and of his promise to meet them later.

He didn't think he could possibly go through with that plan now.

With the minimum of carpet and floorboard corroding spillage, he capped the hipflask and bottle, stashing the bottle back out of sight.

He listened for sounds of the others in the house.

Some drilling, some hammering, some yelling. Noises from another world, in which mundanity replaced profanity, in which the inane filled the shoes of the insane.

The coast was, as much as it could be, clear.

Alex opened the drawer beneath the bed, and reached for the secret it contained.

85

The psilocybe mushrooms had mostly dried, some adhering to the sheet of newspaper beneath them, some curling up into a wrinkled shrivel. There must have been close to a hundred in all, at least three times the amount for a truly psychedelic adventure. It was maybe, emotionally and circumstantially, the unwisest time imaginable for a full on mushroom trip. Maybe, just maybe, it was as appropriate as could be. Either way, Alex knew he could not stop himself now, not ignore the voice within urging him to indulge like never before.

It was close to six, barely an hour before the carnival was set to begin its politely received procession. Quickly Alex set to work, rolling the dessicated fungi into balls, chewing their rubbery texture, ignoring the fecund smell and earthy taste as best he could. Using day old tap water left in a glass beside the bed, he chewed and swallowed the mushrooms as quickly as he dared, half a mind on indigestion, the other on avoiding vomiting onto the carpet. A good five minutes work, blessedly undisturbed, and he had eaten them all. Unless he went into the bathroom and made himself vomit immediately, there was no way he could avoid their aftereffect now.

A few drops of rain tapped against the window, as if a rapping beak were there amid the water beady eyes. He hoped such an unkindness would return to haunt him nevermore.

Without a clue in the world as to how they might mix, Alex took a brave swig from the absinthe. He held the fiery bitter liquid in his mouth, all but gagging on the taste. He struggled, faltered, swallowed half, braced himself as it journeyed down his oesophagus to his struggling fungus-stuffed stomach, throwing his gastric PH factor to a figure that tested the scale.

Surviving that, he swallowed the rest of the contents of his mouth and forced himself to cope and keep it down.

It was time to go, out into the darkening night, out into the gathering storm, out into the heaving streets, the carnival about to start its show.

Things were just about to kick off. Nothing could stop it now.

86

He was out of the house and standing in Alfoxton Road before he knew it, hardly able to remember the descent of the stairs, he could not have even bothered to register or avoid Roy and his father, could not even remember shutting the front door in his wake. He stood screened from the house by the front lawn hedge, looking like he was about to cross the road and was implementing the Green Cross Code like the world's most careful man. He felt the rain, insistent and indifferent, tapping him on the head as if to bring him back to his senses, or remind him such a return journey was something he might have once been able to make.

He didn't want to remain here. He felt like a lunatic landmark, the phantom squatter at last stepping out before his unlegal habitation, presenting himself to any whistle-blowing neighbour as if challenging them to face him now they were faced with his snapped-tethered sight. Roy's father's car was parked economically before the front gate, and if he made one of his regular nip outs for just the right tool now, Alex would be spotted and likely questioned, an interrogation no more bearable than were it conducted by the police.

He stepped out into the road, his mind realising he had performed the act after his feet had seemed to, unsure of whether or not the way was clear or whether or not he had known it was. He crossed at the junction between Alfoxton and Danesboro Roads and, as suddenly and unthinkingly as he had sprung himself out into the streets, disappeared into the cut through between the houses, the scrawny lesser known lane that would eventually squeeze him out onto Quantock Avenue, as if he had made himself disappear before any curtain twitchers could secretly welcome his presence but verbally wish him away.

As he disappeared from human sight between the high wooden fences overgrown with shrubs and trees and ever-growing litter, his feet squelched in mud as if the ever-shaded ground here never really dried. He plunged into the thicket of shadows, submerging himself in a blackness he half-wished he could hide in until the end of time. With arms extended defensively before him, he brushed the vegetation out of the way, squinting lest one of the protrusions should spring back into his face. He paused, as if to rethink, but he was through with backtracking, through with admitting failure and the screaming realisation he was logically at a dead end. He fumbled in his coat pocket and brought out the hipflask, unscrewing the cap with fingers that shivered, with or without the cold. He brought it to his face in the dark, the bitter aroma of the absinthe diminishing that of rain-soaked road and fence and earth. He took a gambler's sip, too much, then spat half of it out before tentatively swallowing the rest. He peered out of and into the dark, a nocturnal beast staring from a makeshift lair, the feral and the desperate vying to be first. Snatches of enlivened noise reached him in waves, carried by a harrying wind like memories of happier times. Voices chattered in urgent expectation, children chuckled and competed to be heard, the undertone of an excited burble punctuated the lonely dark with its taunting carefree joy.

Alex pressed further into the cut through, specks of light filtering through holes in the fences, feeble blotches of colour from empty houses trying to look full. The narrow alley turned to the right, cutting off the view of the lamplit road behind, and Alex entered full dark with barely a second thought. His shoes sploshed in puddles their sound and his dampening socks told him were large. Rain started to patter, heavier by degrees, tapping out a lonely tattoo on the boards of the fences and the leaves of the nettles in his way. His hair was getting sodden and his sleeves were wet through from brushing aside the plant life, but however damned he might anyway be he was if he was going to go back now.

The way snaked left again, revealing a faint glow of white, a vague block he recognised as discarded free newspapers, dumped unread to save their delivery addressees the job. Alex rustled and wrestled the foliage aside, groping his way along the dark foreboding path, knowing the light at the eventual end would be but a shade less dim and symbolic only of enduring despair. He pushed himself through faster, more assertively, wanting to kick the obstructions aside while knowing they were but plant life and he was but a man of straw.

Although he had eaten the mushrooms but what was surely

minutes before, he was certain he felt them begin to do their work. His stomach had been all but empty before their consumption, and his metabolism operated at lightning speed thanks to nervous energy which was often the only kind it had to go on at all. His senses tingled with expectation, his extremities bristled as if conducting signals crackling on a frequency the dial of his mind was gradually turning toward. He recognised the feeling, the tiny burst of what was to come as if an acknowledgement by the body, of the individual and universal, that the line had been crossed, the ritual had been enacted, psilocybe partaken of and the powers that be been informed.

A clattering brought him back, and his head jerked to the right, eyes blinking blindly at the dark and the invisible source of the sound. A sense of something crouched, tensed, seeing him from its perfect concealment, was the heart-stopping embodiment of the monkey about to fasten on his back, the demon poised to sink its claws into his soul.

The jet black beast mewed, scrabbled over the boards of the fence, and was across Alex's path and far ahead, ready to warn the world in wait the hapless luckless man was on the way.

Alex pushed ahead, harder, faster, almost panicking the half-ensnaring foliage aside. His hands were scratched, nettles stung, something caught in and tugged at his hair.

Thirty-five years old, alone and forgotten in an alley if not blind then denying of all sight, battling against invisible foes of which the rest of the world were not even aware.

He had to maintain direction, had to keep to the way. He could not afford to lose it now.

He found the corner where the path turned sharply left, tapering to its narrowest before meeting at last with the big wide world of Quantock Ave. And Alex's foot met with the body on the ground.

Whoever it was, they must be dead. As Alex's foot had trodden on them, they had not stirred or shifted, had not made even a ghost of a sound.

Recoiling, as he only could, breath sucked into his lungs no less violently than it exited them when the Cornhill youth had gut punched him, he stood in paralysed silence.

Rain pattered about him, plopping dully down upon the nettles, a sound as bleak as the night was black.

Alex kicked the lump on the ground, as solid and soft as flesh wrapped in clothes.

There was a crackle from the form that was coming to life, then the sound of clothing spilling out of a bin liner became the noise that he at least thought that he heard.

Alex had had enough. He projected his sodden, scratched body desperately toward where he hoped the alley would end. As the fences closed in on either side, the unkempt vegetation became a flesh-abrading wall, a barrier of near-insentient life that flailed at him like tendrils in a frenzied rage.

Mud or excrement betrayed his step, and he slipped on a substance as slippery as entrails freshly spilled.

Is this the beginning of a very bad trip?

He landed half in a bed of nettles, half a bath of mud.

He had never felt more like a tramp in his life, and he was sure his appearance was now anything but about to disagree.

He burst through the final skin-tearing curtain of green turning red turned black, and was spat into the street as if the dark had thrown him out for being underdressed.

He regained his balance, blinked at the night sky as if it were the sun, and took stock of his depressingly and blessedly visible surrounds.

A group of teenage girls recoiled in shock, possibly fearing he had made to ambush them. They quickly stepped out of the way of the man whom had emerged from where no-one would go, bedraggled, unkempt, looking savage as he was scruffy, a heathen vagabond vomited into Bridgwater's brightest night.

'Weirdo!' one of the girls called after him, presumably imparting information he didn't already know.

The girls ahead were talking with some men whom had turned to see what the commotion was about. It was time to get going again, before getting beaten up and booted for being beaten could be what he would become to boot.

88

Head down, hands in pockets, clothes wet through, mud streaked and weather- and otherwise beaten, Alex propelled himself along Park Avenue, concentrating only on his feet, trying to ignore the world around him as much as it had seemed to ignore him. Pavement and the edges of garden walls blurred in the periphery of his vision, rolling by as if he were on a giant treadmill, which he more than likely was. Arriving at the gates of the primary school, he turned right to take the cut through to Furze Close, carpeted with the mulch of autumn, usage and rain. Others were making their squelching way along the same alley, and Alex filtered into the flow levelled by the shadows into shapes in the night.

Alex emerged beside the Close's green, the openness emphasising the fall of the rain, strengthening and intensifying with the anticipation of the Bridgwater crowds. God the Cosmic Jester was playing the joker card for everyone's benefit or lack of tonight, it seemed.

He turned left, away from the road and the pavement and the people, becoming the sole person crazy enough to wade through the narrow alley that cut between the houses and cricket ground, a thoroughfare by now suggesting he was short of an oar. As the throng were drawn to the carnival lights, Alex submerged deeper into the dark, the black never blacker against the beguilement in the Bridgwater glare.

He wrestled the hipflask back out of hiding into the solitary impenetrable gloom and washed down one bad taste with another. The impact caught him ill-prepared, and he gasped, gagged, then let the gods punish him with the emesis he deserved. He doubled over, one hand holding the flask, the other his stomach, and a thin stream of watery vomitus pooled at his feet and spattered on his jeans. He fought the urge hard, snatching ragged snorts of breath, and managed to retain as much of the poisons seeping into his veins as he could. He remained crouched for many minutes, concentrating on breathing, keeping thought at bay, then eventually erected back to a straight, fucked up, stance.

The alleyway forked and Alex turned right, his myopic eyes by now telling him almost nothing at all. He laboured past the backs of houses aligning Northfield, the cricket ground to his right all but completely screened by vegetation that could not be seen. The ground underfoot became wetter than his clothes and hair, reminding him it was raining, and raining harder as the moments ticked by. Perhaps he had become all but numb to the feeling when all it ever seemed to do was rain on him anyway. He coaxed another brief swig of absinthe out of the bottle and into his stomach, by now as unsettled as his nerves.

He was starting to feel as feral and desperate, as primal and nerve-driven as a stray dog skulking hungry and unloved through a blind back alley of despair. The hairs on his neck seemed to prickle even through the damp embrace of long-soiled clothes. His breathing was coming in ragged pants, as if he was as out of condition as luck. His face felt contorted in a grimace cum snarl, saliva coating teeth eager for any morsel they might find. He plodded on, hunched forward as a lupine form, baying in vain at the moonless starless dark night of the tortured soul.

However good or bad it would become, there was no doubt about it – he had begun to trip.

89

The shadow pulled free of the vast unlit; a dark globular drop rising to the top of a lava lamp's liquid insides. The haunted man, the ghost of a man, spilled like a slick of oil, slipped into the sickly lamplit street like so much waste. Transformed in that slippery lightless channel, he wobbled like the newborn reborn; bastard; orphan; rejected by, ejected like poison from, a womb. He found he could not find his feet, then found he did not need to feel he could find them in order to flounder on. Northfield became West Street; animated scenery ever-changing the increasingly cartoonish surrounds.

Sounds came in snatches, carried by wind whipped into excitement by expectant babbling crowds. A serpentine amphitheatre's audience drooled before the start of the fun and games. Sipping absinthe, stumbling on, Alex made to throw himself further into the ring.

The road ahead stretched itself, focus zooming into a long and lengthening shot. Distance and time were expanding, unfolding, teasing him into a gradual slurring, where slo mo became the real time mode. Wind threw itself at his eyes and face, vision blurring and crystallising as tear ducts coped with blasts and psychotropics and sorrow, eyes with a blinding mist of airborne rain.

Above and beyond the carnival, silencing the cacophony, belittling the growing crowds, thunder drew the attention of all. A guttural growl traced its way across the pitchy sky, like a tear between horizons of the ominous nebulae.

The rain stopped raining and started to pour.

Thunder struck a godalmighty chord.

Thunder, rain, wind. The tempest, the storm.

Absinthe, mushrooms, inebriation.

Psilocybin, wormwood, alcohol, pain.

Depression, anxiety.

Poverty, adversity.

Desperation, humiliation.

A carnival of ills of cruel fate.

Nam-myoho-renge-kyo.
Here we go, here we go, here we go.

90

A wall of human bodies, to Alex more animate than they seemed to be alive, formed a living pavement along North Street and Penel Orlieu. Hi-vis-jacketed mounted and foot police paraded like the procession's first attraction likely to arrest the crowd. Figures leaned from upper storey windows, ready to look down upon the event everyone looked forward and up to all year long. Collecting pots were shaken like maracas by the fancy dressed; rattling donations given, as ever, by the predominantly poor.

This was not where Alex wanted to be. If anything, he wanted to get himself to the High Street, to the fore of the Mansion House pub, where yearly reunions were made by those whom behaved as if they had remained friends for this one moment in the year.

It was still possible to use the pedestrian crossing to North Street, and Alex did so, fighting his way through a throng while it was still possible to. He jostled a route to the alley alongside the tax office, that emerged in Mount Street, getting in everyone's way in order to get out of it. In a few beats of a frantic heart, he was where he had always seemed to end up whenever there was a party: surrounded by people prepared to have a good time, out of his mind on sobriety and intoxication, dizzy on depression and escaping on a personal high, and wishing everyone else could be like and unlike his party-going/pooping self-absorbed self.

A kaleidoscopic carpet of refracted scattered light formed the rain-topped blacktop where his scuffed boots splattered forth. Arms trailing, flailing, pinwheeling for balance or trying to take flight, he launched his precarious gait through perception's yawning doors. Journeying to the end of a road, venturing to the edge of an edge, he was at the bend of Mount Street, the only person left in the hundred thousand crowd attracting carnival thwarting streets.

To his right, the town's sole fleapit cinema endured another audience's long-term intermission. Just beyond, the mini-roundabout that prevented the High Street and Penel Orlieu from coming to blows, was blocked off by the countless gathered as if to watch the fight of streetfights. To the left again, the car park, choked chock-a-block with climate-changing carriages, as yet had not a single alarm bothering to scream a two-note plea to simply be ignored. Left again, the council doomed swimming pool of the Sedgemoor Splash was the farthest building to be seen, at the shallow end of deepening visuals submerging in transparency all to be beheld in the urban scene.

Alex Bishop, Mr Omega, the last man in the line, waded through the contours of light and form and texture, drifting toward the swimming pool, trying to cling to a life saving something the saturated sinking individual was fighting for all of his life to find.

Drawing level with the swimming pool, the only man in his universe turned right, toward the all-encompassing cacophony of the uncountable crowd. The ground of Angel Crescent became a dancing mosaic of puddled confusion; a swirling tirade of raindrop-choppied water on which to walk. Sight had become thickly layered with multitudinous levels, with more to meet the dilated pupil by far than the mind was otherwise prepared to reveal to the eye. The martial beat of snare drums rattled out a self-important tattoo, a marching band paving the way for the all-out assault on the senses. Glockenspiels tinkled in defiance of the ever-sprinkling rain. The warcry had been sounded; whatever the costs, the show was set to go on.

He thought about turning tail, of fleeing the scene before he entered into the crush of the multitudes, anonymously and indistinctly and feeling like the focal point of a trillion scrutinising eyes. But, just as he had pressed on regardless though the cut through, just as he had forced himself through hour after hour of murdering grunt shifts, just as he had crawled out of borrowed beds and faced each face save threatening day, so he owed it to himself to stand before and witness this, the free show that Bridgwater looked forward to more than anything else each repetitive year, whether or not he enjoyed it, however out of his face he was, whatever consequences social contact or the lack of might prove to be. He felt like he had lost everything; a home, a sense of belonging, security, money, work, dignity, respect, hope, faith, plans, desire…even his health must be on the brink of going bad as his mental state, alcoholism, lack of nutrition and anxiety reached a critical state. What the fuck else was there to lose?

One more thing.

He moved into the narrow alley between Barclays Bank and an estate agents, at once revealing the backs of the thick and easily entertained crowd.

Just one more thing he would lose tonight. And a very important discovery that would be as well.

He pushed into the begrudgingly yielding concentration of bodies, forced his way to the fore of the Mansion House in one determined wriggle, exchanging not one word.

He blinked, hard, then gazed around him, at once coming to terms with where and when he was.

There was a carnival procession about to begin.

And the show of shows about to explode.

92

Dazzling light entered the distended pupils of Alex's wide open eyes. Visual information exploded with unparalleled brilliance, igniting like fireworks in his enlightening mind. Illumination of such cold intensity, its quality synthetic as its flavour was dull, invasively spotlit each crudely bathed feature, clinically transforming night to judgement day. Scanning, rolling thirsty orbs of beholders were beheld. Open mouths and animate lips worked of their own accord as muted wonder would be whispered whatever it took for awe. Upturned faces turned and stared, oblivious in their self-absorption, aglow with inner sparkles and a thousand scorching bulbs.

And there, sometimes gaudily, sometimes unconsciously revealed, the story book dynamism of every single spectator, in every single countenance, divine and sublime.

While an aritificial jungle rocked to the rhythm of tribal drums, a steel and concrete wilderness was the truly primal side of the divide. Black body painted natives of a stereotypical cultural void danced before the multi-coloured –textured -layered folk; grostesqueries so unlike the façade in which they were no longer able to hide. As idols teetered and totems towered over and above the performers and crowds, the onlookers turned from the human to a morphing multiple-species montage. While bones and beads and finery of African peoples jiggled and jived, sub- and semi-conscious significance the audience wore symbolically belied.

The audience became the stealers of the show as the crowd outperformed the procession.

A tsunami of sensory input engulfed the eventide.

As masquerade fused with masquerade, the unrealised carnivalesque consumed the carnival realised.

Dale Bruton

93

The mysteries of the Far East mesmerised the South West. Geishas neither danced nor talked nor sang yet drew a loud applause unheard of. The shogunate stood in synthetic silks, the plebeian the labelled garbs of genuine exploitation. Shinto idolatry symbolised the worship of ancients, the Anglo-indigenous epitomised the endless now.

Beyond the lights and costumes and dance, the models and dynamics and craftsmanship and colour en masse, beyond the song and rhythm and tune, the babble and burble and rat-a-tat of claps, Alex's five senses merged with countless more than a sixth. Warmth and radiation, passion and fire, filled his body and his mind and his senses and his spirits, and all that defied labelling in all that passed for his space. Immersing and penetrating and saturating each fibre, cell, pore; the refamiliarised ever-dependable core at the base of the flame of the all. The feeling of being known, the feeling of being accepted, the feeling of being loved, beyond the flux and the ephemerality of human bonds. Downtrodden and beaten though he may have been, such a humbleness gripped him that he realised at once the pride that is paraded in the declaration of the being down and out. And there too, with his mind and senses thrown so nakedly agape, did he see beyond all the self-deceit that is the human condition's greatest trick, the devil at work within us all, so did he see and feel and know that the pulse of faith throbs as surely and reliably as that of life, for life has no crumb of a speck of an iota of a chance to be without it, for no matter how utterly futile, everything depends upon its promises unfulfilled. And within that fractal of chaos, that mess of broken heart and promise of unfulfilled tormenting dream, so there is that part of us that never leaves that faith behind, that keeps undying contact no matter how steep the path, the undeniable admissible only to the straight with themselves when they are being the straight with themselves, the deep-seated part of us beyond the ego and the vain and the burden of proof that harbours a peace ever unaffected by our warring with life. The place and the part of which those who mask their fear as the angry and the dogmatic fashionably declare it unfashionable upon which to dwell or even alight.

Norsemen disembarked from the bow of a ship; a float above a sea of soaking bobbing heads. Valhalla hailing seafaring warfarers once again invaded the island-minded plundering tribes. Viking horns and bloody swords poised in static form, sworn to attack the hordes swearing at the electric storm.

Umbrellas sprouted like the conjuring up of enormous magic mushrooms. Annoyance clouded faces as fabric canopies blocked their view, while nature's did its own, antithetical, job to the same effect. Slickened faces kept countenance they were out of for the rained on parade.

North American Indians hollered at the audience their raindancing caused to see red. How oh how could it rain down now upon their pow wow so? The battle of little point became the big, chief concern sitting in bulldozing arrow-slitted eyes.

A fresh wave of psychotroposis saturated with unplumbed depth. Reality's parameters, perception's doors, exploded beyond all sense of proportion, paradoxically grounding him with dizzyingly heightened awareness effects. In an ultra-ultra-personal world, Alex was his own macrocosmos; a sattelite planet in an infinite mess. And yet, a unification with something defying categorisation became his oneness with the world and all its godlessness and gods. As he surrendered to that delicious harmonic, that intangible progression, that frequency reaching its peak, so he became fused with something that is everything, the infinite that has to be denied to exist, omnipotent beyond materialist futility, the invincible calm impermeable to its denial, to all violence, to all anger, to all hate.

England Olde and new fought to slay a dragon, as immigrant as St George had made it cross. Kings and Queens unknown as unloved looked down upon their regaling pawns. Costermongers traded clichés on pre-capitalism-removed cobbles of the capital's streets.

The human zoo that hemmed him in metamorphosed into a multi-layered confusion of family and form. Eyes sank into sockets like beasts within lairs of beasts, in fear of being raised by the civilised being razed. Hue and tone of skin upon skin blazoned beneath the myriad bulbs. The veneer of domesticity peeled away in a slough en masse, the skulls beneath the skins grimacing, sensing their exposure while baring their teeth. Chitinous brows frowned in hardship allowed for years to weigh on the mind. Beak-like noses pecked at spouses; prows of warships presenting a never paid bill. Pursed lips tightened to prevent their contents spilling into the gutter, a lifetime's unspoken expletives fastening the tongues of the thine offended thee. Feathers ruffled, jaws snapped, derma told stories never untold in faces one could but read. The human became the reptilian, amphibian, insectile, and almost anything but the humane. The real made way for the surreal, but the larger than life lifeforms, Alex realised, were hallucinatory only to the in denial, and a more accurate by far vision of the all too real.

Gold and silver faced celebrants danced in a make believe casino where each and every gambler seemed on a winning streak. Cards, chips and coins whirled, like the confetti of excessive success, the pageantry of successive excess. Roulette wheels paddle-steamed a path down the road paved with pennies collection floats had yet to net.

As Alex's blood swam with an elixir with effects money could never buy, the crowd were wowed by the free show expensively put together by those whose imaginations seemed broke. To Alex, the carnival was now just one particle of all the infinite stimuli pervading his infinite senses with a psychedelic tour de force. Colours exploded, time slurred, sounds were textured visions. Smells were chemical storybooks, thoughts lightning-speed detectives, emotions a tapestry enwrapped in priceless warmth. And all with such an innate flavour of rightness, of the just and the true and the divine, that none who scorned psilocybin as a crime would ever earn the right to know.

Pirates, robbed themselves of all originality, displayed like a treasure trove the clichés they had amassed. With peg legs, parrots, and patches galore, Alex half-expected the words I AM A PIRATE emblazoned upon their tuniced forms. The Jolly Roger managed a sheepish grin, flapping over an effort whose chance was long gone to win so much as a silver cup.

Three-sixty degrees of crowding. A heliosphere of sensory input. The maximum overdrive of incessant omnipresence. Thoughts were seen forming in blueprinted faces, emerging as mutations, bastardising the pure while civilising the profane. Filters of expression were filtered out, the baseness of character leaking through, the id overshadowing the ego, superconsciousness superseding superego to superlative degree.

A tableaux freeze-framed life inside a palace of ice, the weather authenticating the gooseflesh on its inhabitants' forms. A tethered polar bear bared its teeth, beneath stalactice icicles like the fangs of its like.

The audience had evolved into creatures that defied evolution's chains. As emotion and psyche dictated physiology, a circus of horrors surrounded Alex, like a Boscht repainted; the garden of earthly delights removed to the urbane.

Galactic warriors laser zapped a battle against an atmosphere that lacked.

Martial artists kickboxed their way into a box.

Another ship sailed into view, riding on a tide as shallow as the ocean was deep.

Life histories, stories untold, the evisceration of a secretive society, the bare bones exploding from cupboards unlocked, a kaleidoscope of revelation whirled and spiralled within and without the man in the eye of the storm.

It was the first Friday in November, Guy Fawkes' Carnival night.

To Alex Bishop, if to no-one else on Earth, it was *the* fireworks night.

94

And then the carnival had come to its end.

With a nod toward civil order, the crowd began to disperse. At first it felt like a hand that had been fisted around Alex's form was gradually loosening its grip. Those auras and personal spaces and biochemical signals that had enmeshed and jarred with his own, gradually untangled, allowing him at last to breathe with a little more ease. And then a torrent of feet and jostling torsos decided to forge a path toward the west of the town, and Alex was swept up in a current he tried but failed to resist. There was one exit route presenting itself to one side, his left as he began to be frogmarched in reverse, then fore as he crabwalked an attempt to turn around, then starboard of the stream of bodies, looming like a lifebelt as he floundered amidst the tide.

With one determined effort, helped by a handful of others trying the same ploy, he squeezed himself into the alley between the Mansion House and Bridgwater Bookshop, free at last to walk untouched, if not swing his arms in something like a natural gait. To his right, drinkers were glimpsed through windows of the pub, cramming into the front bar in the battle to be served, while in the back bar regulars cavorted in their own more private squeeze. To Alex's left, the window of the bookshop displayed the latest local history hardback; a safe haven niche market, always telling of how it was and never of how it is.

The escapees, fresh from jumping ship, scurried like half-drowned rats down the rain-sluiced canal the alley had become. The way right angled itself to the left, and Alex and the others paddled their way around the back of the town hall, past a takeaway kebab and between pavement pizzas returned. The rivulet of the bedraggled again entangled with the soaking wet sea. Alex kept himself pressed up against Remedies to his right, easing himself around the hull of the building, into the street he wondered how many knew or cared to know its name – the street that most, it seemed, had failed to chart as part of their voyage home.

Alex, ears ringing, head spinning, felt slapped into sobriety by the end of the procession, by the continuing effects of psilocybin, wormwood and alcohol combined. The rain had stopped spilling from the skies, steadily dribbling from guttering instead, sputtering from the choking mouths of overflowing drains. Litter provided flotsam aplenty, carried as effluent along the poorly lit Stygean stream. Ahead, the shadows pooled with the murk, and it was this way that Alex paddled, minus the guide of Charon, into a darkness with all the stench and all the vibration of sin.

95

Alex slipped on a slimy something, spotdanced for balanced, failed, and fell. Taking most of the impact with his hands and arms, he landed in a puddle the length and breadth of the sky from whence it came. He made a semi-spectacular splat, realised he had survived intact, and stood back up like something that could scare the creature from out of its black lagoon.

It could not have been a more perfect pratfall. Almost unconsciously, Alex began to laugh.

Around him, barely discernible amid cloying dark, tattered scraps of crumbling buildings loomed, like antiquarian markers of urban decay. Fragments of walls, facades bowed by dilapidation, fronted time abandoned houses like a century-spanning three-dimensional collage.

Helpless now to quell his giggling, Alex emptied his bladder, perhaps diluting the pollutants in the heel-high surrounding Acheronian mire. Steam rose where the two streams collided, like a tendril emerging from the liquid beneath.

Shouts, jeers and hailing pervaded the night, as one throng ushered themselves homeward and one awaited the squibbing still to come.

Alex moved between and around the houses Jack the Ripper might happily have lurked among, no fear or care in the world in whatever remained of his mind.

He crossed the road at an angle, bypassing the Angel Place car park, bleakly echoing the decadent indulgence, sending back the signal it was the shadow of what it might seem.

Alex carried on, regardless, of even regardlessly carrying on, it seemed.

Again moving against the mill, Alex retraced footstep on step, back in the direction of the constabulary cell. The police station seemed, to far from Alex alone, about as capable of delivering the services it was intended to as a station that was part of the network that was once British Rail. As if the thought of British trains were contributing to the loco state of his mind, so the path that lay ahead seemed like a light year's journey to the next juncture in the dark tunnel that seemed without end – the Labour Club – which lay but a thousand yards away.

96

At King Square, the other unspoken ritual, the other ceremony that coincided with the carnival night, was well underway. Teenagers, and perhaps a few younger, were busily groping each other, some heavily petting, others on the verge or in the midst of a rut. Moving to Queen Street, many more largely underage drinkers trysted in underage multi-limbed knots. In parking areas, doorways, and anywhere halfway out of the way, they writhed and squirmed, under cover of semi-darkness in lieu of the covers of a bed. Uninhibited prohibited acts celebrated severance from parents; couplings from which parenthood might not be far away.

Alex cut across the High Street, kicking through litter it was clearly someone else's job to clear away. A few panhandlers were rummaging through the rubble, searching for coins and booty amidst the papier mache of food wrappings galore.

Maybe Alex should follow their example, but the substances in his bloodstream and weather hardly put him in the mood.

He had his booty with him already, his complete worldly treasure, his entire life's wealth.

Twenty pounds of Her Majesty's finest sterling. God save the queen of this banana republic of island apes.

He felt in his pocket for the purple-hued banknote. As he pulled it free, it tore in two, soaked and pulped to a gluey, barely recognisable, mess.

Alex Bishop laughed and laughed and laughed. He just couldn't help himself. Not any more.

From the Midshires bank where he stood, he continued on his unholy mission, stumbling and splashing, pausing doubled up, laughing all the way to the pub.

97

The Labour Club was holding to tradition, proving to be the freakshow alternative to carnival on the streets. Alex added to its morbid curiosities, another oddity wilfully outcast.

Just as he was entering the bar, Marcus Plenty was, determinedly and obnoxiously, revealed to be on his way out. Unable to pass Alex without letting the newcomer know that he had just finished making everyone else feel like he always did, he opened his sneering mouth like a cobra ready to spit.

'What do you want, you fucking gay twat?' Of the three accents he wavered between – gutter-level-word-laden middle English, wannabee posh, and Mockney, tonight he had gone for loose-fitting option three.

Alex looked into those deliberately obnoxious eyes with their absence of humour and inner joy on that look-at-me-I'm-a-successful-carefree-rogue plastic mask of a face, and could not help but laugh.

Marcus' sneer broadened in discomfort and defence. 'Fucking state of you, you pissed up fucking loser.'

The laughter escaped Alex in such gales that, his face frozen in a grimace exposing an awkward fear, Marcus looked almost worried might blow him away. 'You don't know how happy I am that you think that about me,' he eventually managed to get out, and turned toward the bar, the genuine laughter empowering and elevating him to a place Marcus Plenty seemed to have long left behind.

'Well, glad to see you're in such a *gay* mood,' he delivered, and slipped out of the door like something slimy oozing through a hole.

Ken Cunningham stood behind the bar, eyeing Alex and his ill-controlled giggling. He frowned, nodded toward the door, and asked, 'What happened there?' as if he had not heard the brief exchange or believed there was a lot more to it than could have been overheard.

Alex shrugged, laconically, unable and unwilling to fully stem his mirth. 'Have you ever known Marcus Plenty when he wasn't being funny?' He stepped up to the bar and turned to face its patrons, unable to wipe the grin from his face and looking like the smugly accused.

Almost the entire supporting cast on the humble stage of his Bridgwater existence were going through their paces and repeating tired lines. In the place where the philistine were more like thugs and the arty more like alcoholics, both groups had opted to spend or end the night in here. Daniel and Ian were squeezing every ounce of fun they could out of the pool table. Malcolm and Patrick were trying to find common ground at a drinks table. Big Bob was sat beside his downcast-faced blackeyed wife, looking every excess inch the man he truly was. Eve and her sorority were looking like they were angry they had nothing to get angry about. Half-a-dozen others were lamely getting legless as their trouser pockets said that they could. Sniggering, without a care left in the world, the glared at Alex simply looked on.

'Want a drink then, you loony?' Ken enquired, wondering whether to remain standing or sit this particularly silly spell out.

'G-Guinness, please,' Alex managed through his giggles, propping himself against the bar as the laughter racked him, leaving the barflies flanking him visibly unamused.

'You haven't been and got off your head, have you?' came a voice from behind him, and Alex turned, squinting through his hysterical tears, to find Daniel observing him as if through a microscope's eye.

'Share the joke then,' flanked Ian, allowing himself a small injection of what was affecting Alex himself.

'Believe me, if I could then I would,' he struggled for nearly a minute to voice. 'But I don't get it, Ian, I really don't. That's what makes it so damn funny, I guess.' He half-collapsed against the bar as laughter took him that threatened to never let up.

'Here you are, madman,' Ken said, as he positioned the Guinness a careful distance from its recipient on the bar. 'Two quid to you.'

Alex fumbled the remains of the score from a pocket as if he were exhuming the dead. All beheld the ghost of his wealth; a sorry surrender flag matter-of-factly held.

Ken tutted in theatrical disdain. 'I'll get it,' he muttered.
'I thank you, Ken.'
The door to the bar opened.
One, two, three, four clowns entered.
All Alex could do was to carry on and laugh.

98

As from one dream development to the next, Alex found himself sat upon the table with Patrick and Malcolm, Daniel and Ian having escorted him there, for better or worse. The five sat through the briefest postmortem of the carnival, in which the newcomers at the bar had clearly been participants, that only Patrick and Alex had seen, and only Patrick was capable of constructing a semi-comprehensible sentence about.

Alex's mind whirled from one to the other stimulus within the club's surrounds. The conversations melded into a melting pot of the pathetic and profane. Mumblings and whining, confession and gossip, worms crawling free of cans to writhe amid the spilling beans. Burdens were shifted from shoulder to shoulder, bait was swallowed then regurgitated, deceiving the deceiving into believing their own deceit. Where words were heard, their meaninglessness was for the main part what they imparted, while the static buzz of volume-speaking hushedness told more about the speakers than they seemed aware of themselves. Aggressive laughter beseeched as it imposed, willing unwilling listeners to envy whatever it was on which they would never be in. Boisterous voices in needless noisiness overcompensated for being pointless to hear. As if reeled in by the sudden emergence of a vacuum impatient to be filled, Alex was transported back to the table at which he sat, aware he had been asked a question that would draw him back to the gravity the table flanking clung to in habit if not fear.

Eight eyes beheld him with as much uncertainty as of how they themselves wished to be seen.

'Uh...Pardon?' Alex asked whomever it might have been about whatever they might have said.

'Are you alright, Alex?' Patrick asked, either repeating the already asked, or asking what should have been.

'I'm not dead yet, Patrick,' Alex heard himself say, suddenly aware there must be some reason his vital signs still ticked away.

'How's it all going then?' enquired Daniel, his a no-nonsense look within the club's nonsensical surrounds.

Alex could tell all eyes were on him without having to check, and not just because it was his cue to speak. He could feel the emotional output that would dictate the way the eyes could never lie, whatever the face that framed them suggested they wanted to say. Through all of their concern at however the giggling wreck appeared, which was probably like a giggling wreck, emotions were tempered by that which makes a lifetime's every motive impure. Daniel was hoping to summon advice he could trade for the third party type that one day might mean he would never have to fix his own life. Ian was biting on his tongue and coming joke, afraid of having to focus on problems, of which he was ever afraid. Patrick was hoping a few succinct buoying terms would get the tack back on the track of the more important trivial and inane. Malcolm was trying not to wince too obviously that something exposing emotion could steal the focus from his feelings-concealing wit.

Looking at none of them but seeing them all, Alex said, 'Probably, circumstantially, things have never been worse…'

'Oh good,' Malcolm interrupted, and beneath the schoolboy reflex quip, Alex saw the underbelly of a character and cause that belied what he struggled to portray. All the championing of the peoples' cause through whatever mutation of socialism was currently straining to save face in the face of history and the gut punches it had thrown of late, was the product of refusing to deal with individuals, self and any *one* else. Come to think of it, Alex had never known Councillor Stoodley to be supportive or encouraging of any particular individual not affiliated to a group cause he could not himself control. And maybe it was the very word personal, and its links with sensitive and emotional, that kept one-to-oneness at the back of a sharp-witted, but machismo-complex harbouring mind, and funny but too oft flippantly downputting one-liner mouth.

'…but, for some inexplicable reason, I've never felt better than I do right now.'

'Why?' they all asked in chorus. 'You on drugs or something?' another added.

Alex looked at Daniel, encased in a bubble of troubles of his own substanceless design, tethered to Bridgwater and preventing him from rising above the ground and getting out of town. At Ian, a refugee from the same sorry excuse for a school as Alex, forever letting a lack of education tell him he would never be qualified for life. At Patrick, who made his living in a shop that he paid for at the expense of a life, never leaving his place of work even when somewhere else. At Malcolm and Ken, who tried so hard to appear to be the thinking man's hard man they were oblivious to how pathetic those they knew capable of thinking thought this to be. Then he looked at the rest of the bar, at Eve and her cohorts, forcing the world to notice how they were forcing themselves to think they were having a good time. At Big Bob and his broken toy of a wife, of the clowns thinking they looked exotic and conforming to the lowest com-denom norm.

And then he thought about himself. About his lack of anywhere official to live. About his lack of a job. About the fact he was single. About the fact he had no possessions. The fact he had no money, the fact he had not even a clue how he was going to survive beyond the coming few days.

Wondering how it had got there, he discovered a smile on his face.

'No,' he said, turning back to the others. 'Because I've just realised that at least I'm free.'

Someone smirked, and the others took their own turn to laugh.

'At least you've still got your bonkersness,' said Malcolm.

Alex started laughing at himself as well, and continued feeling free.

99

Pennywise exited the men's a penny lighter, and flashed Alex a look to wither a character from one of King's tales. Though wisdom registered no more than humour within his clown-painted eyes, a knowing glance shot out a warning like a plastic flower a squirt of mace. Returning to the coulrophobe's nightmare at the bar, the circus act shared a secret something like one of the lions was loose.

'What's your next move then?' asked Daniel of the man returned to Ha Ha La La Land. 'Have you got some kind of plan?'

Alex started trying to compose himself, then gave up the fight and with it the will. 'I can't stop laughing,' he managed in the end, and realised it was the most appropriate answer of all.

'Well, not gonna get any sense out of him, are we?' dismissed Ian the comedian, uncomfortable that someone could so openly laugh. The four started a conversation about *Big Brother* instead.

Before he could fit back into a fit of the giggles, Pennywise came back into view, flanked by John Wayne Gacey, then joined by one of their plain-clothed brethren, who did not have a red nose but did a black eye.

'Alright, *cunt*?!' asked Lee, the phantom of the Cornhill, returned for unlucky confrontation number three. Alex guessed his ridiculous-looking sidekicks must have been among the others in the gang that had besieged him on the first day of his return.

Malcolm, Patrick, Daniel and Ian had stopped their conversation, transfixed by the surreal scene in which they sat. From the corner of his vision, Alex noticed the remaining two clowns talking to Eve and Big Bob respectively, clearly on familiar terms with the people who looked almost as ridiculous as they.

Alex the tightrope walker giggled as he teetered on the taught and tight.

100

'Remember me, do ya? Ain't got no fuckin' pigs in here t' 'elp ya now, 'ave ya?'

'Hey!' called Ken Cunningham from his vigil at the bar. 'You're out of here. This is a bar, and the police *will* be here if you threaten customers any more.'

'Shut the fuck up, granddad! Is got fuck all t' do wi' you.'

Nodding at each other in what was anything but a positive exchange, one of the four clowns charged out through the door of the lounge, into the fore of the building.

Ken wavered between a retort and an uncertain glancing after the clown fresh out of the circus cum wrestling ring.

Alex's eyes shifted from the gimlet ones of Lee - shiftily flitting between Alex and the door to the lounge – and his gobsmacked seated counterparts, all now worrying about the prospect of getting smacked in the gob.

There was a loud crash that everyone recognised as the door to the building being slammed with force. It sounded like it belonged in a prison, which was probably what the Labour Club had suddenly become.

The clown returned to the bar, not on a unicycle but swaggering on his big-booted feet. 'Door's locked,' he announced as his punchline.

Ken, in mounting confusion, tried to assume control. 'What do you mean the-'

'You were told to shut the fuck up!' a clown at the bar snarled, and smashed the bottle of Becks he had been drinking against the edge of the bar. The explosion of glass and rage stopped time, shocking everybody into sober realization the stage had been set for a barroom brawl. The clown, green wig, braces 'n' all, held the broken neck of the bottle with menace equally misplaced and absurd. 'Now put a sock in it before I put some'at else in it, got it?' he growled, and none dared believe it was a joke he had just told.

Ken and the heavily made up thug locked stares, but for now at least Ken held his tongue.

Alex, wondering quite how much psilocybin and absinthe had gone to work in his head, searched his mates' faces for a clue to what was what. They all, without exception, looked as stunned and confused as the man in the midst of a trip. Alex found himself wondering if the drugs' effects were contagious, and just how contagious they might possibly be.

The five huddled around the table unconsciously huddled a little more. They exchanged wary glances, pensive and calculating, unwilling as of yet to become more noticeable, none of them daring or knowing what to say.

'Right, mate, you 'n' I 're gonna finish what we started,' the trademark-Bridgwater-bruiser-named Lee declared, as if confident he were making perfect sense.

'Steady on, mate, there's no-' Patrick began in his best beseeching voice, and then Lee cut him short with the viciousness of a streetfighter's knife.

'Someone ask you t' fuckin' speak? Is got fuck all to do wi' you 'n' all, whoever the fuck you are, and I don't give a fuck who you are, right? Got it, cunt?'

This was starting to look less and less like diplomacy and patter might talk its way out of a fight.

'I was just saying-' Patrick could not stop himself saying, and his four counterparts pleaded with their eyes for him to just say no more.

Alex glanced behind him, his position giving the worst view of the others that made up the captive audience trapped within the bar. Uncertainty, apprehension and morbid curiosity were equally shared out among the all enthralled. The clowns, in baggy trousers and loud diamonded shirts, looked as menacing as thugs dressed as clowns could, fresh out of a horror film and into a dark harlequinade. Big Bob and Eve and her cohorts had merged into a smug gloating mass, joining the ill-embroidered droogs in their detachment from sense.

Reality with its ever-redefining unbelievable self to one side, Alex snapped out of a semi-daze into the dreamlike nonsensicality of what was going down. As if coming to in a series of waking double takes, realising he was every tingling inch the focus for attention, for violence and blame, the blinking, giggling-stifling man sensed his own cue to speak drop through the slot in his head and out of his mouth.

'Why exactly are you so upset?' he asked of Lee, his blood's fortification giving him an effortlessly steady voice.

Immediately Lee rounded on his quarry, and Alex believed for a moment he would simply resort to blows and that be that. 'Don't pretend ya don't fuckin' know,' he snapped, and walked smartly up to Alex, Alex rising from his chair in defence. They grabbed the folds of each other's coats, Lee in attack, Alex defence. 'You fuckin' grassed on I, an' no-one fuckin' grasses on me.'

From the corner of his eye, and for certain not escaping the corner of his foe's, Daniel and Ian rose as well, Patrick meeting them halfway, Malcolm remaining in mock repose.

Lee did not flinch at the shaky-legged's rising to their feet. One of the clowns remained guarding the door, the one at the bar looked itching to use the broken bottle to carve a twisted smile. The remaining two approached, flanking Lee, sidekicks looking like, acting like, and as the stooges they were.

'What are you talking about?' Alex rebuked in comical exasperation. 'You attacked me physically without provocation for no good reason at all, as you know.'

'Fuckin' posh cunt,' was spat out of Eve's mouth. 'Who the fuck does he think he is? Fuckin' do 'en over, Lee.'

Lee grinned, grabbing tighter hold of Alex's destruction-tested clothing. Alex remained in a state of check, offering no concession of aggression, no satisfaction of seeing fear. The effect of the substances within his blood combined with adrenaline, and a deep-seated weariness of bowing to aggressors anymore.

'Eve,' Ken said, reminding everyone that he was supposed to be the closest to being in charge. 'That's enough. You'll get yourself barred from here.'

'Oi, Mark,' cried Lee to whoever was Mark. 'You wanna shut that clown at the bar up ur what??'

There was a second of confusion shared by all, and then it became clear that Mark was the clown with the broken bottle, and the clown in question was Ken, frowning and thinking the one just spoken was the leader because he was the biggest clown of all.

The firecracker popping of fresh-lit squibs cut through the

baffled hush from the centre of town. The final official ceremony of the night had just begun.

'Hold up, hold up,' Daniel insisted, capitalising on the sudden confusion and attempting to bring his own order to the scene. He rose, gingerly, to his feet, looking like he wondered what he himself was about to say.

'Oo the fuck asked *you*?!' Lee snapped, and as if elastic had powered him, had Alex flying back across the lounge, tripping over his chair, gracelessly crashing to the floor and taking said chair with him, somehow dodging a broken neck or back or bone, hitting the sticky carpet with more than enough force to wind, limbs akimbo, head spinning, helpless, supine, bruised and forlorn.

Stunned, uncomprehending of just why he had been violently pushed over at that precise moment, and wondering if Lee, with or without his stooges, was about to wade in with a volley of vicious kicks, Alex dared to raise his head to see whatever was coming next.

Lee had apparently tossed Alex aside for the moment to facilitate diving at Daniel, at whom he had obviously seen red for daring to attempt to make him think. Quick as a snake, he lunged across the table and grabbed hold of Daniel's shirt, yanking it hard, lifting it from where it had been tucked into his jeans with a jerk. Immediately retreating the way Lee had leapt, Daniel, aided by Ian, grabbed hold of the cloth and pulled it back the way it had come. Daniel, face red and set in anger, strained with his shirt, trying not to bend forward for this character as his clothing was literally being torn away. Malcolm stood and clumsily gave a token hand, maybe rethinking a bloody revolution now that a simple fray seemed to make him as unsteady to the left as right.

'You stay where you fuckin' are,' threatened Mark, waving the broken bottle like a toy, to Ken who was wavering at the edge of the bar.

The other clowns moved closer, tensing, threatening to turn the slapstick farce into the costume drama kind.

'You fuckin' cunt!' snarled Lee, demonstrating a knack to inscribe his Valentine's cards with irresistible finesse, then the fabric finally decided to divide. The force of resistance balancing the tug-of-war no more, Daniel was flung back, and Ian too, Councillor Stoodley bringing up the rear selflessly serving the public by providing an ample cushion on which they both could fall. Lee cannoned in the other direction, bowling over the henchman clowns minus a cymbal crash but plus a couple of ill-controlled laughs.

A guarded hubbub accompanied the shuffling to get a better view of the tumbled and felled. Daniel, Ian and Malcolm were slowly untangling and tentatively getting back on their feet; Lee, spitting curses and looking at last more incensed than sadistic, sprang back to the verticular like a pop-up toy with a scalded behind. He kicked one of the clowns to help him back to his assumed stance, that looked like its machismo still lay somewhere on the ground. 'Get the fuck back up,' he snarled at his collaborators, as if blaming them for causing him to fall, and hardly reinforcing their muscular support. 'Who was fuckin' laughing?' he hurled as he whirled, turning on his audience as well.

'Tha's one o' the funniest things oi ever fuckin' seen,' bellowed Big Bob. Lee's line of enquiry was discontinued in haste.

'*They* were fuckin' laughin' at you,' Eve helpfully volunteered, pointing at Daniel, Ian and Malcolm, whose faces registered nothing but bewilderment and pain.

Alex remained where he was, discreetly tensed to spring back to his own two feet, but capitalising on the attention for the moment having been directed elsewhere.

'Come on, Lee,' the clown still acting as doorman urged. 'Give this fucker what for an' le's get the fuck out o' here.' Alex presumed one of the F-words acted as a pronoun referring to himself.

'Yeah, come on, oi've 'ad enough of this shit in 'ere,' Mark the Clown the broken bottle brandisher concurred.

'What - you gonna attack someone in front of a million witnesses?' Ken chided, causing Mark to glance at Lee, seeking guidance from the leader of the clowns.

'I don't give a fuck,' spilled out of Lee's mouth, the very same words Alex had heard before his fists had taken over the talking. 'Fuckin' warrant out fer me anyway.'

'Yeah, but what about fuckin' us?' the clown that had taken the kicking from his leader braved. 'Oi don' wan' anyone pointin' the fuckin' finger at I.'

Lee rounded on what appeared to be the weakest link in the chain gang member. Alex, keeping himself cosmetically dazed, raptly watched the ringleader's every move, noticing with a chill the glee that accompanied the ferocity of his glare. 'I'm gonna point my fuckin' *fist* at you if you don' shape up.' The clown flinched as Lee took a step toward him, before he turned to address all the made up buddies in his charge. 'Oos gonna fuckin' recognise any o' you lot anyway, ya fuckin' twats? Ya all look like Ronald fuckin' McDonald anyway.'

The last of the squibs were spluttering away somewhere in the great outdoors, sputtering their dying explosions like the final rounds of an army in retreat.

'You lot must be mad if you think you can get away with this,' Ken kindly informed the clownish, for everyone's benefit and not least his own.

'Don't listen to 'e,' stirred Eve's ladle in the gravy. 'If I was you I'd get they 'n' all while yer at it.' Indicating Daniel, Malcolm and Ian, she finished with, 'They're all fuckin' mates 's bad 's one another.'

'You're getting barred!' declared Ken, with an edge.

'Come on then, get it fuckin' done,' the doorman urged. ''I di'n' fuckin' tell you 'e wus 'ere so we could stand around all night.

'What 'ave 'e turned queer?' chided Big Bob, then robustly laughed to make up for his unfunnyness, as well as emphasise he was the only one present with the bravado to make such a jibe.

'I ain't fuckin' queer,' spat Lee. ''e's fuckin' queer.' He pointed at Alex. 'An' I'm gonna give 'im what 'e's bin fuckin' askin' for.' He made his advance, causing Alex to flex ready to act.

Big Bob smirked at Lee's blundering innuendo. Then he started to laugh. 'Go on then, give 'im what 'e wants, queerboy.' He bellowed at everyone's expense, languishing in the moment no matter who got involved or hurt.

Alex's heart was pumping hard, strained and taxed and pressured by the absence of its kind. Oxygen, glucose, adrenaline, intoxicants, entered his brain with an abundance profound. The chemistry of the air was forming into a compound it seemed would inevitably and imminently explode. As he scanned the faces, keeping Lee in his hyperactive sights, specks appeared to be forming in the air, like embers, soot, charred fragments, a dark intangibility gathering for the come what may. When he looked directly at the swirling moths of decay, they dissolved before he could confirm that they were there, but when he looked again at Lee, he saw them as if they were drawn to him, feeding on or feeding the growing blackness of his mind.

'I. AIN'T. FUCKIN'. GAY!' he swore, rage and desperation striving to threaten the secrets squirming at the back of his mind.

The entire bar seemed to hold their breath. Even Eve quieted her lashing tongue. For an instant that may or not have been in his mind, or both, it seemed all were aware of the particles of rot and decay, free radicals diseasing light, magnetised to Lee like parasites thriving on blight.

'Well, fuckin' get 'en then,' doorclown implored, as if to take control of the hopelessly out of the same.

Lee looked at Alex, lying on the ground, trying to look a target too pathetic to warrant a scored point. He snarled, did he snarl. As if succumbing to the anger of a lifetime's bitter resentment, his face contorted, changed to the physiognomy of hate, in shockingly alarmingly psychotically short a time.

The squibbing had stopped. The night itself felt tensed for the fight.

Something passed between Lee and Alex, and with it the knowledge that the latter would never be spared if his murder were likely to go unsolved. Alex knew that whatever ghosts, demons and skeletons danced on the remains of his wanton twisted mind, Alex had become the scapegoat for everything Lee chose to hate for fear of ever having to face.

Lee screamed, the sound of wounded pride and savagery unleashed, and ran full steam at Alex, not firing on all cylinders but definitely on the ones it was prudent to fear.

Alex rose to a crouch at speed to equal the cannonball of hate.

He launched himself toward the human juggernaut, matching his assailant's strength with needs must might.

There was a cry of something, possibly alarm, possibly excitement, and suddenly the rest of the club came to life. However it had been stirred into being, whatever exactly had been the cause, fighting had broken out between the clowns and those aligned with Alex, with Eve and Big Bob looking like those on the brink of getting involved.

Alex and Lee had each other's arms entrapped, wrapped in obscene proximity, straining for advantage Alex knew he could not afford to lose and would not know what to do with if he gained.

His grunting face kissing distance from Lee's hellbent grimace, Alex attempted a last stab at ending the night without blood of someone's on his hands.

'For god's sake, *think*! You'll end up in jail,' he grunted, using up strength he could but hope had not gone to waste.

Lee, grimace turning to grin, seemed to be tasting a bitter variety of victory.

'I don't give a fuck,' came his hateful mantra and code yet again.

'Oh yes you do,' Alex spent more vital energy vaguely attempting to get across. 'You're completely controlled by what other people think.'

And then came a moment of clarity perhaps unparalleled in all Alex's thirteen thousand days.

Lee's face twisted with pain he endured and tried to inflict in vain. Blackness crowded his features and form like pockmarks on ancient film, apertures into which disappeared hope and light.

This one person, this singular character, however much a grain of sand in a desert of barren despair, was the same essential mask, the same magnet for fear and hate and prejudice, aswarm with the same dark radiance, that manifested in every form of every expression of all that was the heartfelt gutfelt wrong.

It was what soured every relationship on earth, the thing that cheapened marriage, the thing that scoured love. It kept people poor and starving and others rich and ever dissatisfied, and all of us ever in want of more more more. It kept the bruiser and the bonehead on Bridgwater's streets, darkened the shadows with danger and poisoned the sprawl of the urban decay. It was the self-important shortcomings of politics, local to global, nazi right to fascist left, and the world history of every side simply getting it wrong. It made unemployment a necessary evil and work an evil even worse. It was the patriotic and the territorial, the poison pride and glib disdain, the racist and the sexist, that the English upheld by tradition at their own levelling cost to be paid. It was in money and poverty, the spoilt haves and jealous nots, it gave the disadvantaged a complex and the advantaged the illusion of respect. It was in law and it was in order and the free market anarchy reactionaries maintained. It was jobsworthiness and job dedication, the tyranny of the bourgeoisie and the perpetuation of exploitation in sickeningly self-usurping working class pride. It kept Daniel the cosmonaut tethered to the black hole of Bridgwater town. It kept Patrick slaving for tomorrow that was ever another day away. It kept Councillor Stoodley's serving of the people the scraps of a tired idealist's cause. It kept Ian the victim of jokes delivered to force an elusive smile. It kept education feeding the masses ignorance, trained questing minds to certificate their getting on. It keeps us ashamed of our problems, keeps us dressing up circumstance, keeps us dressing down issues and dressing our own wounds. It makes us MI6s through delusion universal problems are somehow unique and overgaurdedly our own. It puts ticks in boxes, keeps rules played by the philistine's book. It kept blue collar workers manacled to serfdom in brusque defence of the one right they upheld – the one to dodge responsibility of taking control of one's life. It keeps invective vomiting from mouth and from orifice, in lieu of words of power, of meaning, of feeling, beyond defensiveness and macho herd instinct, expressions to distract from expressing feelings of which they were fucking well fucking well scared. It is intolerance, it is grudge, it is spite, it is righteous and indifferent, it is bitching, it is gossip, it is threatening and daring, backstabbing, duplicity; it is every facet of our love affair with hate. It is the political milestone that trips up the leftie. It is the dischord that thrashed the hell out of punk. It is the failings of the followers of the obese Siddartha, the disciplines of the esoteric that keep faces less open than strict. It kept associations worlds apart, driving wedges of intolerance and of superiority firmly into the fabric of time-honoured denial and lies. It keeps us looking over our shoulders, through the curtains, down our noses, or checking to make sure an audience is there to find. It is the need to keep secret our profound discoveries, the pressure to propagate banal and inane, quality time wasting DIY, the papering over the cracks in chores that never cease to have no end in sight. It is Bridgwater Carnival's promise and potential, compromised, monopolised, packaged in centuries old tatty gift wrapping again and again and again.

And it fuelled more than anything else on earth what Lee was displaying and Alex narrowly avoiding. Violence and aggression.

The devil had a pseudonym so widely overlooked, so universally accepted and upheld, so taken for granted and residing amongst us, unchallenged, even decorated with pride. No wonder the supreme spirit of evil gained so much, and so ingeniously engineered, so inadvertently awarded, so great a success.

The Devil was Seriousness.

The Devil that keeps us trying to get what we do not want, letting society dictate what we need, keeping our hearts carefully concealed by cards clutched tight to our treasure-craving chests. The Devil that keeps us frightened to show our weaknesses and in thus doing exacerbates them, ignorant of levity being the only way to defeat defeat. The Devil th-

Crack! Lee headbutted Alex in the face, catching him squarely in the forehead, dazing and dizzying him and sending him back to his Cornhill dive. Pain, indignation, anger, rattled through his skull, ears ringing, face numb yet strangely stinging, wrongness and injustice a nauseating cocktail as black as this hate-fuelled attacker was inside.

Alex was aware of the pool table behind him, his back grinding against it with a frightening degree of pain. The pain brought him back to alertness and awareness that this maniac might possibly literally murder him now.

Lee was more than just this crazed individual Lee. Alex felt as if everything dark and evil and malevolent about this town were at his throat now. This was every bonehead the town had to offer aplenty, everyone whose currency was violence, everyone prepared to throw the first punch, everyone who wanted to be a hard nut, everyone whose preferred communication was talking with their – without exception – blood-soaked fists. Anyone who went looking for a fight, anyone who would fight you for looking at them.

All of these characters in Bridgwater's streets shared a secret they quaked at when it gnawed at their minds. Their machismo

was an overcompensatory defence, shielding them from what they would run a million miles not to see.

Sexual ambiguity. In a world of their own disproportionate fear's devising, where non-heterosexuality seemed the most disgusting and shameful disease.

The desire to make physical contact with other men, in the only way they could dress it up as somehow being butch, somehow being straight.

The desire to attack objects of their own attraction, vainly attempting to conquer their desires by targeting what secretly excites them within.

The one single reason one would choose the path of aggression. Because they want to attack what reveals to them aspects of their own nature that fill them with self-loathing and shame.

Lee was reaching for Alex's throat, grip strong, Alex feeling his own start to wane.

It was time to put his theory to the test.

Alex opened his mouth. He knew the kind of thing he had to say to stand a chance of getting the leverage he would need.

'Hey!' he shouted, and his voice did not fail him in its volume of needed might. 'He's got an erection!' rang around the club with the reaction it desired. 'Christ! He's rubbing a fucking erection against me!'

Everyone in the club heard, and for a moment all were shocked to attention. It was nothing anyone had expected to be said, least of all Lee, not even Alex himself.

Big Bob became Alex's inadvertent collaborator. 'Ugh! Gay bastard!' he bellowed, then laughed too loud and hard for reasons unvoiced but clear.

'I'm fuckin' *not*!' Lee rasped, desperate to be heard against the big man's version of a laugh. He half crouched as the clowns at his calling cast glances at his now centre stage crotch.

'I'm fuckin' *NOT*!' he tried to emphasise, the hand close to Alex's throat involuntarily moving to his groin. It was as this happened that Alex suddenly realised what he had said had probably been true.

Alex saw his chance and took it.

He took a pool ball in each hand from atop the table he was crushed against.

He brought his hands together with a grunt, and with the most aggressive force he had ever mustered in his pacifist life.

He had a lot in reserve. More than characters who took violence for granted could possibly hope to know.

The balls hit Lee at either side of the head, the crack punctuating the cracking of the bonehead's skull.

Lee's hands flew to his damaged head, and Alex brought both balls down on it once more.

Then he was on the floor, the place where, had he himself landed, Alex felt sure he would not have been left alone by Lee.

Alex looked up in time to see the baseball bat Ken had wrested from concealment behind the bar swinging at the distracted Mark, colliding with another head, another clown down.

The clown acting as doorman had decided to return to his post, this time opening and exiting said barrier at speed.

The two remaining clowns followed his example, as if to make their getaway in a backfiring collapsing car.

The dust settled on the throng and felled aggressor, forever thereafter to be dubbed as Bender Lee.

Alex shook his head, but the only thing he cleared was the knowledge that none of it had been a dream.

Perhaps he would be able to make sense of things when the drugs wore off.

'What the fucking hell just happened?' Daniel was asking rhetorically.

Perhaps not.

'Right, I'm going to have to call an ambulance and doubtless the police,' Ken informed the witnesses with caution. 'Anyone who doesn't want to be here when they arrive had best clear off.'

Everyone else except Daniel, Malcolm and Ian did.

'Thanks for helping me out there,' Alex expressed to the people he knew had been trying their best.

'Are you alright?' Ian asked him.

He replied with one of the most commonly told lies. 'Yes.'

'You hanging around for the police, are you?' Ken asked, stooping and checking Lee was breathing and not coming around before the cops.

Considering the amount of intoxicants in his bloodstream, plus his current lack of an official abode, Alex suggested a visit to the nick was something for which he wasn't in the mood.

Shrugging off the offer of an escort, Alex stepped out into the cold wet night, alone, distrusting his luck but not to the same degree he valued his own company right then.

He did not dither. He wanted to walk, he wanted to move, he wanted to get somewhere. Out of his head proved not quite far enough away.

At the Cornhill, oblivious to whatever malingered in the landfill streets, a man was doing what could only be described as shagging a woman in a brightly-lit phone box while she, indifferent to his efforts, spat curses at whomever was on the other end of the line.

When he at last reached Alfoxton Road, he continued past it, along the Quantock Road to the edge of the town.

He reached the Welcome to Bridgwater sign, spelling mistake and all.

Tentatively, almost experimentally, he took a step past it, relieved when he did not crumble to dust. Someone should spread the word, he thought.

But he knew it was that old devil seriousness that made people unflinchingly criticise the town. And that made people proud of it as well.

Alex continued on his way out of town, aware that tears of something were welling in his beleaguered eyes.

Far ahead, where the hills met the heavens, he could see the faintest traces of a coming day's light.

About the author:

Dale Bruton is the winner of both the judges' and audience prize in the Prague Playwriting Contest 2009, for his play *Forced Entry*.

To send correspondence, comments, criticisms and computer viruses, please write to dalebruton@seznam.cz

Lightning Source UK Ltd.
Milton Keynes UK
04 September 2009
143369UK00001B/2/P